Sarah Linley lives in Yorkshire and works as a Communications Manager for a housing charity.

She spent two years backpacking around South-East Asia with her husband. Their travels inspired her debut novel, *The Beach*.

When she is not writing, she enjoys walking in the Dales with her dad and his dog.

@linleysarah1

The Beach

Sarah Linley

OneMoreChapter

OneMoreChapter
an imprint of HarperCollins*Publishers* Ltd
1 London Bridge Street
London SE1 9GF

www.harpercollins.co.uk

This paperback edition 2020

First published in Great Britain in ebook format by
HarperCollins*Publishers* 2020

A catalogue record for this book
is available from the British Library

ISBN: 978-0-00-836815-9

Typeset in Birka by Palimpsest Book Production Ltd,
Falkirk, Stirlingshire

Printed and bound in the UK

To Mum and Dad,
who encouraged me to follow my dreams.

Chapter 1

'Stay a while. You know you want to.'

A shaft of sunlight, as sharp and sour as lemon, pierces the curtains and illuminates the bed. Tom wraps his arm around my waist, drawing me in to the warm cocoon of his tangled sheets. For a second, time stands still as I bask in his attention, but our sixty minutes are nearly up.

'You know I can't. I have to get back to school.' I kiss him as I release myself from his hold.

He watches me getting dressed. A strip tease in reverse, carefully orchestrated to leave him wanting more. I grab my mobile phone from the bedside cabinet and check my messages. I've missed a call from my mum, but I haven't got time to call her back.

'Will I see you tomorrow?'

'Can't, sorry. Playground duty.'

I retrieve my ID badge from the floor and swing it around my neck. In the tiny en suite bathroom I reapply my make-up and tidy my hair. I don't want anyone in the staff room to guess what I get up to at lunchtime. I kiss Tom goodbye and promise to call him later.

'I love you ...' My heart jumps, but he hasn't finished. '... coming round like this.'

I try to hide the disappointment from my voice. 'Me too. We'll get together again soon.'

I make my way down the stairs, stepping over discarded Lego and toy cars. I leave by the back door, hoping no one sees me emerge from the side path into the driveway. The suburban street is quiet during the day, but you never know who might be watching behind closed windows.

The school is only five minutes' walk away from Tom's house; I should make it back before the bell rings. The day is unseasonably warm for October. The leaves have turned the colour of popcorn and the nights are drawing in. I walk over the ancient stone bridge, crossing the river which is swollen from recent rainfall. The water flows down from the surrounding fells, breaking over large stones, depositing branches and debris on the banks. Occasionally the river floods, leaving the village cut off from the rest of the world, damaging the riverside properties people pay a fortune for and making the roads impassable. Most people around here drive 4x4s and not just for show.

I can see a group of kids, laughing and showing off on the muddy bank of the river below the bridge. They are too old to go to our school and there is no secondary provision in the village, so they must be bunking off. A teenaged girl balances precariously on a large rock, a can of drink in her hand, as the water streams around her. The others egg her on, perhaps oblivious but more likely exhilarated by the danger. People underestimate the power of the River Wharfe, only seeing its picturesque beauty as it wends its way through the Yorkshire Dales, but the water here is deep with a vicious undercurrent. Almost in slow motion, the girl raises one leg like a ballet dancer and wobbles dangerously. As I walk away, I hear a scream and a splash followed by a cacophony of shouts.

I look over the bridge and see the girl struggling in the water, her arms flailing. Her friends are panicking and shouting at each other. I race down the steps, nearly slipping on the wet limestone, and run towards the group. My brain is on autopilot, focussing on what needs to be done and clouding everything else out. The mud sucks at my heels, slowing me down, and I am forced to abandon them and run barefooted.

One of the boys has stripped off his jacket and looks like he is about to jump in after the girl, but I hold him back. I don't need two of them to rescue.

'Get a branch, quickly,' I say, pointing to the nearby woodland. I lie on the ground, ruining my white blouse, and stretch out my arm as far as I can but I can't reach her. The girl, who looks about fourteen, is now clinging onto the rock but the water is pulling her downstream. Her eyes are wide and terrified, and she's shivering uncontrollably. If she lets go, she will be pulled under, the force of the current throwing her against the rocks like a rag doll.

'What's your name?' I shout at her above the roar of the water, which is ice cold and seeping through my clothes.

'Samantha.'

I recognise her now. Her little brother Nathan is in my class. 'Samantha, I'm Holly. Hold on, it's going to be okay.'

The boy hands me a branch and I test it with one hand to check it is sturdy enough. He has had the good sense to pick up a strong, thick one. I hold it out to Samantha.

'One hand at a time, grab on.'

She looks uncertain, weighing up her options, too scared to release her grip on the rock but knowing the strength in her cold trembling fingers won't last much longer. She doesn't look like a cocky teenager anymore; she looks like a little girl. Gingerly, she releases one of her hands and grasps the branch.

'Now the other one. Quickly.' My steady voice belies the terror racing through my head. I can't let her see how scared I am.

She whimpers and shakes her head, paralysed by fear.

'Come on, Samantha. You can do this.' I try to sound as calm as possible even though I am struggling to maintain my grip. If either of us let go now, the result could well be fatal.

She takes a deep breath and snatches the branch. Her sudden weight pulls at my arms and I slide closer to the water's edge. Adrenaline shoots through my body, every instinct telling me to let her go and save myself. I take a deep breath, dig my elbows into the ground to keep steady and use all the strength I can muster to drag her towards me. Once or twice I think one of us is going to let go of the branch but, somehow, we make it and inch by inch I pull her towards the bank. As soon as they can reach her, the teenagers take over, grabbing on to Samantha's sodden clothing and hauling her to safety, collapsing in a great muddy heap. Samantha lies on the ground, coughing up dirty water.

'Call an ambulance,' I gasp as I help her to sit up. She is shaking so I wrap one of the boys' discarded coats around her and rub her arms to warm her up. Eventually her shivers subside. Apart from the shock, she doesn't seem to be hurt.

'I'm going to be in so much trouble,' Samantha says, looking around at the empty beer cans and discarded tab ends.

'Better in trouble than dead.'

I look down at my clothes. My thin white blouse is saturated, see-through in parts, and covered in grass stains. My black pencil skirt is ripped, and my feet are caked in clay-like mud. There is no way I can go back to school looking like this. I check my watch. I'm already twenty minutes late for class. They will be wondering where I am by now.

The ambulance eventually arrives, parking at the top of the bridge and two paramedics make their way across the slippery bank. I feel a sense of relief as they take control of the situation. One of the paramedics assesses Samantha while the other wraps a foil blanket around my shoulders and asks me questions. As he does, an overwhelming sense of panic rises up from where I had suppressed it. The roar of the water seems to be getting louder and there is a ringing in my ears. My vision blurs and it's difficult to breathe. I can't understand what he's saying.

'Look at me,' a sharp command. I struggle to focus on the handsome paramedic who is crouched in front of me. 'Breathe.'

I can't. It's as if my air passages have been blocked. My breaths are coming out as loud rasps and my lungs hurt as I battle for air. What's happening to me?

'Hold out your hands.'

My hands are trembling and seem strangely disconnected from the rest of my body as he takes hold of them. I look into his kind, reassuring face and force myself to relax.

'You're OK, you're doing fine, now breathe … nice and slow.'

My breathing calms down as I obey his instructions. My vision returns to normal and my heart stops racing. I am so embarrassed.

'Just a panic attack,' he says. 'Have you had one before?'

I shake my head.

'I think you should come to the hospital and get checked out.'

'I'm fine, honestly.'

He checks my pulse and seems satisfied with the result.

'OK, well at least get someone to walk you home.' He shouts over to one of the lads to come and walk with me.

I am acutely conscious of my dirty clothes and bedraggled appearance. I reluctantly agree to the teenager accompanying me home and we all make our way slowly back up the steps like a funeral cortege. The boy looks relieved when I dispense of his services as soon as the ambulance sets off.

I'm shattered and Tom's house is closer than mine, but I turn the other way towards my own cottage. I need to be alone right now. Seeing Samantha in the water has brought the bad memories flooding back. Memories of a different place and a different time, a different body in the water and a very different outcome.

Chapter 2

I strongly suspect it was my boss who tipped off the local newspaper about my 'heroic rescue'. Trevor loves the media and anything that reflects well on the school and, by implication, his leadership.

The following day a reporter and a photographer turn up. The journalist is about my age and nervous. She rattles off questions, barely waiting for my response before firing out another. She insists she needs my age and marital status, though I can't see how they're relevant. Trevor watches me from the corner of his office, a self-satisfied grin all over his face. He is no doubt picturing himself presenting the article to the governors as part of his monthly media report, lapping up the kudos. I pose dutifully for a picture, wishing that I could cover up the ugly cuts and bruises I sustained during the rescue.

'It will be on the website later today,' the reporter promises. 'We want to break the story first!'

I fake a smile. It's hardly the scoop of the century, but I am still dreading the publicity and people gossiping about me. I don't know how my sister stands it. As an actress, Lisa must have to do this type of interview all the time, but at least she has access to a good make-up artist.

'Do you have everything you need? Only I need to get back to my class.'

'Of course, it was really lovely to meet you.' Her voice drips with insincerity as she shakes my hand.

'And you.'

Trevor shows them out. I can hear him pitching a story about the school choir as they close the door behind them.

Rhona is covering my class. She won't thank me for it. She hates dealing with the litany of demands the younger ones bring. This afternoon we're making Hallowe'en decorations. I have laid out sheets of newspaper over the tables and placed glue, tubes full of glitter and colouring crayons in the middle. When I walk back into the classroom, the children are hard at work, tongues sticking out in quiet concentration. They barely notice my return. Rhona is sitting at my desk, watching the clock.

'Wow, what did you do?' I ask, dumping my bag at her feet.

'Threatened them all with expulsion if they weren't quiet.' I can't always tell when Rhona is joking. 'How was your fifteen minutes of fame?'

'Excruciating.'

Rhona gathers her things. 'I think you should be dead proud of yourself. You saved that girl's life.'

'Well, anyone would have done it. I was just lucky to be passing at the right time.'

'Yeah, funny that ...' Rhona says, winking at me. She's the only one who knows about me and Tom. I blush furiously and glance over to where Jack is sitting. He looks so much like his father. 'Are you coming for a drink later?'

I'm about to answer when we are interrupted by a high-pitched shriek. Our heads both turn sharply to see one of the little girls throw her paintbrush on the floor. Her cheeks are cerise, her bottom lip is wobbling, and tears are streaming down her face. Rhona takes the impending tantrum as a cue to leave.

I rush over. 'Hey, what happened?'

Phoebe, a precocious and spoilt five-year-old, holds out one of her curls, now a tangle of white blonde hair, glue and glitter. This is just what I need. Phoebe's mother is a serial complainer and there's not a chance in hell this latest sign of my ineptitude will go unchallenged. I lead Phoebe over to the sink in the corner of the classroom and try to wash it out but it's hopeless and in the end, I have to leave it as it is. I will just have to face the wrath of her mother. From hero to villain in one afternoon; not bad going.

By the time the final bell rings I am exhausted, and I still have a pile of marking to get through before I go home. I stay in the classroom as the sun sets, watching the starlings perform a murmuration against the rose-coloured sky, while correcting the kids' rudimentary attempts at basic sentences. Some of them haven't even mastered the alphabet yet and I notice that Jack is still getting his b's and d's the wrong way around.

Rhona pops her head around the door shortly after seven to ask if I'm ready to leave but I shake my head dolefully.

'All work and no play, Holly ...' she scolds gently. 'I'll be in the pub if you change your mind.'

I'll give it another half an hour and go home. I take out my phone and check the newspaper website. The river rescue is the main story. The picture of me is hideous and the reporter has got half the details mixed up. I close down the browser and check my notifications. There's an unopened Snapchat message from my sister. She befriended me on the app a few months ago but this is the first time she's contacted me on it. I open the message.

I recognise the picture immediately. It was on my wall at university for three years. I am standing between Kristóf and George while Meg is giving the V sign above my head. Kristóf looks bored while George is beaming at the camera, loving life. It was taken the first night of Freshers' Week when we didn't really know each other.

My hands are shaking so badly I drop the phone and it clatters onto the classroom floor. My gut writhes with the mixture of grief and guilt that always arises when I think about that time of my life. Why would my sister send me that photo? I pick up my phone to check the message, but it has already expired.

Chapter 3

'*Teacher saves teenage girl from drowning.*'

Google Alerts draws his attention to the article that appeared on the local newspaper site an hour ago. He set up the alert on Holly's name some time back, but this is the first time it has delivered a result.

He scrolls through the interview, feeling his temper rise. Holly's quotes are steeped in self-deprecation and false modesty; the bitch is clearly lapping up the attention.

'Anyone would have done it. I was simply in the right place at the right time.'

The reporter has made no attempt to challenge her version of events. He looks closely at Holly's photograph. Her face is cut and bruised, and she looks older than she does on her Facebook profile. An honest picture for once, not the stylised, heavily filtered crap she usually posts.

He screengrabs the article and adds it to her folder. It isn't as full as the others but there are still plenty of files. Private messages she thought no-one could read, deleted emails, and photographs she's forgotten taking. Hundreds of images depicting a smiling young woman without a care in the world. It makes him sick.

Mia is clattering away in the kitchen and the heady scent of garlic and tomatoes wafts through the study door. He doesn't have long.

He flicks through the images in her folder and picks one of the four of them. He forwards it to his mobile phone using the encryption software he got from Latvia, opens Snapchat, taps in Holly's username and sends the photo. No message. Not this time. He wants to see how she reacts first. He removes the SIM card and places it with the others, neatly locked away in his desk drawer.

Mia is calling him down for supper. He shuts down his laptop and switches off the lamp. It is getting dark and above the London rooftops, the sky is a wash of blues with the faintest glimmer of daylight.

He will have to wait for Holly's reply. But he's good at waiting; he's been waiting for a very long time.

Chapter 4

Eight years ago

It was the first night of Freshers' Week. Mum, Dad and my sister Lisa had left a couple of hours ago and I was in my room, waiting for the right time to walk down the corridor and meet the people I would be living with for the next year. I didn't want to be the first to arrive. I was dressed for clubbing: heels, short skirt, glittery top, but I had no idea what everyone else would be wearing. Was I overdressed for a student night? I poured myself another shot of vodka and mixed it with cherryade, hoping the alcohol would calm my nerves.

My new room was small and utilitarian, on the second floor of a block of flats that overlooked a courtyard. The only furniture was a single bed and a fitted wardrobe, desk and shelves. The bathroom comprised a toilet, shower and sink efficiently crammed into a compact cubicle. Everything about my new home was built to withstand the rigour of first-year students. I hadn't unpacked properly but I had made up my bed with the pretty duvet cover Mum and I had chosen last week. We had filled the trolley with everything I would need for my first time away from home, getting excited over wooden spoons and tea towels.

In the flat opposite, a hot guy was walking around bare-chested. He caught me looking and winked as he walked to the window and closed the blinds. Back home, the only view from my bedroom was the windswept mudflats of Morecambe Bay. On a normal Saturday night, I would be going out with friends I had known since primary school. Dad would be telling me to "knock 'em dead" and Mum would be slipping me an emergency tenner to keep in my shoe. I would know which pubs would ask for ID and which were full of creepy old men. Gemma and I would share a taxi home at the end of the night, and we would stay awake until the early hours chatting, analysing our night in minute detail and choosing which pictures to post on Facebook. Now there were more than 200 miles between us and she would be making new friends in Cardiff while I was sitting in my room feeling clueless.

My mirror was propped up against a stack of textbooks. They were pristine, unread and despite their abstruse titles, full of excitement and mystery. I was a proper university student, at last. School, and the agonising wait for my A-level results, seemed like a distant memory. I checked my phone: it was finally time to make my appearance. I reapplied my lip-gloss, shook out my hair and checked I had money and keys before walking down the corridor to the communal kitchen. I could already hear laughter coming from behind the door. I took a deep breath and walked in.

The large kitchen had a dining area in the middle of the room. There was a collection of bottles on the table: vodka, whisky, cola, wine and a twelve pack of cheap Belgian beer. Tinie Tempah was playing out of a set of speakers attached to an iPod. The smell of pizza was rising from the oven, making me feel hungry. Laminated notices reminded users to clear up their dishes after them and to use the recycling bins.

A group of students had gathered on the sofas near the window. I added my bottle of vodka to the table, knowing that it would be gone by morning, and walked towards them. A girl with light-brown skin, dark make-up and bright pink hair stood up, swaying slightly, and moved towards me. 'Hey, I'm Meg.'

She gave me a quick hug. She smelt of strawberries. It reminded me of the products I used to buy from the Body Shop, before my friends introduced me to Clinique.

'Holly.'

'Guys this is Holly. From?'

'Lancaster.' I thought it sounded more sophisticated than Morecambe.

'I'm Kristóf,' a guy with olive skin, black hair and intense brown eyes stood up to shake my hand. Kristóf was wearing skinny black jeans and a faded Jack Daniels t-shirt. He was tall and thin and sported a goatee beard. I could see that he was handsome, but I preferred my men with more muscle.

The other boy didn't stand up, but lazily held out his hand. He looked like he had just stepped off his father's yacht: sun-kissed skin, sandy curls and preppy clothes. His hands were soft, and his nails looked manicured. He introduced himself as George in a posh accent that I thought was sarcastic but turned out to be genuine.

'So, what's the plan tonight?' I asked cheerily, trying not to sound nervous.

'Well we're supposed to meet at the Union bar at seven,' Meg said in a strong Geordie accent that I was struggling to understand. 'But there's plenty of time. We don't want to get there first, like a bunch of saddos.'

I poured myself another drink, trying not to think of the empty calories I was pouring into my body; I would make up for it tomorrow. I perched on a kitchen stool as we exchanged personal information. Kristóf and I were the only ones studying the same subject: English Literature. We chatted a bit about our favourite books, but his tastes were more highbrow than mine and I soon felt out of my depth. Meg was an engineering student and had won a scholarship on the back of a solar-powered device she invented in sixth form that was being used by the Red Cross in Africa. She played it down, saying it was just common sense, but I was impressed. George was taking Business Studies.

'Keeping my parents sweet until my inheritance kicks in,' he declared, to Meg's obvious disgust. 'Of course, they wanted me to go to Cambridge like my older brother, but I didn't get the grades.'

By the time we reached the Union bar, it was heaving with students making the most of the free shots on offer. Meg grabbed four plastic glasses filled with unidentified neon liquid and handed them around.

'Here's to a night to remember!'

Kristóf and Meg downed their shots while I sipped mine cautiously. It tasted of lime and it went down OK, but it was sickly sweet and probably filled with sugar. I had to be careful drinking shots. I didn't want to puke on my first night. I noticed George surreptitiously abandon his on the table behind him.

'I'm going to get a proper drink,' he shouted in my ear. 'Coming?'

I followed him, pushing through the crowd of students at the bar. He ordered a whisky for himself and a glass of prosecco for me and paid for them with a £50 note. None of the boys at home would have done that. They thought they were flash if they paid with a tenner. The bar man handed him his change and he slipped it into his wallet without even counting it.

Going into Leeds was like being sucked into a hurricane. There were more shots, more bars, more bodies pressed against me as we made our way around the city centre. I was accustomed to seeing groups of students act like this in Lancaster: self-assured, noisy, oblivious to anyone who wasn't part of their world; but this was the first time I had actually been part of it. It was exciting and scary at the same time. The alcohol had anaesthetised my nerves and I found myself chatting to random strangers, asking them where they had come from and what they were studying. Most of the time I couldn't hear their responses over the loud music, but it didn't really matter. I bumped into the man I had watched getting dressed earlier that evening. He was very drunk and trying it on with every woman in the group. You had to admire his tenacity in the face of so many rebuffs. There might have been a time when I would have let him snog me, pathetically grateful for his attention, but there were so many gorgeous men here that I could afford to be picky. I didn't want to get a reputation. George and Meg were in their element, taking selfies and organising rounds of drinks. Kristóf was more reserved. All evening he remained aloof, watching us from a distance like an anthropologist observing an intriguing tribe. He looked so out of place and miserable in this crowd, I wondered why he had bothered coming.

We ended up in a grungy club where they sold tequila shots for £1. The floor was sticky and the music reverberating from the speakers made my ears ring. I felt over-dressed and self-conscious under the gaze of the older men who were standing around the dance floor appraising us like farmers at an auction mart. Where had all the gorgeous men disappeared to? My chances of finding Mr Right here were diminishing by the second. I was tired, my feet hurt, and I wanted nothing more than to go to bed, but I didn't want to be the first one to call it a night. I wasn't even sure how I was going to get home.

I found a seat in one of the few booths that were not occupied by snogging couples and took out my phone to message Gemma, but there was no signal. It was past two o' clock and I wondered when the club closed. Surely then we would head home. Meg shimmied over.

'What's up?' she shouted. Her breath stunk of cigarettes and beer. She slumped in the seat next to me and placed her head on my shoulder.

'Just taking a breather.'

'Here, try one of these. Got them from that guy at the bar.' She held out her hand. Nestling in her palm were two small yellow pills. I had never done drugs. I wasn't prudish about it, but I didn't like the idea of not being in control. I reminded myself I didn't know Meg that well, and I definitely didn't trust a random stranger in a bar.

'No thanks.'

'OK, your loss.' She took one and washed it down with my bottle of water. I instantly regretted my decision. I was at university now; I needed to live a little.

'Oh, go on then. Why not?' She smiled and handed over the pill. I hesitated again – picturing the headlines in the media, Mum and Dad identifying my body, the memorial page on Facebook – and swallowed it.

Fifteen minutes later, I was back on the dance floor,

jumping up and down to the music without even thinking about what I looked like. An hour later, I was declaring my love for everything about the club. The lights were painting everyone yellow, red, blue and pink. It was all so pretty. I told Meg that she was my new best friend and tried to pull Kristóf on to the dance floor. A man who looked old enough to be my dad taught me how to moonwalk. George picked me up at one point and twirled me around, making me dizzy. It was the best night of my life and I didn't want it to end.

The next day my phone was full of messages and Facebook updates. I seemed to have made a lot of friends overnight. I checked through the pictures I had been tagged in and was relieved to see they were all fine. There was a lovely one of the four of us, Meg pulling a V sign above my head. I didn't look like I was off my head, thank God. I swore that was going to be the first and last time I took drugs. Gemma had posted some pictures of her night out and I liked them and privately messaged her to check she was OK.

I took a long shower and deep cleansed my face. I spent ages on my make-up and straightened my hair before I ventured sheepishly to the kitchen. I could smell bacon cooking and my stomach growled but I had consumed so many calories last night, I was determined to stick to black coffee for breakfast. Meg was sitting at the kitchen table, still wearing her pyjamas. She looked younger and prettier without all the heavy make-up. George was frying strips of bacon while Kristóf popped slices of bread in the toaster with one hand and gulped down a cup of tea with the other.

'Oh my God, you're actually dressed and wearing make-up!' Meg said. 'That's just not normal!'

I could have taken it as an insult, but it wasn't meant that way. It really didn't seem to matter to any of them what I looked like. George placed a bacon sandwich and a cup of tea in front of me before I could decline. I took small, delicious bites as Meg relived the evening, laughing at the funny parts and making plans for the rest of the week. We were a disparate bunch, but I had a feeling we were going to become the best of friends.

Chapter 5

I can't sleep, thinking about the message and who might have sent it. It wasn't my sister. I checked and she isn't even on Snapchat so someone must have created a fake profile using her name and picture and, like an idiot, I fell for it. The photograph has obviously been taken from my Facebook page – it was my cover image for most of my first year – but I changed it a long time ago. Is someone from uni trying to get back in touch? But why bother setting up a fake account?

I haven't been in touch with anyone from university since I left. I decided to draw a line under what happened and move on with my life. I assumed the others had done the same. I think about responding but I don't know what to say. In the end I block the sender and switch off my phone.

But the memories won't stop flowing. It's as if a room inside my head, that has always been firmly bolted, has been unlocked and my past is spilling out. Good memories that I had forgotten about; bad memories that I haven't. I try to push them back in the room, lock the door behind me, but there's nothing I can do except endure it.

Dragging myself out of bed and into the bathroom the next morning, I groan at the sight of the huge bags underneath my eyes and my pasty white skin. I use my most expensive foundation, the one I usually save for special occasions, and take my time over my make-up, meticulously crafting the mask that will need to stay in place all day. I put on a pretty floral dress and some leggings and look in the mirror. It's one of my favourite outfits but today it looks childish. I get changed into some black trousers and a cream silk blouse. Then I worry the kids will splash paint on it, so I change again. I eventually settle for a navy dress and team it up with a scarlet scarf Rhona bought me for my birthday. I put on heels even though they will be killing me by lunchtime. I look older, more professional. I may look fierce, but my stomach is churning, and I can't face any breakfast.

A light drizzle coats my face as soon as I step out of the door. It is colder than I was expecting, and I wish I had thought to put on my gloves. The mist is hanging low over the hills, obscuring the landscape. My tiny cottage is in a beautiful location at the edge of the village with picturesque views of the Dales, but it's secluded. My parents bought it as an investment and charge me a minimal amount of rent. Either side are holiday cottages which are only occupied in the summer months, and occasionally over Christmas and half-term. There are no streetlights along the path which leads from my house into the village centre and it's still not light, so I have to be careful not to step in any dirty puddles, or worse. Walkers regularly use this route to access the moors and they don't always clean up after their dogs.

It's taken me a while to get used to living in a village. I've had to adjust to the more sedate pace of life and the proclivity for gossip. As the first new teacher to arrive in several years, I attracted a lot of attention and plenty of invites to community meetings and groups. There was much speculation about my marital status and which of the eligible bachelors from the neighbouring farms would snap me up. It was like stepping into a Thomas Hardy novel.

At first, I felt a bit isolated. It was my first job after graduating from teacher training college and I didn't know anyone in the village. After a while though, I started to feel part of the community. I got friendly with Rhona and her husband, Rob, and they introduced me to everyone and now I have Tom. It may not have much in the way of nightlife or high street shops, but the village is friendly and safe, and everyone looks out for one another. I can't imagine ever wanting to leave.

As usual, I meet Rhona outside the pub. She is checking her phone and smoking a cigarette. She waves enthusias-tically as I approach.

'You'll never guess what happened yesterday,' she says, launching into the latest tale about a boy in her class who she has nicknamed 'Orrible Oliver. He is the bane of Rhona's life. A precocious ten-year-old with a gob the size of Yorkshire and an ego to match. 'Brought in a box of matches. Trevor caught him trying to set fire to the blinds. He told him it was a science experiment. Can you believe it?'

'What did Trevor do?'

'Oh, you know our illustrious master. Doesn't like to deal with anything that might get back to the governors. Confiscated the matches and gave him a verbal warning. He should have expelled him, the little shit.'

I smile sympathetically. I've managed to avoid having Oliver in my class, but the other teachers are always moaning about him. It sounds like he's more trouble than half my five-year-olds put together.

'You're looking a bit peaky. Are you OK?'

'Didn't sleep that well.'

'Oh aye. Tom wearing you out, is he?'

I wink at her. 'A lady doesn't tell.'

Rhona likes to tease me about Tom. She was with me when we first met and has taken a keen interest in our relationship ever since.

'Still going well though, is it?'

'Yeah, I think so. I just wish we didn't have to keep it a secret. I mean we're not doing anything wrong.'

'Give it time.' This is Rhona's favourite phrase, as if giving anything time has ever made it better. I know that Tom doesn't want to announce our relationship to the whole village yet, and I understand why, but I think there's also a part of him that wants to continue to play the wounded husband, the long-suffering partner of a cruel wife who walked out on him and their child. He doesn't want people thinking that he's moving on too quickly. Besides, I have reasons of my own not to broadcast it. Rhona said the last head would have turned a blind eye, but we're both pretty sure Trevor would have a fit if he found out I was screwing one of the parents.

'Still up for a walk at the weekend?'

'Definitely.' I've always enjoyed walking in the country-side, it helps me clear my head. Dad used to take me to the Lakes when I was a kid and we've tackled most of the peaks together. I was less familiar with the Yorkshire Dales when I moved here but over the past three years, I have covered the major climbs and discovered a few more off the beaten track. Surrounded by rolling hills and limestone pavements which date back to the Ice Age, this area is a walker's paradise. I used to go walking on my own, but since Rhona got a Fitbit for her birthday, she's been joining me to get her steps up. It's nice to have her company, although she's hopeless at reading maps and we're constantly getting lost and having to climb over barbed wire fences to get back on track.

'Rob says he's coming in later. You know, to give them *the talk*.'

Rhona's husband Rob is what the local newspaper calls a 'bobby on the beat', the last bastion of community policing. His patch covers a collection of villages in a largely rural area with a very low crime rate, apart from the odd burglary and a few drink drivers. He likes to visit at the start of each school year to meet the kids. 'Catch 'em early before they get into trouble,' he says, although I suspect it's more because the children hero-worship the emergency services at this age and treat him like a celebrity.

'Yeah, it usually goes down well.'

Rhona stubs out her cigarette before we reach the school gates. She doesn't like the kids seeing her smoking. As we turn the corner, there are already some parents waiting to drop their children off early before they go to work. Rhona greets them with a cheerful hello. She is far friendlier than I am; I keep my head bowed and try to sneak through the crowd unnoticed. Parents always want a 'quick word' about their child's progress.

I spot Phoebe's mum among the throng. She is bending down and fastening her daughter's bright pink coat. I speed up, hoping to get away from her, but she looks up as I place my hand on the gate and makes eye contact.

'Ah Miss Metcalfe, have you got a minute?' Phoebe's mother places great emphasis on the word 'Miss'. She is a tall woman with a sharp black bob and the hint of crow's feet around her eyes. I would guess she's about forty. I fake a smile and walk over.

'Good morning, Mrs Abbott. Hello Phoebe.' I can see that a lock of her hair has been cut and pinned to one side: a visual reminder of what a terrible guardian I am.

'Phoebe told me that she had glue in her hair yesterday. And that one of the other children deliberately stuck it there.'

This is blatantly untrue. I look down at Phoebe who stares back at me, wide-eyed and innocent. I'm impressed; not many five-year-olds are that accomplished at lying.

'I'm afraid Phoebe did get glue in her hair, but I'm not aware that any of the other children were involved.' My voice is steady and calm even though my heart is beating fast. Will Mrs Abbott make an official complaint? Will I be sacked over a little girl's lies?

'Well, perhaps you need to be a bit more aware of what is happening in your classroom, Miss Metcalfe. After all, isn't that your job?'

I bite my tongue and swallow my temper. Rhona is always complaining about parents who treat teachers like glorified babysitters.

'I can assure you that the children are very well supervised, Mrs Abbott. Which is why I am one hundred per cent certain that no other pupil was involved.'

'Phoebe doesn't lie. The other children may well be jealous of her intelligence.'

'I agree that Phoebe is a very intelligent little girl; which is why I was hoping that I could chat to you at some point about ways we can keep that creative imagination of hers channelled. Perhaps you would like to make an appointment to discuss the matter?'

Mrs Abbott flushes and looks at her watch. 'Well, I am rather busy at the moment.'

'I totally understand. I'm sure it must be very difficult with two little ones to manage. How old is your son now?' I nod towards the baby boy tucked up in blankets and fast asleep in the pram beside her.

Her face softens. 'Six months.'

'That's a nice age.'

'He's absolutely no trouble at all. To be honest I think Phoebe may be a little jealous of the attention he's getting.'

'That's perfectly understandable.'

Phoebe, sensing her moment in the spotlight is over, releases her mother's hand and runs off to join her friends in the playground and no doubt complain about her unfair treatment.

'Honestly, that child will be the death of me,' her mother says under her breath. 'Do you have children yourself?'

'Not yet.'

'Well, take my advice and enjoy your freedom while you have it!'

I breathe a sigh of relief as she turns the pram and walks away. I feel a bit better now about the day ahead. Surprisingly, handling Phoebe and her mother has given me the boost of confidence I needed. If I can handle her, I can handle anything.

*

'We're here to talk about honesty,' Rob says. 'Now, who can tell me what that means?'

The kids are gazing up at him in rapture.

Phoebe's hand shoots up. 'Telling the truth?'

'That's right. Anyone else?'

Jack shyly raises his hands. 'Not telling lies?'

'Absolutely!' Jack beams. Rob is great with the kids, he seems to have no end of patience as they ask him many, many questions. The whole thing is making me feel a bit queasy. I don't know what it is about Rob, but I always feel flustered in his presence, like he can see right through me. I always feel an urge to confess everything I have ever done wrong in my life when I am around him. He must be great at his job.

'Do you put people in prison?' Bilal asks.

'Only when they've done something really naughty.'

'Nathan's dad went to prison.' The room falls silent as all the kids turn to stare at Nathan who is sitting in the back row, sucking his thumb. Liam Whitaker, Nathan and Samantha's dad, went to jail last year for burglary. It's not something we talk about in the classroom, but the kids pick up the gossip from their parents. I think sometimes we underestimate how much life experience these kids already have by the time they get to school.

'Come on kids, have you got anything else to ask PC Osbourne?' I ask brightly before Nathan gets upset. I can already see him blinking back tears.

Jack saves the day. 'How fast does your car go?' Jack is obsessed with cars.

'Oh, very fast. But only in an emergency and only when I have the blue lights flashing.'

'How long have you been a policeman?'

'Do you have a gun?'

I switch off and relax as Rob tells them about how he joined the police after leaving school. I consider pulling Nathan to one side to check if he is OK, but I think that would attract more attention. He's a quiet, nervous boy at the best of times. The kids seem to have moved on and pretty soon they are pestering Rob to let them ride in his car which is parked in the playground. Finally, he manages to extricate himself from his fan club and says goodbye to the children.

'Thanks for coming in.'

'My pleasure. Are you coming over for tea later, or have you got other plans?' I can't tell if this is an innocent question or if Rhona has told him about Tom.

The truth is, I don't know when I will be seeing Tom again. It's always him that contacts me, not the other way around. I don't want to seem too needy or desperate to see him. My only plans for tonight involve a ready meal and watching crap telly, but I don't want Rhona and Rob to know that. If they want to think I have a night of passion ahead with my lover, I'm not going to disillusion them.

Chapter 6

The week passes with no more messages and I convince myself that I over-reacted. Over the years I have learned to get used to these sudden jolts of memory, the little things that send you hurtling back into periods of time you would rather forget. This is no different from seeing someone on the street that looks a bit like Meg or hearing a track that was playing that night. Nostalgia's a bitch.

On Sunday, I go walking with Rhona. The Yorkshire Dales is usually packed with tourists but now that the holiday season is over, and the bad weather has set in, there are only walkers and mountain bikers using the car park at Malham. I manoeuvre my car into a parking space and we pull on our walking boots and waterproofs. It's forecast to rain later. At the other end of the carpark, a crowd of teenagers pile out of a minibus, reluctantly put away their mobile phones and set off along the popular route to the cove.

'Did you see Tom last night?' Rhona asks, as she double knots her brand new and high spec boots. Mine are knackered and starting to leak but they're as comfy as a pair of slippers.

'No, I guess he doesn't want Jack seeing me around too much and getting ideas.'

'Fair enough, I suppose.'

I disagree. I'm pretty sure Tom is using Jack as an excuse to take it slowly. Rebecca hurt him badly and I think he's afraid to commit to another relationship so soon. Her things are still all over his house; her expensive cosmetics cluttering up the bathroom cabinet, her designer clothes hanging in the wardrobe, preserved in dry cleaner's covers. Sometimes, when Tom is in the shower or downstairs making coffee, I open the wardrobe and look at her dresses. They reflect the taste of an older woman with plunging necklines and beaded detail. They vary in size from an eight to a fourteen but it's confusing because some of them are from America and sizes are different there. Her shoes are a size six and impossibly high. I tried a pair on once and it was like being a child again, playing dress up in my mother's heels.

There's a picture of Rebecca in Jack's room. In the photograph, Jack is still a baby with chubby arms and the slightest hint of ginger hair. Their faces are pressed together, Rebecca's long dark hair tumbling over her shoulder, and she is dressed casually in a pair of jeans and a Breton t-shirt. Even without make-up, Rebecca looks glamorous. I know Tom only keeps it there for Jack's sake – he has removed all the other pictures of her from the house – but it still feels like a place marker, a warning that she could come back at any time and reclaim her family. I want to smash that picture into little pieces.

'I just wish we could spend more time together, be a proper couple,' I say. 'I only get to see him at lunchtimes. He doesn't want me there on an evening in case Jack sees me.'

'Well, it is still early days. You've only been seeing each other for a couple of months.'

We lock the car and walk up the path towards Malham Cove. The footpath is wet and slippery from overnight rain and grey clouds gather overhead, obscuring the view. Ahead of us, the teenaged walkers in brightly coloured anoraks climb the steep path like a row of tiny ants heading into the clouds.

'I know, but I don't see why we can't hook up after Jack has gone to bed. I could leave before he wakes up.'

'He might be a bit confused if he gets up in the night and sees his teacher in bed with his dad!'

'I suppose. Tom says he does sometimes climb into his bed in the middle of the night.'

'Poor kid, it must be hard for him. He'll be missing his mum.'

I know she's right. It must be so confusing for Jack and I don't blame Tom for putting him first. I just wish I didn't have to keep treading on eggshells around the subject of Rebecca. Everyone acts like she was some sort of saint or something. She left him, not the other way around.

'I know, I'll try to be patient.'

It's thanks to Rhona that I met Tom. He's a black belt second Dan in ju-jitsu and was teaching self-defence classes in the village hall over the summer. Rhona, in another aborted attempt to get fit, had persuaded me to give it a try. The class was almost entirely composed of middle-aged women, immaculately made-up and dressed in Lycra. As soon as Tom walked in, they flocked to him, helping him to set up the mats, paying their subscriptions and flicking their hair flirtatiously. Even in his white gi that looked like a pair of pyjamas, you could tell his body was ripped.

'He's a bit of alright, isn't he?' Rhona whispered. 'I wouldn't kick him out of bed.'

I tried to focus as Tom took us through some basic strikes and releases but there was something about his smile, his confidence and those crinkly eyes that made my heart pound. I felt an instant connection. Even though we were in a dusty hall full of people, it felt like there were only two of us in the room. His physical proximity as he straightened my arm or moved my leg into a different position was like a delicious form of torture. I was glad when the session finished, and I could cool down.

Most of the class headed to the Black Swan afterwards to ruin our hard work with a few drinks. I didn't think Tom would notice me, surrounded by all these gorgeous women, but he kept catching my eye and smiling. As we were leaving, he asked for my number.

I had been single for a while before I met Tom. I had

had a few short-term relationships since moving to Yorkshire but they never amounted to anything. Men my age just didn't seem interested in settling down and I wasn't prepared to be casually thrown aside when they'd had their fill of me. They told me I was too clingy; one had even described me as a 'bunny boiler' when I challenged him about the amount of time that he was spending with his ex. I had tried internet dating, but it was full of morons that were only interested in one thing. I was holding out for the full package: a man who would treat me right, who was in it for the long haul, who wouldn't cheat on me as soon as my back was turned. Tom was sweet and kind and the chemistry between us was undeniable. Even though he was a lot older than me and carried a lot of 'baggage' (as my sister would say), I really liked him.

I didn't tell Rhona at first. I knew she would warn me off. She would have said it was too soon, that he was on the rebound. Tom's ex-wife Rebecca had walked out on him a few months before and gone back to her native New York. When I did tell her that we had started seeing each other, over one too many glasses of wine, she promised not to tell a soul. I didn't want people judging him for moving on.

'Has Rebecca been back in touch since she left?'

'I don't think so. Tom doesn't like to talk about it. I know she didn't send a present for Jack's birthday because it really upset him.'

'I don't know how anyone can walk out on their kid

like that. She must have had some sort of breakdown.'

'Maybe.' I try not to be annoyed by Rhona's comment. Why does everyone feel the need to find excuses for Rebecca? People are always speculating about what drove her to it, whether Tom was to blame, but I don't listen to village gossip. Tom will tell me the full story when he's ready.

Rhona tactfully changes the subject and starts talking about Parents' Evening which Trevor has organised for next week, and how she's going to break it to Oliver's parents that he's a monster.

'I mean they must already know, right?' she says, more to herself than to me. 'No-one can be that deluded.'

I concentrate on the path ahead of me, occasionally stopping to take in the scenery and a swig from my water bottle. In defiance of the forecast, it has remained dry, the sunshine breaking through the clouds in shafts of warm gold. The route is an easy one with spectacular views from the top of the cove. We find a grassy spot next to the vast limestone pavement to take off our rucksacks and eat our sandwiches, breathing in the cold air and looking down at the village and tiny houses. From here, the world and all its problems seem to lose their significance. I wish I could stay up here forever and not have to worry about blasts from the past and competing with ex-wives.

We begin our descent, treading carefully on the lime-stone steps which feel as slippery as marble underfoot, and saying hello to the occasional walker passing by. When we get back to the village, we head straight to the Black Swan for a well-deserved drink. I strip off my jacket and hat and get warm by the blazing fire while Rhona goes to the bar and orders large glasses of Malbec. My cheeks are probably bright red, and my hair is damp with sweat, but I feel happy and invigorated by the exercise and fresh air.

I root through my bag to retrieve my mobile phone and my heart jolts as I see there is another message, this time on WhatsApp. I don't recognise the number. I think about deleting it unopened, but curiosity gets the better of me. With trembling fingers, I open it. Once again, it's a picture message but this time I know for sure that it hasn't been taken from my social media accounts.

I don't need to look at this picture again to remember it; every single detail is etched in my memory. The white sandy beach, the moonlight reflected on the water, the sky lit up by lasers and the couple locked in an embrace. To an outsider, it might look like a photograph in a travel magazine, advertising romantic getaways. The two people are in shadow and their faces are turned away from the camera. You would have to know them as well as I do to recognise them. Their bodies are entwined, his lips pressed against hers.

Memories I had consigned to the back of my mind flood back: the sound of dance music pumping from the large speakers, the waves crashing against the shore, the smell of grilled chicken drifting from the food stalls, the feel of the warm, sultry air on my bare shoulders. My heart is beating so fast I can feel the blood pulsing through my veins. I feel light-headed and I wonder if I'm going to faint. I take deep breaths, trying to calm myself before Rhona comes back to the table.

She is walking over now, carrying two glasses brim full of red wine. I quickly drop the phone in my rucksack as she puts the drinks down.

'Hey, are you OK? You're as white as a sheet.'

I fake a smile. 'I'm fine, just a little cold.' I take a big gulp of wine, which hits the spot and calms my nerves.

I wait a few minutes and then make an excuse to go to the loo. In the privacy of the toilet cubicle, I take out the phone and look at the message again before deleting it. I will have to change my number. The first picture may have been a mistake, an unlucky coincidence, someone from my past just wanting to get in touch, but there's no misunderstanding here.

This picture could destroy me.

Chapter 7

He sifts through their lives like a prospector panning for gold, not even sure what he's looking for. A private message perhaps, an email.

He must have flipped past that image a hundred times without appreciating its significance. It looks so ordinary: just a boy and a girl kissing in the moonlight. It was only when he took a closer look at the time stamp that he realised what he had uncovered.

He could have taken it straight to the police, but there would have been questions about how he obtained it. He would have to admit to hacking into their accounts. It might not even stand up in court. Besides, he's trusted the police before, and they let him down.

No, he's on his own now. It's down to him to expose their lies.

He cannot sleep, he cannot work, he cannot eat. His mind is full of shadows. A simmering rage circulates around his body, threatening to erupt at any point. His desire for answers feels like an insatiable thirst.

Holly haunts his dreams. She doesn't deserve to be happy, to find love, to have a future. How can she get up in the morning knowing what she's done? How can she clean her teeth, brush her hair, go to work, as if nothing has happened? How can she live with herself?

He can't.

All the pain they inflicted to save themselves. All those years wasted, believing their lies. What could possibly compensate for that? An eye for an eye? A life for a life?

He is not unreasonable. He will give her a chance. If she admits what she's done, he will let her live. All he wants is the truth.

Chapter 8

Eight years ago

'You do know I'm afraid of heights, right? I mean, really afraid of heights.'

'You'll be fine,' I said, signing my name on the sheet and pushing it towards Meg. 'Just trust me.'

'I do, you know I do.'

Meg and I had become the best of friends during our first term at uni. On the surface, we had nothing in common. Meg was self-confident, opinionated and not afraid to rock the boat. I was more conservative, happy to stay in the background, avoid confrontation. But she was funny and caring and I knew I could trust her with my darkest secrets.

I had told her how I felt about being adopted, and the day I had tracked down my birth mother. I hadn't even told my sister Lisa about that. I was sixteen and had been rowing with my parents about something stupid. I can't even remember what it was now. Mum and Dad had always

45

been upfront with me about my adoption, had promised to help me connect with my birth mother when the time was right, but I went behind their backs and traced her to Liverpool. I don't know what I was expecting. A tearful reunion? That she would fall to her knees and beg my forgiveness? But the woman who opened the door was a stranger; a middle-class, middle-aged stranger with a family of her own who didn't want to be reminded of her past. She made it abundantly clear that I should never turn up at her house again.

In turn, Meg told me about her dad who had died fighting in Afghanistan three years before. His death had knocked her for six, and she had nearly failed her GCSEs as a result, but her mum had pushed her to keep at her studies and make him proud. Her most prized possession was a charm bracelet he had given her on her twelfth birthday. She wore it all the time and would tell me the story behind each charm when she was drunk and maudlin.

She had persuaded me to leave my comfort zone so many times during our first three months at university that it was only fair that she got a taste of her own medicine. I had seen the skydive advertised on Facebook. I had never done anything adventurous before and I thought it was about time I started. I didn't want to leave university having only ever studied and gone to the odd fancy dress party.

To say Meg wasn't keen was the understatement of the century.

We were standing in the foyer, surrounded by students dressed in pink and giving out ribbons and balloons. I scrabbled in my pocket for some loose change to throw in a collection bucket that had been thrust in my face and returned my attention to Meg. She was staring at the disclaimer form as if I had just pressganged her into a space mission.

'Come on, Meg. It's for charity.'

'Can't I just give them my kidney or something?'

The third year organising the Jump for Cancer fund-raiser hid a smirk. He was really fit; I wondered if he had a girlfriend. I smiled at him as Meg hesitated.

'We'll be together the whole time,' I reassured her. 'Just think how proud you'll be afterwards.'

'If I live to tell the tale.'

'It's really safe,' the third year intervened. 'I've done it three times already.'

'You must be very brave,' I said coyly.

He shrugged. 'It's just good fun.'

Meg didn't look convinced but she reluctantly took my pen and filled out her details. I knew she would capitulate eventually; she just needed a bit of persuading.

'I don't see George and Kristóf signing up,' she grumbled.

'Well you know what Kristóf is like, charity begins at home, and George has plans for that weekend.'

'Hmph, very convenient.' She linked arms with me. 'Come on, you owe me a pint for that.'

We made our way to the Student Union where we found

Kristóf and George playing pool and arguing about politics, again. The four of us had become inseparable during our first term. We lived in each other's rooms, sharing stories, laughing at videos on YouTube, debating the meaning of life, and drinking far too much. Kristóf and I spent a lot of time together anyway because we were on the same course and Meg and I could always find something to talk about at the end of the day. George was so relaxed and friendly that you couldn't help but warm to him. He could charm his way in or out of any situation.

I found my shyness dissipating the more I hung around them. They were all so confident and didn't seem to care what anyone thought of them. George loved to be the centre of attention and Meg never said no to a party. Kristóf was more reserved and carried an air of intellectual superiority about him which could have been off-putting if it wasn't so well deserved. We didn't really have room in our social cluster for anyone else, although George had a string of girlfriends that he was always introducing us to. They became pretty interchangeable after a while.

Kristóf potted the black and finished the game as we joined them.

'Another round, mate?' George asked, indicating towards Kristóf's empty glass. We knew he would be paying for them all night. Kristóf never bought his own drinks.

'Cheers. So, have you two signed your lives away then?'

'There's still time to back out,' Meg said ominously.

'Don't you dare! Anyway, we have fundraising to do.

They're relying on us now. Are you going to sponsor us, Kristóf?'

He looked flustered and muttered something about being skint. I dropped the subject. Apart from George, none of us had any money. I was living off my student loan and what my parents gave me; and Meg had a part-time job in one of the bars in town. I only hoped going to university was going to be worth the ridiculous level of debt I would accumulate by the end of three years.

'You mean we have to pay them to do this?' Meg said incredulously, picking up the leaflet again and scrutinising the small print.

'That is kind of the point.'

'Well, rather you than me,' Kristóf said. 'I hope you've got insurance.'

'It's all perfectly safe. They do these jumps all the time.'

Meg rolled her eyes and changed the subject. 'So, what did you get up to at Christmas? You didn't really fill us in.'

'Not much. Caught up on my reading.'

I didn't want to tell Meg the truth in front of Kristóf. Going back home after my first term at university had been as awkward as hell. Everything seemed small and parochial compared to my life in Leeds. I had met my former school friends in town on Christmas Eve and swapped tales of drunken escapades over glasses of rosé, but their stories didn't mean very much when you didn't know the people involved. I found my old friends fickle and self-involved, overly concerned with their appearance and how many followers they had on social media. I didn't feel like they understood the new me.

Nothing had changed at home. My sister had a starring role in the local pantomime and was out most of the time rehearsing. She had fallen in love with one of the cast members who Dad thought was a bad influence. Mum and I kept out of the way as Dad tried to convince her to concentrate on her schoolwork and worry about boys when she was older. They argued about it constantly. I spent most of the time in my room reading and counting down the days until I went back to uni.

'What about you, Kristóf? Any hidden girlfriends in the Isle of Wight we should know about?'

Kristóf flushed bright red. We had never seen him with a girl. George thought he might be gay and Meg had speculated he was asexual, but I just thought he was shy around women. He could learn a lot from George, who was, true to form, now flirting with the woman behind the bar. He had seemed genuinely upset about missing the skydive and part of me hoped that he would cancel his plans. It would have been great to have him by our side.

In the weeks leading up to the skydive, Meg prayed for bad weather, hoping that it would be called off, but the day dawned sunny and bright. We piled into the minibus and said hello to the other students who had signed up.

'I honestly don't think I can do this, Holly,' she whispered, as the minibus pulled out of the city centre and into the countryside. 'What if I pass out?'

'You won't.'

She bit her lip and looked out of the window. It was a surprise to see Meg like this. She was usually the brave one, the one who never said no to a challenge. I guess her fear of heights was stronger than I thought. She looked like she was going to be sick and we hadn't even got to the airfield yet.

The day started with a long and boring safety talk. Meg was listening intently, particularly when the instructor took us through all the potential risks. I could see her hands shaking as he demonstrated the right position to be in when we left the aircraft. He showed us the different toggles on the suit, and what they did, even though we were jumping in tandem and would be safely strapped to an instructor.

'Just lay back and think of England,' one of the women joked.

Meg didn't look amused and I felt guilty that I had dragged her into this. I had been so excited about the skydive I hadn't realised how genuinely frightened she was. It was a testament to our friendship that she was willing to go through with it.

We were given hugely unflattering red boiler suits to wear which stank of sweat and God knows what else. As the plane took off, I felt a jolt of uncertainty. Up to this point, I had been so concerned about how Meg was feeling,

I hadn't allowed myself to be scared, but for a second I thought about what we were about to do and what might happen if it went wrong.

I considered chickening out, but Meg would have killed me.

The instructors were joking about it being their first time as the plane slowly ascended through the clouds to the clear blue sky above. As the plane levelled, we were given a three-minute warning and they opened the sliding door. There is nothing more unnatural than being in an airplane, 13,000 feet above the ground, with an open doorway. The ground looked very far away and the buildings and cars below looked like children's toys. The noise of the wind buffeting against the aircraft was deafening. I reached over and squeezed Meg's hand.

'You can do this,' I whispered. 'It's going to be fine.'

She nodded. I watched my best friend and her instructor edge their way to the door and receive some last-minute instructions. She looked back at me, terrified, and the next second she was gone. A tiny red speck swallowed by white cloud.

It was my turn.

We manoeuvred ourselves to the doorway and I stared into the abyss. There was no turning back now. My mind was totally blank; I couldn't remember anything they had told me during the safety talk.

Suddenly we tipped forwards and I was plummeting. We were falling so fast I couldn't even scream. The instructor held my head back as the cold wind stung my cheeks. In the absence of anything to hold on to, I clenched my hands into tight fists.

The freefall only lasted around thirty seconds, but it felt like a lifetime.

I had left my stomach somewhere on the plane and I could barely breathe as I saw the instructor reach to his chest and tug at the parachute. I closed my eyes and prayed it would work. Then suddenly we were jolted upwards and above us I could see the heavenly sight of the rainbow canopy inflating above me.

'Whoah!'

The instructor said something in reply but his words were lost to the wind. I could feel my heart return to a normal rhythm and the adrenaline slowly wear off as we floated gently towards the ground. I could see the fields below like a patchwork quilt and the tiny outline of the skydive centre. Everything looked so beautiful. I could see Meg in the distance preparing for landing.

It wasn't long before we were doing the same. I changed my position and braced myself for the impact but my instructor was a pro and landed us with relative grace.

'Enjoy that?' he said as he unfastened me from his suit.

'It was incredible!'

As soon as I reached the others on the airfield I was engulfed in a hug. 'Oh, my God, that was amazing!' Meg's eyes were lit up and there was a huge beam on her face. 'I want to do it again!'

'See, you should listen to me more often.'

'Holly, I am always going to listen to you in future. You are my guru.' She gave a mock bow and we made our way back to the centre. 'I honestly thought I was going to wet myself when we were in the plane though.'

'Don't tell the others, but I may well have done.'

Chapter 9

During the day, I can distract myself by work, but every night this week I have been woken up by nightmares, my heart racing and my back swathed in sweat. My brain is like a newsfeed serving up a continuous stream of stories from my past. Lying in bed, in the early hours of the morning, I try every technique I can think of to get back to sleep. Deep breathing, visualisation, meditation, but nothing works.

I can't stop thinking about the message and what it means. How did someone get hold of that picture? I'm the only person who knows that image ever existed. I got rid of it years ago and I made damned sure there weren't any copies. What do they want from me?

I need to pull myself together. Whoever sent this message wants to scare me and I don't intend to let them. They can't know what happened that night. If they did, they would have gone to the police a long time ago. I will just have to wait for their next move. In the meantime, I have a life to live. I refuse to be dragged down by my past.

It's Parents' Evening tonight which is like speed dating with piranhas. Trevor insists that we hold it before half term, even though it's still too early in the academic year to form an opinion about how the children are handling starting school. They change so much in the first few months: the shy ones grow in confidence; the bolshie ones settle down. Each parent has ten minutes with me and in that time, I am expected to deliver a thorough assessment of their child's needs. It's a system designed to frustrate everyone concerned. Every parent is convinced their child has special qualities that I am yet to discover. Most of the parents are older than me and regard me with great suspicion, clearly doubting that I have the experience or qualifications to look after their little darlings. Sometimes I think they're right.

Still, I'm looking forward to seeing Tom tonight. I haven't seen him all week and I'm missing him like crazy. He's been busy with a project at work and I have been struggling to get away from school without my absence being noted. We're not exactly prohibited from leaving the building, but most of the teachers stay in at lunchtime, catching up on paperwork or reluctantly supervising the kids. It's not easy to get away without people commenting. I wish they would mind their own business. If only there were a fast-forward button that I could press to take our relationship to the next level or Tom would sit down with Jack and tell him about us. At least then I could go over there in the evenings. All I want is for us to be a proper couple, a family. I'm fed up of sneaking around like we've got something to hide.

I go home after work to quickly change my clothes and by the time I get back to the school, the parents have already started arriving. I pass Rhona's classroom and I can see through the window that she is in the middle of what looks like an intense discussion with Oliver's parents. I wonder whether she is managing to keep her temper. I give her a quick wave and walk to my classroom where a line of parents has already gathered in the corridor.

'I'm so sorry to keep you waiting,' I say, sounding like a doctor's receptionist as I unlock the door and usher the first set of parents in. Phoebe's mother is cold and frosty as she settles herself down on the small chair in front of me. I pull out my folder and outline that while her daughter may be academically gifted, she doesn't pay attention in class.

'I think she finds the work you give her boring. A girl of her abilities should be challenged.' Her husband fiddles with his watch and doesn't say a word.

'I don't disagree, Mrs Abbott, and we will be starting her on some higher-level work next term,' I lie. Perhaps her mother is right? Maybe I should be challenging Phoebe more? I will need to discuss it with Trevor though. He doesn't like us deviating from the curriculum.

Mrs Abbott spends far longer than ten minutes telling me how to do my job so it's good in a way that the next parent fails to turn up. Emma Whitaker is a bit of an enigma. I see her occasionally when she comes to pick

Nathan up from school, but she stands at the end of the road, away from the other parents, and barely speaks to anyone. I wonder if she feels intimidated by the 'yummy mummies' that dominate the village. She has never even thanked me for saving her daughter's life. I don't want her gratitude, but I do wish she had made the effort to come tonight. I have been worried about Nathan recently. He comes to school sleepy and doesn't concentrate in class. I want to get to the bottom of why he's slipping behind. I'd like to bring the educational psychologist in to run some tests, but I wanted to discuss it with her first. I mark her absence on my list.

Pretty soon it's Tom's turn and I can feel a fluttering in my tummy as he walks in and closes the door behind him. I have to hide the huge smile I can feel forming on my face.

'Good evening, Miss Metcalfe,' he says in a stupid voice, pretending to be one of the kids.

'Good evening,' I roll my eyes at him, as he pulls the chair up close, our knees nearly touching. I talk about Jack's progress this term, as I would with any other parent, but of course Tom already knows all this. His hands are resting on his knees and are tantalisingly close to the hem of my skirt. I move my legs away.

'Stop looking at me like that,' I whisper, looking over to the door. Trevor is patrolling the corridors.

'Yes, miss.' He gives me a wicked grin and I can tell he is probably imagining us sneaking off to a broom cupboard somewhere. I feel myself getting flustered and my discomfort get even worse when Trevor decides to walk in and observe our interaction. I find Trevor intimidating. He is one of the youngest heads in the country and a rising star of the teaching profession. He loves statistics and league tables and likes his staff to compete against each other. He gives pep talks in meetings about raising our game and aspires to get our tiny school an 'Outstanding' Ofsted. Rhona calls him the 'young pretender' and says he won't be here for long; but he's the only boss I have ever had, so I don't have any one to compare him to.

I have to hope Trevor doesn't pick up on the sexual tension between me and Tom, although it must be glaringly obvious. Fortunately, Tom knows better than to misbehave in front of my boss. I drink a glass of water quickly to try to cool down as Tom departs and Trevor continues to make notes in his folder.

'I see that Mrs Whitaker didn't turn up for her appointment,' he says, looking at my attendance sheet.

'Yes, I was planning to give her a ring tomorrow. See if she can come in another time.'

'You know the family's circumstances, I presume?'

'Yes, of course.' There's no-one in the village that doesn't know about Nathan's father.

'Well, follow the procedures and I'm sure it will be fine.'

I hide a smile. Rhona does a fantastic impression of Trevor telling us all to 'follow the procedures'.

My phone beeps with a notification and I blush as I

reach into my bag and make a big show of turning it onto silent. Trevor shoots me a warning look before leaving the classroom. As soon as he has gone, I take the opportunity to check the message. It's from Tom.

'Coming over later?'

Inviting me over while Jack is in the house is a big step for Tom. I am about to reply when the next parent takes a seat in front of me. I try to remember whether it is her child who is still not properly toilet trained. I make a half-hearted attempt at giving my report, getting the child's name wrong twice, and the parent leaves, shaking her head in disgust.

As soon as I get a chance, I sneak off to the loo and text Tom back, spelling out what I plan to do to him later. It feels like an eternity until it finally reaches half past seven and the last parents leave the building. I walk out of the school with Rhona.

'Phew! I need a drink after that,' she says, pulling me in the direction of the pub.

'I can't tonight, sorry. Tom's invited me round.'

She raises an eyebrow and then breaks out into a laugh. 'That's progress.'

'Hmm, took him long enough.'

'Well, have fun. Don't do anything I wouldn't do!'

'Have a good evening, ladies.' My skin crawls as Trevor walks past us. He must have overheard our conversation and I can only hope that he doesn't know who we are talking about.

'Oh shit, do you think he heard us?' I ask Rhona as soon as he is out of earshot.

'Don't worry. Probably not, and even if he did, he won't know who Tom is. There are loads of Toms. He might think you're talking about Tom Fletcher.' Tom Fletcher is the school caretaker and about seventy. I pull a face.

'Gee thanks.'

'Well, I'm going to catch up with the others. Seriously, have a nice time. And I want all the details tomorrow morning!'

I walk quickly towards Tom's house. It's a beautiful night, the sky is full of stars and a thin crescent moon casts its light over the river. A dog walker emerges from the stone steps and bids me a good evening as I walk across the bridge. Tom's estate is quiet, doors locked, and curtains closed. The sound of broken glass breaks the silence as a woman throws an empty wine bottle into her recycling bin. Everything is peaceful and reassuringly suburban.

Tom opens the door before I can ring the bell.

'Shh!' he says, pulling me into the hallway and kissing me. 'I've only just got Jack to sleep, it took him ages to settle.'

I giggle. 'I couldn't wait.'

'God, me neither. You looked so hot in that classroom, all prim and proper.'

I look up and see a little face peering at me through the banister. Jack looks sleepy and bewildered, which is hardly surprising. It's confusing enough for children his age to see their teachers out of school, let alone standing in their hallway, kissing their father.

'Daddy!'

Tom turns and pushes me into the shadows. He looks horrified and I wonder if he realises that Jack has already seen us.

'I can't sleep,' Jack whines. 'Will you read me a story?'

Tom rolls his eyes and looks torn but, with a resigned smile, turns his attention upstairs. 'You get back into bed and I'll be up in a couple of minutes.'

'Promise?'

'I promise.'

Jack goes back to his room, trailing behind him a blue blanket that looks well chewed.

Tom runs his fingers through his hair as I readjust my clothes. 'Sorry.'

'It's OK. Do you want me to wait? Come back later?'

'He's going to be up and down all night, I think. Maybe another time?'

'Of course.' I try not to sound too disappointed.

He kisses the tip of my nose. 'I'll tell him. Soon. I promise. No more sneaking around.'

I make my way home, past the school and towards the inviting lights of the village. I hesitate outside the pub, debating whether to join Rhona and the other teachers, but it would be too humiliating. Rhona would know I'd been rejected, again, and it's hard enough without her pity. I turn my back on the laughter and warmth spilling out of the inn and take the tiny side street towards my cottage. It is pitch black and a bit spooky. A cat runs across my path, making me jump. It halts in the middle of the path, staring at me, before sneaking back into the shadows. I look behind me to check I'm alone – I think those messages have creeped me out a bit – and I am relieved when I reach the front door of my cottage.

It's still early but I can't be bothered to light a fire. I snuggle under some blankets on the sofa instead and think about ringing my sister but I'm not in the mood to hear about her exciting life in London. I really don't understand Tom's problem. Jack seems to like me as his teacher; I'm sure he would accept me as his dad's new girlfriend. Why does everything have to be so complicated?

Chapter 10

I was planning to go down to London at half term to visit my sister, but she hasn't replied to any of my messages. Lisa has recently joined the regular cast of a popular TV drama and has become something of a celebrity. The money is obscene, but the hours are long. It's weird seeing my little sister on the cover of magazines in the supermarket. In some of the photographs, she is barely recognisable from the girl I grew up with. She's naturally beautiful anyway but by the time they have finished styling her, making her up and then Photoshopping out any flaws, she looks picture perfect.

Since she moved down to London to pursue her acting career, her life has become a whirlwind of parties and long days on set. Our relationship has been reduced to a series of social media posts, one-line messages and broken promises to catch up soon. It took her a while to get a serious part and she has done her fair share of thankless auditions, non-speaking parts and naff commercials. With her blonde hair and pale skin, she used to get typecast by directors, but it sounds as if her days of playing beautiful corpses on daytime TV may be over.

She updated her Facebook status last night with a selfie taken with some celebrity on the red carpet. My sister looks thin and elegant, pouting into the camera to show off her cheekbones. I don't recognise the celebrity at all; he's probably from one of those reality shows that catapults ordinary people into fame for five minutes. I'm a little bit cross that she can find the time to post a selfie but not message her sister, but I guess that's the life of a TV star.

I had been looking forward to going to London, shopping in Oxford Street and maybe catching a show but, as I haven't heard back from her, I decide to go to the coast to visit my parents instead. I was hoping Tom would come with me, so he could finally meet them, but he fobbed me off, saying he had a big project on at work. His parents have agreed to look after Jack over the holidays and are coming up to collect him. He didn't offer to introduce us. I worry that he's not really serious about our relationship; that this is just a bit of fun for him.

Mum and Dad have lived in Morecambe since the 80s. The ebb and flow of the estuary, its tea shops and guest houses, coach parties and comedians, formed the backdrop of my adolescence. My memories of growing up are full of moody walks in the early morning, picking up shells and watching the sun rise over the horizon, turning the sea golden; the sound of gulls crying overhead; the dangerous tides and the treacherous quick sand; spending my pocket money trying to win cheap toys in the amusement arcades and huddling in bus shelters with my friends to escape the lashing rain that whips across the promenade. The Yorkshire Dales is lovely, but I miss the sea. Morecambe will always feel like home.

My parents still live in the same house that we grew up in. It's on the outskirts of the town with a spectacular view of the bay. My sister and I would spend ages at the shore, making up stories about pirates and smugglers, then writing up our adventures in little notebooks like the Brontë sisters did. I don't know where those books are now, probably buried in a box in the attic somewhere. Lisa and I always got on as children. I know some sisters that fought over everything, competing for their parents' love and attention, but we always had each other's back. We're not biological sisters – I was adopted when I was a baby and Lisa came along three years later – but it's never made a difference. Mum and Dad have always made it clear that they love us the same. It's hard not to be jealous of Lisa sometimes though; she's naturally pretty and attracts attention wherever she goes. I've got used to feeling like the Ugly Duckling in comparison.

As I pull up to the house, my parents' chocolate Labrador runs up to greet me. I get out of the car and pat him on the head as he jumps up, splashing mud across my skinny jeans. I'm not overly keen on dogs but I pretend to like him for my parents' sake. There's a big stack of leaves in the corner of the tidy garden and a rake rests by the wall.

It's a nice crisp Autumnal day so I don't know why Dad isn't outside making the most of it. He's usually a permanent feature in the garden. A thin trail of grey smoke rises from the chimney.

I make my way around to the back of the house, shouting 'hello' as I push open the backdoor and walk into the kitchen. The scent of baked apple and cinnamon hits me and makes my stomach growl. I never bake at home; it seems pointless when you live alone, but my mum is a fantastic cook. She is crouched over the oven, peering at a golden-brown pie, and I make her jump when I walk through the door.

'Holly, sweetheart!' She seems so pleased to see me and I feel a pang of guilt that I don't come home more often. She gives me a big hug, leaving floury handprints on my cashmere jumper. I don't know why I bothered putting on my best clothes. She has cut her hair since I last saw her, and the new short, spiky style suits her.

'Hi Mum.'

I dump my bags at the door. I can hear Dad chatting to someone in the living room.

'Have you got visitors?'

'Go and have a look.' Mum's eyes twinkle with excitement and I wonder what she's hiding.

I make my way into the living room and am almost knocked over as my sister launches herself at me.

'Hey Hol, Mum said you were coming home for a few days, so I thought I'd surprise you.'

My sister looks perfect as usual. She's dressed in skinny

jeans and a jumper like me, but they fit her better. I recognise her perfume as a brand I would love to be able to afford and a Mulberry handbag has been slung carelessly on the end of the sofa. Even with no make-up and her hair scraped back in a ponytail, she outshines me.

Dad is sitting in the seat closest to the wood burning stove. He looks older and thinner than before and I wonder if there is something wrong that he's not telling us. I worry myself sick about my parents dying. I don't know how I would cope without them. They have always been there for me through thick and thin. Life without them would be unbearable.

'Both my gals, home for the weekend,' he says. 'It's like old times.'

It is like old times. We fall back into familiar patterns, sitting in the same seats at the table, arguing over who gets the last parsnip. Over dinner, Lisa tells us about the latest development in her career: a new storyline featuring one of the soap's biggest stars. She's banned Dad from watching it for the next few weeks as there are some steamy scenes coming up.

'Is he as hot in real life?' I ask.

'Hotter,' she says, helping herself to a second slice of Mum's apple pie. I don't know how she manages to retain her figure. 'But he's got a boyfriend. He says kissing me is like having to snog his grandma.'

'Charming.'

'So, we won't be seeing you both on the front of *OK Magazine*?'

'Ha! You never know. There's always plenty of speculation about my love life. Do you know some reporter had the cheek to ask me if I had a baby bump last week? Honestly, I was on my period! I was just a bit bloated!'

'And have you met anyone down there yet?' Mum asks, trying and failing to be subtle.

Lisa laughs. 'Well, there is someone I've been seeing ... but it's early days. I don't want to jinx it. That's all I'm going to say.'

'You girls and your secrets. We've not met your sister's boyfriend yet either. I'm beginning to think you've made him up, Holly.'

Mum's words cut like a blade. Typical. No-one ever suspects Lisa of making boyfriends up, but I couldn't possibly have managed to find anyone to love me.

'I've told you, he's busy this week.' My words came out harder and more brittle than I intended but I can't take them back. The tension hangs in the air as Lisa flashes me a warning look.

'All I'm saying is that you need to be careful going out with a married man.'

'Mum ...' Lisa tries to defuse the situation, but it doesn't work.

'They've split up. She lives in America now. It's not like I'm his mistress or something.'

'Yes, but they're not divorced yet and there's a child to think about.'

'We do think about him. All the time. You don't understand.' I sound churlish and sulky, like a teenager. Mum always seems to bring out this side of me.

'Well, maybe you could bring him next time you come, and we can actually meet him. And his son. They'd be very welcome,' Mum says stiffly.

'Yes, I'd like to meet this chap,' Dad adds. 'See if he's good enough for my princess.'

'Dad ... I'm not a little girl.'

Lisa smiles at me over the table. 'He sounds great and I'm sure he's much better off with you than his bitch of an ex-wife.'

Mum purses her lips and clears the dessert plates. Lisa tries to change the subject and talk about Dad's cauliflowers, but I am still cross. We were having such a lovely time and I've ruined it by being over-sensitive. I know they think Tom is too old for me, and that I don't know what I'm letting myself in for, but I do. Once they see us together, they will realise we are right for each other, that I'm ready to be a step mum, to commit myself to Tom and Jack.

Chapter 11

The tension diminishes over an evening game of Scrabble and by the time Mum and Dad go to bed, things are almost back to normal. Lisa pours us generous helpings of Dad's port and we settle down on the sofa to catch up properly. I find myself telling her all about Tom and my fears about his lack of commitment.

'It's like he's holding back all the time,' I say.

'Are you worried Rebecca's going to come back?'

'No, I don't think so. And he wouldn't let her just walk back into Jack's life anyway. Not after what she did. I suppose I feel a bit insecure. Everyone tells me to give it time, but all I want is for us to be a couple. There's nothing wrong with that, is there?'

'You need to tell him how you feel, sis.'

'But what if I push him too hard and he dumps me?'

'Then he isn't worth it. You should have more confidence in yourself, you're a catch. He's lucky to have you.'

I wish I had Lisa's faith. 'So, tell me about your new man. Is he famous?'

'No, he doesn't even work in the industry! He actually works in IT. He's called Alex and I met him online. It's really early days though, we've only been on a few dates. I don't think we're even exclusive yet, well, I'm not any way! But you know what Mum and Dad are like. They'll be talking about marriage and grandkids and that is so not where we are right now. We're keeping it casual, you know?'

I'd forgotten how nice it was to be around my sister again. When we're around Mum and Dad we seem to revert to our teenaged selves, but when we're alone, it's more like having a best friend. Lisa tells me all about her life in London; the good and the bad. Amid the glamour and the VIP parties, she tells me there's loads of pressure, particularly on the younger women in the cast, to keep in shape.

'I'm thinking of getting a personal trainer,' she says. 'Most of the other girls have them. One woman goes to the gym for four hours a day. I mean, God, can you imagine anything more tedious? Don't get me wrong, it's lovely that you get sent stuff to wear all the time but sometimes you want to bung on your jeans and a hoodie and go to Tesco like everyone else.'

Lisa confides that most of the cast regularly invest in Botox to look younger and there's a lucrative sideline in modelling and sponsorship deals if you have the right look.

'Which basically means blonde hair and big tits,' she laughs. 'I'm thinking of getting mine done actually.'

'Doesn't it bother you, people judging you all the time?'

'Oh God, you should see what they say about me on social media! I don't know, you can't let it get to you. Besides, *those that mind, don't matter …*'

'*… and those that matter, don't mind!*' I finish off the quotation for her. It is one of Dad's favourites.

She tells me that she is saving for a deposit on a flat in London but the house prices, particularly compared to the North, are horrendous so it's going to take her years.

'Then I might do something a bit different. Theatre perhaps.' I admire my little sister. She has so much drive and determination that I know she'll achieve anything she sets her mind to.

Lisa has to get back the next day, but I stay on for the rest of the week, helping Dad with the garden and catching up with my lesson plans. Dad convinces me to stay for Sunday lunch, which seems to go on forever, and then insists on packing me up with a box full of vegetables from the garden which delays me even longer. Mum wraps up some leftovers and tells me I need to look after myself a bit more.

'I'm sorry if I upset you, darling,' she says as she hugs me goodbye. 'I only want you to be happy.'

'I know Mum, and I am, honestly.' I promise to ring them next weekend. I know they both want what's best for me, but they have been overprotective ever since I came back from Thailand. It's like I'm a fragile piece of porcelain that they are terrified will shatter into pieces any second.

They have no idea how strong I had to be to pick myself up after what happened.

It's late afternoon and getting dark when I finally set off. By the time I turn off the busy A65 on to the smaller country roads that lead to the village, I need full beam to light up the way ahead. The road is lined by dry stone walls and full of sharp bends and narrow passing places. The rain, that has been a persistent drizzle all afternoon, turns heavy and hammers down on the windows, obscuring my vision. I drop my speed down to thirty.

I consider pulling over until the storm has passed but there is no telling how long that will be, and I really need to get back and prepare for school tomorrow. I'm not that far from home now. I switch on the radio to distract me from my rising anxiety as I make my way down the solitary country road. I sit upright in the seat, clenching the steering wheel tightly, willing the rain to ease. The windscreen wipers can barely cope with the incessant downpour and my car is sliding on the slippery surface of the road. Puddles are forming at the sides of the lane, threatening to meet in the middle, and once or twice my car aqua planes. I try to remember what I learned in my driving lessons; whether to steer into or out of a skid.

I glance down at the fuel gauge. The needle is pointing to empty and I curse myself for not filling it up before I set off. My dad is always telling me off for embarking on long drives without a full tank of petrol. I am miles away from the nearest service station. I turn up the radio and try to concentrate on the presenter's voice. I am about ten minutes away from home. Hopefully there will be enough petrol left to make it back. I don't fancy walking in this weather.

A rabbit dashes in front of my car and dives into the dark hedgerow, causing me to swerve. I slam on my brakes and come to an emergency stop, grateful that there is nothing behind me. Taking a deep breath, I release the brake and immediately stall. I turn the key with trepidation hoping the ignition doesn't fail. There is no mobile phone reception out here. If my car breaks down, I am completely stuck until it gets light or another car comes this way.

'Please, please, please ...' I pray as I turn the key. The engine splutters, the warning lights flash but the car eventually starts.

I set off again at a steady pace, calming my nerves by breathing deeply. Relief washes over me as I see the lights of another vehicle making its way along the road behind me. At least if something happens now, there will be someone to come to my rescue. The vehicle is approaching fast, and I can see through my mirror that it is a large vehicle, a Landrover perhaps, which is having no problem dealing with the weather conditions.

It catches up with me, driving close to my bumper, pressurising me to hurry up. I look at the driver in my mirror, but their face is in silhouette. I can tell from the profile that it is a man and I feel a surge of fear. Is this the person behind the messages I've been getting? Or am I being paranoid? Either way, I am out here, alone, with a man who is driving aggressively but making no attempt to pass me. If I pull over, will he stop or carry on? I daren't drive any faster in case I have an accident. I take a deep breath and with one hand scrabble in my handbag for my mobile phone. There is a single bar of reception, flickering on and off. Should I try to ring someone? But what could they do?

The car behind me flashes its lights as we approach a passing point by the side of the road. I take a deep breath and pull in, hoping he doesn't stop as well. I see him shaking his head at me as he drives past. I switch off the engine and try to control my breathing. The rain is easing off now and I can see the moon peeking from behind the dark clouds which are moving further down the valley. Suddenly, all the emotions I have been keeping suppressed all week get the better of me and I burst into tears.

The messages are making me feel paranoid. Someone out there knows what happened in Thailand, I'm sure of it. Otherwise, why would they send that picture? And how did they get hold of it in the first place? What do they want from me? And why now? I don't know what to do, I don't know who to trust. Perhaps I should have told Lisa, but then I would have to tell her the full story, and I made a promise I would never tell anyone what we did that night.

There are only two people I can speak to about this and I haven't been in touch with them for five years. It's not a friendship I am in a hurry to rekindle.

Chapter 12

From the bedroom window of the holiday cottage, he can see brooding hills cast in shadow against an indigo sky. Yorkshire looks nothing like the postcards. It is cold and dark and miserable. The wind seeps through the thick stone walls and it never seems to stop raining. The internet is patchy at best and he can only get mobile phone reception in certain parts of the house. It's like being cast back in time.

He misses London. He misses the frenetic activity, the anonymity of the Tube, the crowds of people from all over the globe pressed together in a constantly evolving eco-system. There is too much space in Yorkshire. It's eerie to look out of the window and see miles and miles of nothing. He has hired the cottage for a month. It should be long enough. Holly's not like the others; she's weaker, more compliant. She won't hold out on him for long. Not when she realises how far he will go to get the truth.

He returns to his laptop where he is reviewing the contents of Holly's inbox. Her email account wasn't difficult to hack. He sent her a phishing email several months ago asking her to confirm her password and the stupid bitch fell for it. Her messages are mostly advertising from various retailers. She has accounts on Boohoo.com, ASOS and PrettyLittleThing. She banks with Barclays. Yawn. There's not much personal stuff although she uses the same password for her social media accounts and that gives him access to her friends and family. Her cloud storage is a treasure trove of forgotten pictures, messages and documents. He has installed a tracking device on her car and attached a small camera to her front gate so that he can monitor her movements remotely. He needs to build up a picture of her life before he starts his campaign in earnest.

He rests his cheek against the cool plaster, feeling the thick stone that separates hunter and prey. He imagines her just a few feet away from him getting undressed, applying moisturiser, performing the daily rituals women undertake to make themselves more attractive. He imagines her slipping between the cool sheets, perhaps picking up a book to read before she goes to sleep, but more likely checking her mobile phone for those last traces of human contact before the internet falls silent. He wonders if she can feel his presence, if she knows how close he is to her.

Chapter 13

Seven years ago

We shared a house in the second year of university. The Victorian terrace in the middle of Headingley looked small from the outside, but inside it was huge with high ceilings and original cornices. Kristóf immediately claimed the attic room; he wanted to be a writer, so it suited him to pretend to be a starving artist living in the garret. Meg and I had bedrooms on the second floor and George's bedroom would normally have been used as a dining room. We played at being grown-ups, planning dinner parties that would make Mrs Dalloway proud and window shopping for posh furniture, but it was the first time any of us had taken responsibility for a house and we quickly discovered that none of us had a clue how to go about it.

Split between us, the rent was cheaper than halls, but we had to find money for things like electricity and a TV licence which caused loads of arguments. Bills were supposed to be shared four ways, but Kristóf was hopeless at budgeting and never seemed to have any money left at the end of the month. George was forever bailing him out. Meg juggled her studies with long hours at her bar job which made her tired and bad tempered. For the most part we got on fine but every so often there were explosive rows which usually ended with either Kristóf or Meg storming out and declaring the other impossible to live with.

George drove us all crazy. He was completely oblivious to the mess he left everywhere. He would eat a sandwich and spill crumbs on the carpet, leave half-drunk cups of tea all over the house and couldn't cook a meal without using every pot in the kitchen. He never washed up and always left plates piled in the sink until either Kristóf or I, fed up with the smell or not being able to find any crockery, gave in and washed up. George was a great cook though and made up for his slovenly behaviour with lavish feasts on Sunday evenings. The leftovers kept us going all week.

No-one on my course could believe that I would choose to be flatmates with Kristóf. He could be quite sweet at home, but in seminars he came across as aloof and arrogant. I don't think anyone in our study group liked him. Sitting back in his chair, his legs outstretched, he second-guessed the tutor and patronised the other students. His arrogance was, unfortunately, well-placed. He quoted from Aristotle and Thucydides, shot people down with ease and entangled people in protracted arguments that they couldn't possibly win. Kristóf loved to make other people look like fools. He thrived off our stupidity.

During the first semester we were studying Victorian literature and it was the module I'd been most looking forward to. Thackeray was on the list, along with Dickens and George Eliot but my absolute favourite writers were the Brontë sisters. Kristóf, of course, thought he was some sort of expert on them. He had studied *Wuthering Heights* for A-level and got a special commendation for his analysis of Heathcliff as a Marxist hero, but I thought, for once, I could give him a run for his money.

We were squashed onto one of the sofas in our tutor's office, which smelt of old books and illicit cigarettes. Outside, the wind was howling, and the sky was slate grey. Kristóf was holding court, lecturing us about the religious symbolism in *Jane Eyre* and the way it reinforced patriarchal ideals. He had been droning on for about ten minutes and most of us had switched off. Ignoring the feeling of anxiety that was rising from my stomach, I raised my hand and tentatively offered a counter-argument.

'But surely Brontë is using Bertha's insanity as a warning against the subjugation of women? And isn't Rochester's blindness a form of emasculation before balance can be restored?'

The room fell quiet. Kristóf looked at me as if I had committed murder. The tutor gave me an approving smile.

'Now, that is something we need to talk about further,'

he suggested. 'Why don't you two workshop those arguments and deliver a presentation next week?'

I could sense Kristóf glowering at me as I gathered my things quickly, leaving the room before he could berate me. If I had known that this would be the consequence, I would never have spoken up in class. I had landed us a shed load of work, on top of everything else we had to get through this week.

A low rumble of thunder sounded as I walked towards the library to get some books before heading home. Meg and George were holding a Hallowe'en party that night for George's birthday. They had been planning it since the start of term and had spent hours choosing the decorations and their outfits, what cocktails to make, what music to play. The party had been getting more elaborate by the day and they had invited loads of people. I had promised Meg I would get back early to prepare but I needed to make a head start if I was going to get this presentation done in time. It wasn't long before I heard footsteps behind me.

'Nice one.'

'Sorry, you know I didn't mean for that to happen.'

'Well, it might not be so bad if we split the reading. Shall we?' Kristóf held the library door open for me. Relieved that he didn't seem as cross as I thought he would be, I accepted his gesture. Meg would have no doubt told him she was perfectly capable of opening doors for herself, but I had no problem with gentlemanly behaviour.

Even by university standards, the Brotherton library was spectacular. Tall marble columns stretched up to a domed ceiling through which sunlight was streaming, bathing the wooden desks in honeyed light. The room smelt of furniture polish and dusty books. The silence was only broken by footsteps echoing across the cylindrical vault as students perused the specialist collections. The computers cataloguing the rare editions appeared anachronistic in these surroundings, more at home in the main library a few steps down the road. In this room, you lost all sense of time and place. I logged on to the online catalogue and typed in the key words for the books we needed.

Kristóf was surprisingly fun to work with. I had expected him to keep his best ideas to himself, but he contributed as much to my side of the debate as his own. We divided the theoretical texts between us, sketched out a broad outline of the issues we would cover, and what we would exclude from the discussion. Kristóf was completely focussed on the task in hand, which inspired me to work just as hard. It wasn't until I looked up at the clock and realised it was nearly seven that I had to put a stop to what had turned out to be an enjoyable afternoon.

'We need to get back for the Hallowe'en party.'

'Oh God,' Kristóf groaned. 'I'd forgotten about that.'

'How can you forget? They've been banging on about it all week.'

'I thought it might have been cancelled or something.

Can't you tell them I've got a headache? In fact, I think I can feel a migraine coming on just thinking about it.'

I rolled my eyes at him. 'I'm not telling them anything. You can ... if you dare.'

Kristóf hadn't shown the least bit of interest in the party. He had initially refused to dress up, which had really annoyed Meg, but had eventually conceded to wearing a Dracula t-shirt. It was only because he admired the book. I had considered dressing up as Miss Havisham, but I didn't think anyone would get it, so had settled for a sexy witch costume with purple and black stripy tights and a black corset. Meg said I looked like a slut but added that she meant it as a compliment.

'It's so clichéd of you to be a Charlotte Brontë fan,' Kristóf sniped as we walked to the bus stop. 'Champion of the underdog, isn't she? I suppose you're waiting for your Mr Rochester to turn up and rescue you, are you? Me, I prefer Emily Brontë. She refused to conform, to bow down to social expectations.'

I glared at him, trying to decide whether to even bother engaging in another argument, and concluded that it wasn't worth my time. Kristóf may see himself as a Romantic hero, on a higher intellectual plane than the rest of us, but he was a grumpy, condescending arse when he wanted to be. As soon as we got on the bus, he pulled out a book and ignored me all the way home.

It was a relief to get back to the house and the far less complicated companionship of my other friends. Meg greeted me at the door, removed the books from my arms and immediately led me to the kitchen where she and George had made up jelly vodka shots and a vat of lethal green cocktail.

'I need your opinion,' she said, handing me a paper cup, brim full. 'Too much booze or too little? What am I talking about? Can you have too much booze?'

Meg had managed to swing a discount from the bar where she worked so most of the spirits had come at cost price. George had bought a couple of cases of decent wine that would probably be wasted on most of our guests and I had chipped in for the party food and decorations. Kristóf hadn't contributed anything; another source of friction in the house. He disappeared upstairs as soon as we got home.

He didn't reappear until the party was in full swing. He spent most of the evening standing in the corner viewing the party guests with thinly veiled contempt and making no effort to talk to anyone. I wasn't going to let him spoil my evening. George had put together a Hallowe'en playlist and invited all the girls from his course, including a red head that he had fancied for ages. It didn't take long before she was following him into his bedroom.

A pang of jealousy shot through me like adrenaline. I necked my glass of vodka and coke and went into the kitchen for a refill. As I poured myself a drink, I was collared by one of the geeks from Meg's engineering class, who was obviously trying out some new chat up lines that he had found on the internet. I was so drunk, and they were so bad, that I took pity on him and flirted back. I noticed Kristóf standing by the back door, nursing a beer and watching us with a sneer on his face. In defiance, I grabbed hold of the geek and started to snog him. His breath tasted of pepperoni and garlic and I thought I was going to gag. He stuck his tongue down my throat and started to paw me like a pubescent teenager while a dark red colour crept up Kristóf's neck like a line of mercury. It reached his face and exploded.

He covered the room in a few strides and grabbed the guy's collar, yanking him away from me and nearly knocking him out on the open cupboard door.

'Oi, what's your problem?'

'She's drunk and you're taking advantage.' I had never seen Kristóf look so angry. He was like a modern-day Heathcliff towering over a gibbering Edgar Linton. My paramour didn't seem to fancy his chances in a physical fight and walked away, his hands raised in mock surrender.

'Oh Kristóf, my hero!' I mocked. 'Thank you, I needed rescuing!'

He turned his glare at me and I realised he was in no mood for my jokes.

'It didn't look like it. You were all over him.'

'I was only being polite.' I poured myself another drink and sat on the counter, swinging my legs like a little girl. 'What do you care anyway?'

'I don't particularly. I just didn't want you to do something you would regret in the morning.'

'I was only having fun; you should try it some time.'
Where was Meg when I needed her? Last time I saw her
she had been in the living room leading a group of students
in *The Time Warp*.

'Didn't look like fun from where I was standing.' Kristóf
grabbed the paper cup from me and threw the contents
down the sink. I tried to stop him and fell on the floor.
Kristóf lifted me back upright. He was surprisingly strong
for someone so lean. 'I think you'd better go to bed.'

I started to protest but couldn't get the words out. He
put his arm around me and helped me up the stairs.

'Thank you, Kristóf,' I slurred. 'You're a nice guy really,
most of the time.'

'Yeah, well, don't get used to it. You're a pain in the arse
when you're drunk.'

'I'm sorry.'

We reached my room and I stumbled into bed, fully
clothed and still wearing my heels. 'I'll have a little nap
and then I'll get back up.'

'Yeah whatever.'

'Are you cross with me? Why are you cross?'

'I'm not cross. Go to sleep.'

'You sound cross.'

'Well, I'm not. I just don't know why you degrade yourself like that. You're better than that, Holly.'

He looked at me so intensely, and our faces were so
close together that, for a second, I thought he was going
to kiss me. I didn't know how I felt about that, but I

thought I should at least find out. I moved towards him but before I got any closer, he stood up abruptly and walked out of the room.

'Get some sleep, Holly,' he said gently, closing the door behind him.

Chapter 14

The next message comes early Monday morning. This time it's a text.

How's Mum and Dad?

So not only does my stalker know where I've been last week, they also have my new number. How is that possible? I only gave it out to a few family members and friends, and none of them would do this to me. The only people who knew I was going to my parents' this weekend were Rhona and Tom and they have no connection with my university mates. The thought that there is someone out there who can seemingly infiltrate all parts of my life makes me feel vulnerable. Have they somehow tracked my phone? Or are they spying on me in person? And if they can gain access to my personal life so easily, what else do they know about me?

I don't reply, but this time I decide to keep the message. If I do go to the police, I will need evidence. But what could they do? A couple of pictures and a text message hardly constitute threatening behaviour. And I would have to explain to them why I am being targeted and that could put me in far more danger. No, this is something I am going to have to handle on my own.

Rhona has offered to come in early with me today to help decorate my classroom for Hallowe'en. She did hers over half term. It's a gloomy day, perfect for the occasion. The morning mist swirls around us, painting the buildings a dull grey and obscuring the path ahead. I snuggle into my winter coat as we walk quickly towards the school, feeling my bones thaw with the heat of the exertion.

Rhona links arms and tells me all about her dining room, which she redecorated over half-term.

'You and Tom will have to come over for dinner!' she suggests, and I agree, although I don't know how he will feel about that. He'll probably come up with another excuse.

Rhona is the closest friend I have had since Meg. She was my mentor when I first arrived at the school as a newly qualified teacher and we quickly became friends. We share the same sense of humour and she always has my back. If I was going to confide in anyone, it would be her, but I can't take the risk. She's married to a policeman and has a loose tongue when she's had a few drinks.

'Anyway, enough about me, how was your half term?' she says.

'Good thanks, Lisa came up for a surprise visit.'

'Ooo any gossip?' Unlike me, Rhona loves her soaps and is an avid viewer of Lisa's programme. I started watching it when she first got the part but quickly got bored. Now I only watch it when she tells me there's a big scene coming up.

'Nothing I'm at liberty to share,' I tease.

'Did Tom go with you?'

'Sore point.'

Rhona takes the hint and changes the subject. I reach into my pocket and feel for my phone, thinking about the latest text and what it means. Maybe I should tell Tom? Perhaps he could help me trace the messages? Tom is good at IT. He might know what to do and maybe I can find a way of telling him without disclosing the full story. I spoke to him last night on the phone and he said he missed me. I hope that means he regrets not going to my parents'.

The school is deserted when we arrive and I'm glad Rhona is with me. It feels eerie without the kids. Rhona unlocks the front door and disables the alarm while I wait outside. Inside it is dark and quiet; even the cleaners haven't arrived yet. The old boiler cranks up and the room starts to get warm. We set about decorating the classroom with spiders' webs and pumpkin lanterns before changing into our costumes. Rhona has come as a zombie bride while I have gone for a boring but safe witch costume with a long black cloak and a pointy hat. Even Trevor has promised to don a Frankenstein mask for the occasion although he is getting twitchy about our half-term attainment targets and hasn't got time to waste on frivolities. He's not keen on having fun unless there is a specific objective attached.

I remember meeting Trevor at the interview. He was

with the Chair of Governors, a stunningly pretty woman in a pink hijab. They sat side by side behind a table while I perched on the edge of my chair, my hands in my lap and answered their questions with as much confidence as I could muster. I had researched the school, studied the latest OFSTED report, looked Trevor up online and knew about his interests and his background. I had a good degree and a glowing report from my tutors. I had stretched my credit card limit and bought myself an outfit at Oasis. I had practised answering difficult questions. Nothing was going to stop me getting this job. My determination must have shone through at the interview. They called me that evening to offer me the position.

It was my first job after leaving teacher training college. I had planned to take a year out after university, get a flat in Leeds with Meg, and save up to go travelling again but everything changed after George died. We never spoke about it, but we knew we wouldn't be living together after what happened. She moved to London and we lost touch. It seemed better that way. I don't know what happened to Kristóf. I doubt he returned to the Isle of Wight; he always described it as the place that time forgot. When I think of him, I imagine him in some dark smoky café in Paris or Berlin, writing his poems.

'Da-dah! What do you think?' Rhona has ringed her eyes with black face paint and her lips are crimson. Her clothes are torn and covered in fake blood. 'Do you think I'm going to scare the kids?'

'Maybe.'

'Ha! Good.' She grabs her bag and heads out of my classroom. 'Have a good one. See you at break.'

The bell rings and the kids tumble in: an eclectic mix of witches, zombies and skeletons with the odd Disney Princess and Bat Man thrown in for good measure. I take the register, noting that Nathan hasn't come to school today. His mum hasn't rung in so Diane, the school secretary, will have to chase her up. It isn't the first time a parent has forgotten to notify the school when a child is ill, but we have to be careful just in case. Trevor takes our safe-guarding responsibilities very seriously.

I have been a bit worried about Nathan recently; he seems even more withdrawn and quiet than usual and I wonder if he is missing his dad. I know his mother has taken him to visit the prison a couple of times and I wonder what it must be like to be five years old and visiting your dad in jail. Does he even understand what's happened?

It was the biggest scandal to hit the village in years. Liam was caught red-handed burgling one of the holiday cottages not far from where I live. It caused uproar. Usually there is very little crime around here and most people leave their doors unlocked. The local newspaper covered the story in great detail, relishing the fact that the culprit was one of their own. A lot of residents rely on tourism for their livelihood and they were worried it would deter holiday makers.

Nathan lives with his mother and Samantha in one of

the cottages attached to the farm where Liam worked as a casual labourer. They were lucky to keep the house when Liam went to prison, but I suppose the farmer felt sorry for them. You would have to be pretty heartless to kick out a mother and two children, although plenty of people would like to have seen them leave the area for good. I've seen the looks people in the village give Emma behind her back. I wonder if she's struggling to manage on her own.

At lunchtime, I get a message to go to the head's office. Expecting to be reminded of the deadline for this month's stats, I am totally unprepared for Diane to hand over a big bunch of red roses.

'Got an admirer?' Diane asks, winking at me.

I can feel my cheeks go the same colour as the bouquet. I can't believe Tom has sent me flowers at work. He must be really sorry about missing the weekend to make such a public declaration. Diane looks at me expectantly as I search for a note but there's no message, just a blank card from the local florist. As I lift the flowers something silvery catches the light. I look closely at the stems and there's a bracelet wrapped around them. It's a funny way to send jewellery and I begin to realise these are not from Tom.

The bracelet is silver and delicately wrought. From the chain hang tiny charms: a tree, a key, a rocking horse. I haven't seen Meg's bracelet for five years, but I would know it anywhere. I slip it into my pocket and keep smiling until I reach the bathroom. I throw the flowers in the sink and take deep breaths to calm myself. I run cold water over my wrists to cool down. I search the flowers again to see if I've missed a message but there's no indication of who they're from.

What does this mean? Is Meg trying to contact me? It doesn't seem like the sort of thing she would do. If Meg had something to say to me, she would come out and say it. Besides, she would never have let that bracelet out of her possession. But if it isn't Meg sending these messages, who is it?

With shaking hands, I pick up my phone and look at the last text. I press reply.

'Who are you? What do you want?'

I wait a few minutes. No response. Leaving the flowers in the sink, I go into the staff room and make myself a cup of tea. I make myself sip it slowly, exchange small talk with Rhona, and then look at my phone again. Nothing. I go back to the bathroom and search the flowers again for any clues. It looks like they have been hand delivered; maybe the florist can tell me who they're from? But does that mean my stalker is here in the village? Are they out there right now? A cold chill makes its way down my spine. What do they want from me? I throw the flowers in the bin and return to the classroom.

The kids run rings around me all afternoon and I almost lose my temper with Phoebe when she refuses to do what I ask for the third time. Finally, it's half past three and I say goodbye to the kids, glad to see the back of them. Walking home with Rhona, I keep glancing over my shoulder. I don't feel safe here anymore and I wish I didn't live alone. If I asked her, I am sure Rhona would let me stay over but then I would have to explain why. She doesn't pick up on my mood as she chats about her plans for the evening, which seem to involve drinking wine and watching soaps.

I leave Rhona at the corner, feeling more and more anxious as the light falls and the shadows creep across the footpath to my house. There is a car parked outside the holiday cottage to the left of mine. It's unusual for it to be let at this time of year but perhaps someone is taking advantage of the off-season rates. I walk quickly, my shoulders hunched, my fingers playing with the keys inside my pocket. I wonder if I need to get some sort of alarm.

I get back to my house and lock the door behind me. I turn on every light and take the bracelet out of my pocket. It is definitely Meg's. But why would she send it to me after all this time? If she wanted to talk to me, she obviously knows where I am. Besides, Meg would never treat her precious bracelet with such little care, which means there is only one explanation why it is now in my presence: whoever is harassing me has also got to her.

There is a knock on the door. I jump, startled, and look around for something to protect myself with. I run to the kitchen and grab a knife. There is no point in pretending I'm not home with all the lights blazing. There is another knock and the letterbox rattles. I make my way to the door, the knife behind my back, and fasten the chain. Taking a deep breath, I open the door.

'Trick or Treat?'

Tom is standing on the doorstep with Jack peeking out from behind him. He steps out and presents his plastic pumpkin which is already full of sweets.

Feeling like a complete idiot, I unfasten the chain and open the door wide. Tom notices the knife in my hand.

'Expecting someone?'

'I was just chopping vegetables.'

I am ill prepared for trick or treaters but manage to find a chocolate bar in the cupboard. I return to the door, dropping it into Jack's collection.

'Do you want to come in? Stay for a drink?' I try to hide the desperation in my voice. If only Tom and I were together properly then I wouldn't have to worry about being in the house on my own.

'Maybe another time? It's nearly bedtime for this young man.'

Jack pulls a face in protest and I feel like doing the same. But I have to be a grown up. 'Well, I'll see you tomorrow then, Jack.'

'Bye miss.'

'Bye Holly.'

'Bye Tom.'

As I close the door, I look behind them into the dark night. Is my stalker out there? Are they watching me right now? Planning their next move? I close the door behind me and double bolt it. Why are they doing this to me? If it's to scare me, then it's working. I retrieve my phone from my bag and check again for a reply. This time, finally, there is an answer.

I want your confession.

Chapter 15

They say Hallowe'en is when the veil between this world and the next is at its thinnest, when departed souls wander the earth looking for answers, but Mark isn't given to superstition. When you're gone, you're gone, and that's all there is to it. Nothing will bring his brother back.

Mark doesn't believe in ghosts, but he is still haunted. He watches the man leaving Holly's cottage, clutching the hand of his little boy, and the injustice claws at him. It's not fair that Holly gets to play happy families when she's ruined his. She deserves to know how it feels to lose a loved one, to have someone she cares about taken away from her.

It would have been George's twenty-sixth birthday this week. Last year, Mark spent the day with his mother, raking over the past. She's no longer interested in the living, only her ghosts. Her grief, omnipresent, threatens to engulf her at this time of year. He watches her visibly shrink under its grip. She refuses to go to counselling or seek help; he suspects she doesn't want to let go. Bereavement is the only thing keeping her going.

Grief is etched on her face. She's only just turned sixty but looks ten years older. She used to be glamorous, a social butterfly, the life and soul of a party. She used to be the kind of mother his friends envied. She had poise, grace, class. Now she potters around a dusty house surrounded by memories, muttering broken sentences that never seem to string together.

Mark tries to avoid visiting her these days. The living room is full of pictures of George. The rest of his family are growing older, but his little brother will be forever twenty-one. Mark can't bear to look at his face: staring at him, accusing him of not doing enough to avenge his death. He wishes he could talk to him. Explain. That they believed the authorities when they said it was a tragic accident. That they had no reason to be suspicious. It's only recently that the truth has started to emerge. But you cannot argue with the dead; they always occupy the moral high ground.

He hasn't told his mother about his investigation; he wants to wait until he has the full story and then he will present the truth as a gift. All Mark wants is to lift the dark cloud that has enveloped his family these last few years. It won't bring his brother back, but it might help them all move on.

Chapter 16

Six years ago

I woke up to shouting. It sounded like George was going to get murdered if I didn't intervene. I dragged myself out of bed and ran down the corridor, nearly bumping into Kristóf who was standing at the top of the stairs, pulling a dressing gown around his lanky body. He had just got out of the shower and his hair was springing from his head in multiple directions like a cartoon character.

'What's going on?' he groaned.

We ran down the stairs and headed towards the kitchen. Meg was waving a wooden spoon in George's face and screaming at him.

'You're a disgusting pig!'

'Oh, for God's sake, chill out,' George pleaded. 'I've got a major hangover and I don't need this drama.'

'What's happened?' I asked, prising the spoon from Meg's hand.

'This Neanderthal was peeing in the sink.'

We all turned to look at George, who lifted his hands up in surrender. 'Oh, come on, we've all done it.'

'No, we haven't.'

'I couldn't be bothered to go to the bathroom. Besides Kristóf was in the shower so what was I supposed to do?'

'Try being civilised for once in your life and waiting!'

It was like watching something out of a Punch and Judy show. I couldn't help it, I started to laugh.

'Do you think this is funny?' Meg turned on me. 'Do you think this is OK?'

'No, but ...' I looked at Kristóf and he broke into a smile. Pretty soon we were both in hysterics which only served to get Meg angrier. She threw the spoon against the wall, narrowly missing my head, and stormed out. We heard the front door slam as we collapsed in fits of laughter.

'George, you're disgusting. We all have to use that sink.'

'I know, it's horrible. I'll bleach it, I promise.'

'Please tell me you moved the washing up first.'

'Of course, I'm not a complete animal.'

'For God's sake, why didn't you go in the garden, or in a bottle?'

George looked at Kristóf as if he was some sort of genius. 'Now, why didn't I think of that?'

I handed George the marigolds and the bleach. 'You'd better do a good job.'

He gave me a mock salute and set to work. Kristóf went back to the shower and I helped George clean up the kitchen. I took a picture of George scrubbing the sink and sent it to Meg with an apology for laughing but she didn't reply. I didn't know why she was that bothered; she barely ate anyway. She seemed to live off cigarettes and caffeine, occasionally supplemented by a ready meal heated up in the microwave or a take-away from the curry house down the road.

Fortunately, Meg was mollified with a heartfelt apology after George had sobered up. He did seem to be genuinely sorry and not only cleaned the whole kitchen from top to bottom but the bathroom as well. This was an impressive feat for a man who didn't even know how to clean a toilet when he first moved in.

I was pleased that Meg had made up with George. He'd invited us all to spend New Year's Eve at his family home in Hampshire and I didn't want their silly row to spoil things. I really wanted to see what George's house looked like and I was looking forward to dressing up and meeting his family and friends. I imagined them all to be incredibly posh. Kristóf had taken some persuading, even though his journey from the Isle of Wight was the shortest. He didn't like parties at the best of times and I knew he liked to spend his holidays reading and working on his poetry.

We knew George's family was loaded, but we still hadn't expected him to live in a place that would give Downton Abbey a run for its money. The elegant manor house stood at the end of a long driveway surrounded by perfectly manicured lawns. I was half expecting a line of servants to greet us at the door as Meg and I climbed out of the taxi. George opened the door and took our bags. He seemed different somehow in his home environment: his accent more clipped, his clothes more sophisticated, his mannerisms more refined. It was hard to reconcile this version of George with the one who had pissed in our kitchen sink a couple of weeks ago.

'Oh my God,' Meg said, her mouth agog as we stepped inside. A huge Christmas tree, tastefully decorated in blue and white crystals, dominated the vast entrance hall, a sweeping staircase divided the room and the ceiling was crowned by an actual chandelier. It looked like something out of a black and white Hollywood film.

George smiled. 'Bit OTT isn't it? Don't worry, the rest of the house is falling apart. Can't get the staff.'

He led us up the steps and through a long corridor lined with paintings. I had been expecting portraits of the family's ancestors, but they were mostly landscapes of white stone houses nestling among cypress trees.

'My mother paints,' George explained. 'Spends most of her time in Italy these days.'

'They're really good,' I told him, but George had already moved on and opened a door at the end of the long corridor.

'You're sharing,' he said. 'Hope that's OK. There are loads of people staying tonight so we're all bunking up. Anyway, I'm on official meet and greet duty. I'll leave you to it.'

As soon as George left the room, Meg let out a squeal of delight. 'Can you believe this place?' We ran to the window and looked out at the view. A small cottage garden was covered in frost and a groomsman was walking along a row of stables, inspecting the horses.

By the time we had dolled ourselves up and I had changed into the dress I had bought in the sale at Debenhams, the other guests had started to arrive. I was worried that my full-length gown might be over the top but if anything, I felt underdressed. One woman arrived wearing a full-length fur coat and a tiara.

'Get a load of Cruella de Vil,' Meg whispered. She was wearing one of her own creations: a deep red velvet dress which clung to her curves and was split to her upper thigh. I could see the men checking her out as she sashayed past them. I felt invisible beside her.

'Shh, that's probably George's grandmother or something.'

Meg grabbed a couple of flutes of champagne from one of the circling waiters and handed me one. I sipped it nervously, trying to spot Kristóf in the crowd of people. George was at the other side of the room, standing next to a stylish woman with sleek ash blonde hair and vertiginous heels. Finally, I located Kristóf in the corner of the room, wearing a tuxedo and a red bow tie. I waved, and he came over.

'Evening ladies.'

'You're looking very dapper, Kristóf,' Meg teased.

He gave a little bow. 'Rented especially for the occasion.' Up close I noticed he was wearing a pair of silver cuff links with the letter G on them which I guessed he had borrowed from George. I thought he would be the one feeling most out of place, but he looked perfectly at ease in this environment.

'You're both looking very beautiful tonight,' he said, staring at me. I blushed nervously and took another sip of champagne.

George finally approached us, the elegant woman still in tow. He kissed us both on the cheek and shook hands with Kristóf.

'Guys, this is Fee, my ...'

'Fiancée,' she finished smugly as I tried to hide my shock. 'You must be George's friends from uni.'

'That's right. My friends from the North,' George said in a fake Yorkshire accent, which always made me laugh when we were back in Leeds, but here it sounded cruel and patronising.

'Really? I have an uncle that lives somewhere in Derbyshire. Is that close to you?'

'Yes, sort of ...' I said, diplomatically before Meg could answer. She must have been reeling from Fee's revelation as much as I was otherwise she would have been faster to respond.

'It's so nice of you all to come. George speaks very highly of you.'

'And he's told us all about you,' Meg replied mischievously. 'Haven't you, George?'

George gave us a knowing grin before moving on to

another group of guests. He seemed completely unfazed by the situation.

'OMG,' Meg mouthed. 'Can you believe he kept that quiet?'

I was trying to hide the gnawing pain in my stomach. George had never as much as hinted at being engaged and he most certainly hadn't been faithful to her at university. I wondered if they had some sort of 'arrangement'. I downed the rest of my champagne and grabbed another one. It was going to be a long evening.

Despite the amount of money that had obviously gone into making the party perfect, it was actually pretty dull. At dinner, I ended up sitting next to George's uncle who stank of cigars and kept peering down my cleavage. The dinner itself was fancy and the rich food and the heavy wine made me feel bloated. I picked at my roast beef, wishing I was back home with my friends and family, greeting the New Year in the local pub instead of having to listen to George's uncle make increasingly sexist comments. I was desperate to switch seats with Meg who was swapping banter with a pair of twin brothers who were topping up her wine glass at every opportunity. I looked over to Kristóf who was listening politely to George's mother boasting about her elder son, Mark.

'He's in Singapore at the moment. Wonderful city, penthouse apartment, all paid for by the company, of course.'

'Come down to the lake house later. That's where the

party really starts.' George had crept up behind me and made me jump. He was so close to me, his breath on my ear, that I felt myself go red. Did he mean just me and him? I watched him slip back into his seat and put his arm casually around Fiona's back. I tried to concentrate on the chocolate torte the waiter had placed in front of me, but all I could do was stare at George and Fee and try to understand their relationship. How could he have kept her quiet for the past two and a half years? How long had they been engaged? Was he actually going to marry her?

I joined Meg and Kristóf after dinner. The drinking had now moved on to cognac but there was still some wine left on the table, so we grabbed a bottle of red and split it between our glasses. Meg was staggering a little and Kristóf looked pained. I wondered if he regretted coming.

'Did George tell you about the after party?' Meg slurred.

'Yeah, at the lake house?'

'The lake house! Who has a lake house?'

'I'm going to bed,' Kristóf announced. 'I don't think I can stand this any longer.'

'It's not even midnight yet!' I protested.

Kristóf begrudgingly checked his watch. 'I'll stay 'til midnight and then I'm done, alright?'

Midnight came in the traditional fashion with even more champagne and a rendition of Auld Lang Syne. I watched George kiss his girlfriend slowly on the lips. Kristóf gave me a stiff hug while one of the twins grabbed

Meg around the waist and swung her around in an extravagant embrace.

'Put me down,' she screeched as everyone looked at them.

Kristóf disappeared five minutes later. As the older guests chatted about property portfolios and the prospects of a general election this year, I realised the younger ones were starting to sneak off. I grabbed Meg and we made our way outside with the twins still in tow. They led us down a network of slippery paths into woodland. Away from the party, it was quiet and still, the only sounds coming from the crunch of snow beneath our feet. We were poorly dressed for a trek through the woods and I hoped that the lake wasn't far. Finally, we followed the sound of muffled laughter and found a wooden chalet and a decking area, looking over a tranquil and moonlit lake. Some of the boys had stripped off and were daring each other to jump naked into the steel grey water.

Inside the chalet the air was thick with sweet smelling smoke and a bottle of Grey Goose vodka was being passed casually around. George was slumped on the sofa and Fiona was curled up with her head on his lap. They had been inseparable all evening. Meg and I squeezed into one of the armchairs and George introduced us to his friends, who all seemed to go by childish derivations of their names. Most of them had gone to boarding school together and loudly exchanged tales of childhood memories and teenage pranks. Meg fell asleep while I listened patiently, accepting the vodka shots and the joint that were being passed around. George seemed oblivious to our presence and I wondered why he had invited us in the first place.

Meg finally woke up and said she needed air. We made our way outside and claimed one of the swings overlooking the lake. It was freezing outside but strangely peaceful, the sky ablaze with tiny stars and the frost glistening on the trees. I wrapped my pashmina around Meg to keep her warm.

'I can't even imagine being this rich,' she said. 'It's obscene. I mean, what do they do with all this money?'

'George says they give a lot to charity.'

'Oh please, probably only to avoid paying any tax. That's the problem with this country; the rich look after themselves.'

I knew better than to discuss politics with Meg. I thought having loads of money would be nice; you wouldn't have to work, you would have beautiful clothes and go on luxury holidays, you wouldn't have to worry about anything; but this lifestyle seemed unattainable to the likes of me and Meg. It was no wonder George didn't work hard at uni. He didn't need to when he had all this behind him.

'Do you think we will always be friends?' I asked.

'Of course,' Meg said, resting her head on my shoulder. 'You're my bestie, always will be. Nothing will push us apart.'

'What about the boys?'

'Oh, I think Kristóf needs us more than he lets on. He doesn't really function without us, does he?'

I laughed. 'I don't think the same can be said for George.'

'No,' she said sourly. 'I think George will fall on his feet whatever happens.'

Chapter 17

The florist opens late on Thursdays, so I head there after work. It is the only one in the village and does a brisk trade. The manager, a fussy woman in her early fifties, hoards secrets like a squirrel in winter. She knows which husbands are in trouble, and why, and the exact bouquet to mitigate their sins. She runs the Village in Bloom society and woe betide any business that does not keep its carefully co-ordinated flowering basket fed and watered. As I walk through the door, I check for CCTV cameras, but I can't see any. I doubt she would let me look at the footage anyway, but if I can pique her interest then it's worth a try.

The bell rings to announce my presence but the shop assistant doesn't turn around. She is crouched down checking elaborate arrangements of white and yellow flowers, one of which spells out the word MUM. My nostrils tingle from the pollen. I hang around awkwardly, waiting for her to notice me, until I can't stand it any longer.

'Excuse me?'

The girl looks up and I see that it is Samantha. I haven't seen her since the incident at the river. She stands up and brushes herself down, her face flushing as she recognises who I am.

'Oh hi, Miss Metcalfe.'

'Call me Holly, please. How are you doing?'

'I'm fine. I just wanted to say, like, thanks for everything. You proper saved my life that day.'

'It was nothing, don't mention it.'

'If there's anything I can do ...'

'Well, as a matter of fact, there is.'

She looks like she wasn't expecting me to take her up on the offer. I follow her as she walks behind the counter and stands by the till. Her nails are long and painted in different colours, completely impractical for work.

'How can I help?'

I can hear movement in the back room and I guess that she's not alone. Perhaps I should ask to speak to her manager? Samantha looks as uncomfortable as I feel. However, Samantha owes me one and that could work in my favour.

'Well, the thing is I received some flowers this week. Some red roses? And I was wondering whether you could tell me who sent them?'

'Didn't they have a card?'

I suppress my irritation at her stupid question. 'No, nothing. Unless it fell off? Perhaps you could check your system? They were delivered to the school.'

She taps the keyboard and looks at the screen. She seems to take ages waiting for the information to upload and I resist the urge to tap my feet. Finally, she peers at the computer. 'Nah, we didn't do any deliveries to the school this week.'

'Are you sure? Look, it's your card.'

Samantha shakes her head. 'They weren't delivered by us. Did you say it was red roses?'

'That's right. They must have been expensive. I only want to thank whoever sent them, that's all.'

Samantha screws her eyes at the screen. 'Yeah, here it is. He came in on Saturday. Paid in cash and took them with him. I remember cos he gave me a fiver tip, and no-one ever does that.'

'So, it was a man? What did he look like? Was it someone from the village?'

'Doubt it, they're all right tight around here.'

'Did he leave a name?'

'Nope. Nothing. Like I said, paid in cash.'

'Well, what did he look like?'

'Is everything OK, Samantha?' comes a voice from the back room. I don't want to get Sheila involved. It will be around the village in no time.

'Everything's fine,' Samantha replies, although her eyes shift towards the abandoned arrangements and I can see she is desperate to get rid of me. 'I dunno. He looked ordinary.'

I clench my fists and release them, keeping my voice steady. 'How old was he? My age or older?'

'Yeah, about your age, I think. Maybe thirty or forty?'
I try not to take offence. Everyone over the age of twenty-three is ancient when you're Samantha's age.

'Tall? Short? Dark? Fair?'

'He had short hair. Erm ... tall, I think. But not like too tall. Quite good looking, for an older guy.'

I am getting nowhere with this. 'Do you have CCTV?'

She laughs. 'Here? Are you joking? There's nothing to steal.'

'Was there anything else you remember? Did he have an accent? A tattoo perhaps?'

Samantha looks like someone under interrogation. She shakes her head. 'He was just ordinary; maybe a bit posh, like.'

I sigh. 'Thanks Samantha, you've been very helpful. How's Nathan by the way?'

'Fine, why?'

'Only he hasn't been at school this week.'

She hesitates. 'He's had a bad cold, Mum kept him off so that he wouldn't pass it onto the other kids.'

She's a terrible liar.

'Just tell your mum to let the school know, will you?'

'Yes, miss. Bye, miss.'

'Have a good evening.'

I walk home despondent, noting that there are a few CCTV cameras in the village but I can just imagine the reaction if I asked to see the recordings on the basis that a stranger bought me flowers. Samantha says they didn't deliver them, so he must have come to the school himself. Maybe Diane will be of more help.

One thing I do now know for definite is that Meg didn't send the flowers. But the question still remains: how did this guy get hold of her bracelet? Why send it to me? And why now? I need to speak to her. Maybe she knows what's going on.

Meg has never been one for Facebook, but I try it first anyway. There are hundreds of Meg Crowthers in the world but none of them resemble my former best friend. I log out and go on to Google and put in her name and Leeds University into the search box.

A few pages come up. Some are relevant, some are not. However, one listing stands out from all the others. I almost daren't open the link, praying that it is the wrong person, but it's there on the website of a local newspaper. Margaret 'Meg' Crowther, died six months ago. There's a picture of her that I don't recognise. There are no details about how she died but her mother is raising money for a drugs charity in her memory. I put two and two together. Meg always dabbled in drugs at university but never to dangerous levels; I can't believe my clever, bright, beautiful best friend would lose her life to drugs.

It feels hypocritical to grieve when you weren't even close enough to someone to be told they had died but I still feel it, along with gut-wrenching guilt that I wasn't there for her. When we should have been stronger than ever, we fell apart. I had assumed that she was like me: moving on with her life, building a career, making new friends. It never occurred to me that she might be struggling too.

Chapter 18

I need to know what happened. I take a chance that Meg's mum Naomi is still living in the same place and on Saturday, I travel to Newcastle. I don't like driving around strange cities, so I take the train and arrive shortly after lunchtime. Naomi lives on the outskirts of the city, in a small semi on a well-kept estate. I wonder whether I will even recognise her; but when she comes to the door, she looks much the same, only older. Her hair, which used to be jet black, is now streaked with silver, and there are tiny creases around her eyes. She looks surprised and a little suspicious when she first sees me standing on the doorstep but when I give her my name, she remembers me and invites me in.

'I thought you might be one of those reporters. They come sniffing around occasionally,' she says in a strong Geordie accent that reminds me of Meg.

'I'm sorry, I should have called first.'

'You're fine, pet. It's good to see you.'

She takes me through to the living room. It is pristine with cream carpets and patterned wallpaper around the chimney breast. Everything is chrome and glass and sparkles in the afternoon sunshine. The television is on; a group of women are sitting around a table talking about the menopause. Naomi switches it to mute and the women continue gesticulating and laughing silently. On the mantelpiece there is a photograph of Meg's dad looking handsome in his RAF uniform next to Meg's official graduation picture. She hated that photograph. The black gown and the cap with its swinging tassel were far too austere for her. Her hair is conspicuously green against the formal outfit.

'Tea?'

'Yes please.'

She goes into the kitchen. I walk over to the picture and examine it closely, remembering how Meg used to love changing her hair colour. She looks young in the photograph, her eyes bright with ambition, her whole future ahead of her.

'Do you remember that day?'

Meg's mum hands me a cup of bright orange tea.

'Yes, of course.'

'I was so proud of Meg. The sky was the limit with those brains of hers. That hair though! The little minx. She never was one for conforming.'

I smile and sit down on one of the sofas, opposite her. Meg was an only child, she meant everything to Naomi. A wave of guilt and sorrow hits me like vertigo. This is all my fault. I should have been a better friend.

'I'm sorry to intrude. I've only just found out, you see. Otherwise I would have come sooner. We lost touch.'

'Ay, I know. She came back from Thailand a different person. That friend of yours dying like that hit her hard. I suppose you don't expect it at your age.'

I feel a fresh surge of guilt. I swallow my tea and try not to show my discomfort. I don't like to think about that summer, but I have to face this.

'She came back home for a while, but she couldn't settle,' Naomi continues. 'She applied for a few jobs but nothing came of her applications and after a while she stopped looking altogether, started hanging round with some of her old friends from school. Disappeared for nights on end. I mean she was an adult, what could I do? But I knew there was something wrong. By the time I realised what it was, she was already an addict.'

So, it was true then. Not a one off, an accidental over-dose, but a prolonged addiction. Poor Meg, she must have been suffering. All these years, I hadn't really thought about how anyone else felt about George's death. I hid away like I was the only one who mattered.

'I tried everything I could. I begged her to stop, had to throw her out of the house eventually. I kept seeing her in town, begging for money. Then she went to London. She phoned me from time to time, but she wouldn't tell me where she was living. I didn't realise how bad it had got.'

I bite my lip, trying to imagine how desperate Meg must have been. 'How did she die?'

'Overdose. Heroin. They found her in this squat she had been living in. I suppose at least she died peacefully but

I can't bear the thought that she was on her own.'

Tears slide down Naomi's face and I wish I hadn't come. I should go over and hug her, but I am wracked with guilt. I finger the silver bracelet in my pocket. Should I give it to Naomi? But how do I explain where it came from? I don't want to upset her even more.

'Excuse me,' Naomi walks out of the room and I hear her open the door to the downstairs toilet and blow her nose. I take the opportunity to slip the bracelet behind Meg's graduation picture. She'll find it after I've gone.

Naomi comes back into the room as I sit down again.

'It's strange. You're the second one of Meg's university friends to get in touch recently. There was a lad came to visit the other week. Lovely looking but a bit ... awkward. Looked like he didn't get out much.'

'Kristóf?'

'Ay, that was his name. Went to Thailand with you, didn't he?'

'Yes. Do you have his number? I'd like to get in touch with him if possible.' Has Kristóf been sending these messages? My brain is running at a million miles per hour. Naomi described him as awkward, Meg always used to say he wasn't capable of functioning in society without us. Perhaps his shyness has spiralled into something else? Something more sinister?

'He left his business card somewhere.' She opens a drawer and roots through some papers while I try not to let on how much I need her to find this number.

Finally, she hands it over. 'It's nice to know that she's missed. It's a comfort. Stay in touch, won't you?'

On the doorstep I give her a quick hug goodbye. 'Take care.'

I walk quickly to the train station, playing with the business card in my hand. I am terrified of losing it. Kristóf is now a Lecturer in English Literature at a university in the Midlands. There is a work email address and a landline number. It doesn't surprise me that there is no mobile phone number. Kristóf hated technology.

I take out my phone to add the number to my contacts and see there is another anonymous message. Why won't this guy leave me alone? I open it. It's another picture. It's of me and Naomi hugging on the doorstep.

I look behind me quickly. The light is already fading, and the streets are full of shadows. There's no-one there.

'What do you want?' I shout into the empty street. 'Come out, talk to me. Stop being a coward.'

Is it Kristóf? Is Kristóf the person I should be afraid of? But how would Kristóf be able to get hold of photos I destroyed five years ago? How would Kristóf be able to track down a mobile phone number that I only gave out to a handful of people? And why? Kristóf has as much to lose from this as anyone. Why would he want to dredge up the past?

I look down at my phone again and store the message. My hands are shaking as I type out a reply.

Fuck off. Leave me alone.

I reach the station and look over my shoulder to see if anyone has followed me. The platform is crowded and, amid the safety of other people, I start to calm down. He can't hurt me here. I pull out my phone. There is another picture message.

It's a picture of Meg. At first, she looks like she's asleep, lying on a filthy mattress. But on closer inspection there is a thin line of vomit coming from her mouth. Next to her hand is an empty syringe and she's wearing the bracelet.

The world tips and I have to hold on to the wall to stay upright.

'Are you OK, pet?' An old woman asks me, her lined face full of concern.

'I'm fine,' I manage a smile. 'Just felt a bit dizzy.'

'There's a bench over there. Sit down for a while and let it pass.'

'Thanks.'

I look at the bench, but it seems too far away for me to reach. I don't want to make a scene. I stay where I am until the train arrives and then make my way to the carriage. I fall into my seat and release the tears that have been threatening to fall since I left Naomi's house. A young man with a thick ginger beard and blue headphones gives me a funny look but doesn't say anything.

Was Meg stalked before she died? Was she given an opportunity to confess and refused? Is this what's going to happen to me if I don't tell the truth?

Chapter 19

'Your brother's death was no accident.'

With those words, Meg had him hooked. She had been calling his office repeatedly for weeks until Mark capitulated and told his PA to put her through.

'Who are you? And what are you talking about?'

'I know what really happened to your brother.'

Mark felt the blood drain from his body. He could barely grasp the phone as the words infiltrated through his brain. What the hell was she talking about? Was this some sort of sick joke? Was she some sort of psycho who got their kicks by ringing up bereaved people with ridiculous stories?

'How could you possibly know that?'

'Because I was there.'

She'd wanted money. No surprise there. Mark knew he couldn't trust her. For all he knew, this woman had never even met his brother. Perhaps she had seen the media coverage, realised they were wealthy, and was trying to make some easy money. But he was so desperate for answers he would have given her anything she asked for. Money was nothing compared to knowing the truth. The amount she had asked for was pitiable; he could make that in a day. Was that all his brother was worth?

They met in a greasy café near Euston train station. One look at Meg and he could tell she was an addict. Her hands were shaking as she clutched a cup of tea, she looked like she hadn't had a good meal in weeks, and her eyes had the haunted look of someone desperate for their next fix. George would never have had anything to do with someone like that.

But when she spoke, her North-East accent triggered a memory from the funeral. He had been too distraught to take much notice of the other guests, but he remembered Meg. She had been with a gaunt looking guy. George's university friends; the ones that had gone with him to Thailand. There had been three of them, but the other girl hadn't even bothered to turn up.

Mark slid the padded envelope full of cash across the table. Meg made no effort to hide what she was doing as she greedily checked the notes. The waitress came over and he ordered a cup of tea. He offered her a refill, but she shook her head.

'Well?' he demanded, as soon as the waitress was out of earshot.

'It was an accident, I swear,' she sniffed. 'We didn't mean to kill him.'

Mark's brain whirred, barely able to take in Meg's words. 'You killed my brother?'

'It wasn't me. Well, I was there, but I didn't ... We panicked. We moved his body to make it look like an accident. And we lied to the police.'

She cried crocodile tears, but when he demanded more details, she clammed up.

'You have to come with me to the police, tell them what you know.' His voice was measured but he was struggling to handle the rage that was rising within him.

She shook her head vehemently. 'No, no police. I just thought you should know what really happened.'

He didn't believe her. Meg hadn't told him the truth because she felt guilty. Oh no, nothing like that, but because she wanted his money.

She stood up to leave but he grabbed her wrist and restrained her.

'Let me go,' she pleaded. 'You're hurting me.'

'Not until you tell me everything about what happened that night.'

'I've said too much already.'

She looked terrified but he didn't care. He had to find out the truth.

'Is it money you want? You can have all the money you want. How much do you want?'

'I don't want your money. I don't know anything else.'

'Yes, you do. How did he die? Who killed him?' He was shouting; people were turning to stare at them. Meg tried to pull away from him, but he had a firm grip.

'I don't know. Let me go.'

'Who else was there that night? That guy from the funeral? What about that other girl you went with? What were their names?'

'Leave them out of this.'

'It's too late for that now.'

He pulled her towards him and grabbed her by the throat, feeling the delicate bones yield to the pressure of his fingers. He would have strangled her there and then if the café manager hadn't intervened. Meg scarpered while he pleaded with the manager not to call the police. By the time he left the café, there was no sign of her.

Mark had only just started to handle his grief. It wouldn't go away, he knew that, but time and therapy had brought it to manageable levels. He could get up in the morning, go to work, make love to Mia, without thinking about his brother. Meg's words brought Mark's world crashing down around him. Everything he had believed about his brother's death had been a lie. Now his grief came back with an intensity that scared him. It was raw and painful and destructive. He could no longer control it.

He thought about going to the police, but what could he say? He had no evidence, only the word of a lying bitch who would no doubt retract everything she had told him. He didn't even know if he believed her. She hadn't seemed remorseful; all she'd cared about was the money. Was this just some sort of elaborate extortion?

He didn't care; he just needed answers.

Meg wasn't hard to track down. She was living in a

grotty squat not far from the café and it only took a couple of twenty-pound notes pressed into the hands of the druggies outside to gain access to the property. He found her a few hours later passed out on a filthy mattress, vomit around her face and neck. She had obviously wasted no time spending his money. He shook her but there was no response. He checked her pulse and cursed. Should he call an ambulance or get the hell out of there? Whatever happened, she was in no fit state to give him answers.

He was about to leave when he caught sight of the charm bracelet. She had been desperate enough to approach him for money, but not enough to sell it, so it must mean a lot to her. She had tried to blackmail him, maybe it was time to turn the tables? Demand to know the truth in return for her precious bracelet. He took a picture of her with his mobile phone and then bent down to remove it from her wrist.

He walked out of the flat with no questions asked or answered. A few days later he returned only to be told that she was dead. Mark watched from a distance when her mother came to collect her things, leaving the flat with a paltry supermarket carrier bag filled with clothes and a few possessions. He had the bracelet in his pocket and thought about giving it to her. But he had other plans for it.

Chapter 20

Tom has invited me to spend some time with Jack on Sunday. I am still reeling from the shock of finding out what happened to Meg, but I have to act normal. This is a major step forward and I don't want anything to ruin our plans. I push all my fears to the back of my mind and concentrate on being the perfect girlfriend. I feel like I am on trial and Jack is judge and jury on whether our relationship will succeed.

I go around at lunchtime, bringing a bottle of Pinot Noir for Tom and an over-priced Lego set for Jack. He beams with delight as he leads me into the living room to open it.

'Score one to Miss Metcalfe,' Tom says, looking pleased. 'Glass of wine?'

'Maybe later.' Even though I realise that I am going to need to reconfigure my relationship with Jack, it would seem strange drinking alcohol in front of one of my pupils. One day he could be my stepson. The thought makes me feel giddy and a little scared. Maybe Tom and I will have a baby of our own and we will be a proper family. I would love that. I know I could grow to love Jack like my own son. He's a sweet kid.

I sit down in the middle of the floor and help him build the kit, realising when I open the box that I have bought something that is far too old for him. He doesn't seem fazed and figures it out with incredible speed.

'He loves building things,' Tom smiles. 'Wants to be an architect like his dad.'

'Or an astronaut,' Jack contradicts. 'Or maybe a fireman.'

'Well, you've got plenty of time to make up your mind.' I love the way kids see no limits on what they can be when they grow up.

Lunch is a basic affair, ham salad with baked potatoes, and I wonder whether this is for Jack's benefit or whether Tom can't cook. We sit around the table in the dining kitchen. It's not a room I've been in before. Like the living room, it is slightly messy with piles of newspapers in the corner and a bookshelf overflowing with paperbacks. I take the opportunity to look through the titles: they're mostly thrillers, which I assume are Tom's, and a few chick-lit books which must have been Rebecca's. There are no classics or books of poetry.

Tom hands his son a plastic bottle of honey which Jack liberally squeezes over his salad. I give him a quizzical look.

'He has honey on everything,' Tom explains. 'I know I shouldn't indulge him, but you learn to pick your battles.'

I bite my tongue, thinking of all the times I have told the kids off for eating with their fingers or not finishing their vegetables. Rhona says that if it's one rule at home and one rule at school, they will never learn. But it's not my place to say anything … yet.

'Well, I think I should try it,' I say, grabbing one of Jack's honey-soaked tomatoes. He looks up at me in amazement as I put the sweet and sour mixture into my mouth. It is, of course, disgusting and I have to resist the urge to spit it back out. Jack is giggling, delighted at the sight of a grown-up acting silly and even Tom is laughing. It was worth it. I can't imagine Rebecca would do something like that. I imagine her to be the height of sophistication and elegance, but absolutely no fun.

'You're as bad as he is,' Tom scolds and I drop back down to earth. The last thing I wanted was for Tom to see me as a child. I need him to realise that I am ready to be a parent. I need to act more mature around Jack. I'm trying too hard to be his friend.

'We should go for a walk after dinner,' I suggest. 'Burn off some of these calories.'

Jack pulls a face, but Tom nods his head. He likes to keep in shape and I like that we have that in common. Tom said I was a natural at ju-jitsu. I might take it up again properly one day and I have been practising the moves. Tom takes Jack to 'Tiny Tigers' on a Saturday morning and I imagine us competing in tournaments as a family, cheering each other on in our different classes.

Tom collects the plates and gets out ice cream for dessert. Jack tucks into his with relish, smearing chocolate over his face.

'Come on then boyo, wash your hands and face and get your wellies on.'

Tom takes the dishes and throws them into the sink. I offer to wash up, but he tells me to leave them. Instead I help Jack with his wellies which he has put on the wrong feet.

'Can I bring my scooter?'

'Of course,' I say, then realise I should have asked Tom first. This is going to be tricky. How do I know when and where to be a parent?

We set off for a walk to the park. As Tom tucks his arm into mine, I wonder what has initiated this transformation. The playground is bound to be full of families on a Sunday afternoon; anyone could see us together. I didn't know Tom when he was with Rebecca. I imagine them, walking arm in arm, pushing Baby Jack in his pram and feel a pang of jealousy. This is her life, her family. She had everything I've always wanted, and she walked out on it. Tom says she lives in New York now, but he only knows that because of withdrawals from their joint bank account. She hasn't been in touch since, not even to ask for a divorce. I can't imagine what must have driven her to walk out on her family. Tom doesn't talk about it much, but I doubt any of it was his fault.

We reach the playground and Jack runs ahead, his face

flushed with exhilaration as he climbs the ladder leading up to a big slide.

'I remember the first time he went up there,' Tom says. 'My heart was in my mouth the whole time thinking he was going to fall. I suppose that was the moment I really understood that you can't wrap them in cotton wool. You have to let them take risks, push boundaries, otherwise they will never learn anything.'

'It must be hard though.'

'Well, it's true what they say, kids don't come with instruction books. But I don't know how you manage with a room full of five-year-olds every day. Don't they drive you mad?'

'Ah, it's not the pupils I have trouble with, it's the parents.'

'Would you like children?'

I hesitate. If I tell the truth, will he think I'm being pushy? What if I say yes, and he doesn't want any more? 'One day, maybe. If the time is right.'

'Rebecca didn't. Jack was a happy accident. Well, happy for one of us anyway.'

He smiles sadly, and I wish I knew what to say. We stand in silence for a while watching Jack find new and increasingly dangerous ways to climb the labyrinth of play equipment in the park. There are only a few kids in the playground today and none that I recognise. I am disappointed because it means no-one will see us together. The drizzle turns into steady rain and Tom gives Jack a five minutes' warning.

'So, I was thinking, maybe we could go to the bonfire tonight?' he says.

Bonfire Night is an important date in the village calendar and everyone attends. Going there as a family will make a big statement. I don't actually like bonfires or fireworks, but right now I would agree to go anywhere with Tom and Jack. 'Yes, if you want to.'

'I think it's time we went public, don't you?'

'Definitely.' He calls to Jack who pretends not to hear him and hides in the playhouse. Tom runs up to the house and grabs him, tickling him until he squeals. Then he lifts him high on to his shoulders and we walk home together.

I used to love Bonfire Night. Wrapped up, holding my dad's hand, writing my name with a sparkler. Baked potatoes in silver foil and the heat from the roaring fire. Watching the effigy burn. The thrill of being a little afraid by the bangs and the whizzes but mostly the excitement of all the colours and the patterns. My sister was the scared one. She would stay indoors with the dog and my mother, watching the display from behind the glass. Now, the fireworks, the crowds, the smell of gasoline, all bring back bad memories of that night on the beach. But I push them to one side for tonight. This is too important to let the past drag me under.

It's already dark by the time we make our way towards the field the farmer begrudgingly hands over once a year for the festivities. We have had such a lovely day. Tom and I each hold one of Jack's hands as we walk, swinging him between us. It feels like we're a proper family. As Tom pays our entrance fees to get into the field, Jack jumps up and down with excitement.

The fire is already going strong. The heat is intense, and I can feel myself getting flushed as we wait for the fireworks to start. I can see people looking at us, turning quickly away when I meet their eye.

'Are we the talk of the village?' Tom asks mischievously.

'I'm sure we will be.' I try to hide my satisfaction.

Just when things couldn't get more perfect, Jack spoils it by whining for a toffee apple. Tom tells him he can have one later, but this doesn't satisfy him, and he starts to sulk, kicking up the mud and complaining that he wants to go home. I try to distract him by telling him the story of Guy Fawkes, but I can tell he is fixated on the toffee apple and isn't listening. I know enough about kids to know the best thing is to ignore their tantrums, so I talk to Tom instead, asking him about his new project. He loves talking about work and starts telling me about the new eco-friendly technology he is incorporating to make the site carbon neutral. I look down to see if Jack has stopped sulking, but he's no longer standing next to me.

'Where's Jack?'

'I thought you had hold of him.'

'I thought you did.'

Tom drops my hand. Fear and panic take over his face as he looks around. 'He was here a few minutes ago. He can't have gone far.'

I spin around, searching for Jack's little green puffer jacket and black bobble hat. The blaze from the bonfire is casting shadows everywhere and it's difficult to make out faces among the crowds of parents and their youngsters. Everywhere I look there are hazards. Surely, he wouldn't have wandered close to the fire? He's only five; he doesn't have any sense of danger. What if he picks up a sparkler and burns himself? What if he wanders out of the field and steps in front of a car? What if someone has taken him?

Tom calls his name and asks the parents standing around us if they have seen him. Soon a search party gains momentum. I don't know what to do. I don't know whether to stand still in case Jack finds his way back to us or join Tom and move through the crowd. Tom is pushing people out of the way in a desperate bid to find his son.

Amid the fear that something might happen to Jack is another danger lurking at the back of my mind. What if this is something to do with me? What if the person who killed Meg has snatched Jack? What if something happens to him and it's all my fault? I turn my gaze to the adults, searching for the enemy, but I don't even know who to look for.

The field is sodden and the mud sucks at our boots, impeding our progress. People's faces are lit up like ghouls in the light coming from the bonfire. A solitary firework spirals upwards then explodes into a kaleidoscope of red, blue, green and purple which makes the audience gasp in unison. I search the faces of all the children standing with their parents, gazing in wonder at the display, but I cannot see Jack. Where could he be? The noises will frighten him. Will he run off and hide? What if we don't find him and he is left out in the cold? Will he try to find his way home? It's probably only been a few minutes since we lost him, but it feels like hours. There's a sick feeling in my stomach that we will never see him again, and it is all my fault. I can't even see Tom any more. Suddenly I feel very alone, an outsider in this world full of responsible adults.

'Lost someone?'

I turn around to see Rhona walking towards me holding Jack's hand. He looks immensely proud of himself as he munches on a toffee apple, completely oblivious to the chaos he has created.

'Caught this little scavenger prowling round the food stalls, eyeing up the merchandise like a sly fox.'

'Oh, thank God!' I give Jack a big hug. 'We were so worried about you.'

'Jack!' Tom pushes past me and grabs his son. 'Oh my God, never do that again.' He picks him up and swings him high. Father and son are cast in shadow against a backdrop of a multi-coloured sky. Later, we will laugh about the time we nearly lost Jack on Bonfire Night. The story will be rolled out at dinner parties and his eighteenth birthday. It was one of those close calls with catastrophe which leaves your heart pounding with anxiety and worse case scenarios playing out in your head long after the danger has passed. It happens to everyone. But it is also a reminder that your life can change in a heartbeat.

Tom throws Jack on to his shoulders so that he can get a better view of the fireworks. He takes my hand again, but all the romance of the occasion has fizzled out like a damp sparkler. Rhona stands next to me but doesn't seem to notice the tension between us. This was supposed to be our special night, going public about our relationship, but it feels tainted now. How can we be a proper family when I'm constantly looking over my shoulder?

Chapter 21

Five years ago

I don't know who came up with the idea to go travelling after uni. We were probably drunk at the time. But I remember it was George who suggested we went to South-East Asia. I had never stepped foot out of Europe before – my parents holidayed in France every year – and it seemed an exciting and exotic destination. I imagined lush jungles, golden temples and white sandy beaches. I had seen documentaries about Thailand on the television and it looked incredible, but I was worried about being kidnapped or duped into drug smuggling. Meg told me I had an over-active imagination.

Surprisingly, Kristóf agreed to come. I couldn't imagine him as a backpacker – he would probably fill his bag with a load of books and forget to bring any clothes. I was glad he was coming though. Underneath the pompous exterior, he could be quite sweet really. He had been helping me revise for my finals and my grades had improved no end since he encouraged me to look at texts more critically, not to be afraid to express opinions or to disagree with the tutors. His relationship with Meg could be strained at times but he often stepped in when she and George were having one of their frequent rows.

'I thought you'd be too busy planning your wedding, George,' Meg teased, unaware that her words cut me like a knife.

'Plenty of time for settling down when I'm old,' George replied, barely looking up from his iPad. The others had been quizzing him about Fiona ever since the New Year's Eve party, but he wouldn't rise to the bait and I still had no idea how serious he was about her. It seemed inconceivable to me that he could be engaged to someone and yet still fool around. Did she know what he got up to at uni? Did she care?

Over the course of the third year, our dreams began to take shape. We planned our route, arguing over whether to include Bali (over-commercialised according to George, the only one of us who had actually been to Asia) or start in Vietnam. We all wanted to see Thailand but disagreed whether to go to the beaches in the South or the mountains in the North.

I got a part-time job to save for my ticket. Mum and Dad weren't happy about it, they wanted me to concentrate on my exams, but they had put everything they had into paying for my tuition fees and I couldn't expect them to pay for me to go travelling as well. They were distracted anyway by my sister's announcement that she was moving to London after her A-levels to become an actress. My dad was worried sick about his little girl going to the big city but there was no arguing with my sister when she had made up her mind. I knew they would want to help her out: the rent in the city was phenomenally expensive and she had no guarantee of a job. They talked about it for hours over the phone and I alternated between listening to their concerns and hearing my sister's excited plans for her future. As always, Lisa had plenty of confidence that everything would be fine, and I had no reason to doubt her. She was the type of person who always managed to make things work out in her favour.

Toward the end of my third year, Lisa came to visit. We had been working hard, cramming like mad for our finals, and were due a break. My sister had recently turned eighteen and had discovered drinking and clubbing. She was eager to go out in Leeds; already frustrated with the limited club scene in Lancaster. She arrived by train on Friday afternoon, running across the crowded concourse and flinging herself dramatically in my arms when she saw me. She looked stunning as usual.

The others were out when we got back to the house. I was pleased because I knew George would monopolise Lisa as soon as he got home. He had already seen pictures of her on Facebook and thought she was fit, although I hoped he would respect the fact that she was my little sister. She dumped her bags on the airbed I had bought specially for her visit and immediately noticed the dress hanging from the wardrobe door. Emerald green, it shimmered in the afternoon sunlight. It had a halter neck and was clinched at the waist with a gold belt. Folds of fabric cascaded and pooled on the floor in delicate waves.

'Is that for the grad ball?'

'Yeah, isn't it beautiful? George bought it for me.'

'He bought you a dress?'

I couldn't tell if Lisa was appalled or impressed. I found myself blushing. I hadn't told anyone how I felt about George; not even Meg, and she was my best friend.

'So?' My voice came out sharper than I intended.

'A man buys you a dress like that with no strings attached? It must have cost a fortune.'

'It's not from any old man. It's from George. He's my friend and besides, he can afford it.'

I put the dress away, suddenly desperate to change the subject. It was a mistake leaving it out like that. I thought Lisa would share my enthusiasm, but her comments made me feel like some sort of gold digger. It wasn't like I had asked George to buy me clothes but when he offered to take me shopping, I wasn't really in a position to refuse. My credit cards were up to their maximum limit and I was saving all my money for travelling. I didn't have Meg's needlework skills and there was nothing in my wardrobe that was classy enough for the Graduation Ball. I couldn't afford an expensive dress and I really wanted to look my best. It was easy for the men. All they had to do was hire a tuxedo, and no-one judged them, but for me it was everything. I wanted to dazzle.

George had taken me to a small boutique in the Victoria Quarter of Leeds. The designer was allegedly one of Kate Middleton's favourites. He had chosen the dress for me. I had never worn anything so beautiful. Feeling the silky material on my skin made me feel sexy and elegant. It was a grown-up dress. He told me I looked fantastic and that the smile on my face was worth it. I tried not to think about Fiona and whether he bought her dresses. Fiona was a long way away and besides she probably had some sort of personal shopper or stylist that did it all for her. In George's world, it was normal for men to spend hundreds of pounds on a dress and for a woman to accept such a present with grace. Why shouldn't he treat me?

'It means he wants to shag you.'

'Don't be daft. If George had wanted to sleep with me, he would have tried to before now.'

It was true. George had had plenty of opportunities to seduce me, but I was evidently not his type. I had grown accustomed to George treating me as a friend and nothing more. Buying me a dress was the first time George had indicated he even noticed me that way, and I liked it. I fantasised that he would ditch Fiona and ask me to be his girlfriend. I could see myself hanging on his arm at film premieres and elegant balls, going to the opera and drinking champagne at parties, mixing with royalty and celebrities and announcing our engagement with an advertisement in the *Times*.

Fortunately, Lisa got bored of teasing me and started talking about the latest love triangle between her friends at school. I made her Chilli con Carne – one of the few recipes I could make from scratch – before we got ready to go out. We were going to one of the super clubs in Leeds and had VIP tickets. Lisa was nervous and worried about what to wear and whether she would get in. Although I had no more idea than she did, it was nice to act the older sister and help her with her hair and make-up. Meg and Kristóf had point blank refused to come to the club with us, baulking at the ticket price, and George had other plans. They had all promised to stay home on Saturday night and we were going to have a chill-out night playing board games and eating take-away.

It was the first time I had been out with Lisa properly and it was an eye opener. Everywhere she went, she turned heads. Men were constantly coming up to her and chatting her up. Some of them literally pushed me to one side in their desperation to dance with her. Lisa batted them away like flies but some of them were extremely persistent. I tried not to be jealous. I knew I could never compete with Lisa, but it was hard to be the one pushed to one side as the men vied for her attention. By 4am the constant approaches were getting irritating and we called it a night. It had never occurred to me before that there might be a downside to looking beautiful, but I don't think Lisa enjoyed her night.

She seemed much happier the following evening when

we were sitting in the living room, playing Trivial Pursuit. Kristóf was winning, although Meg was putting up a good fight. I had given up a long time ago and was sitting in the corner reading my book, occasionally being pulled in to adjudicate. George and Lisa were playing together and irritating Meg and Kristóf by not taking the game too seriously. They were sitting very close and I saw a familiar look in his eye as he whispered something in her ear. I knew it was a matter of time before he made his move on her, and I hoped that she would have the sense not to fall for his charm. I had no idea whether my sister was a virgin, but I did know that George would only see her as another notch on his bedpost. Lisa was eighteen, old enough to make her own mistakes, but I still didn't think I could bear it if she slept with him.

They finished the game and started another. I stood up, swaying slightly, and went into the kitchen to fetch another bottle of wine from the fridge. It was past midnight and I wanted to go to bed but I didn't want to leave Lisa on her own with George. When I got back into the living room, they were gone.

'Where's Lisa?'

Meg and Kristóf looked up.

'I dunno, they were here a minute ago. Has she gone to bed?'

'Where's George?'

There was a heavy silence. Meg bit her lip as if stopping herself from stating the obvious whereas Kristóf seemed to be genuinely oblivious to the tension hanging in the air. For a literary genius, he was crap at reading the subtext. I placed the bottle of wine on the floor.

'I'm going to bed.'

'Holly, don't.'

'It's fine. Really.'

'They're probably just talking or something.'

I left the room and walked down the corridor past George's closed bedroom door. I could hear muffled giggles and had to blink back my tears as I walked up the stairs. Jealousy and anger were bubbling up inside me and I could barely control it. How could she? How could he? I closed the door behind me and let the tears fall. Life was so easy for Lisa; why did she have to take everything from me?

There was a pair of scissors on the table. I picked them up, running my finger across the blade, wondering whether to hurt myself like I had as a teenager. I just wanted to make the feelings go away. I opened the wardrobe and the dress mocked me. How could I ever have thought George wanted me? He liked pretty girls, easy girls. I took out the dress and hung it on the wardrobe door again, berating myself for reading too much into the purchase. He must have just felt sorry for me. I opened the scissors and slashed the dress in two, feeling the pain recede as the fabric ripped apart. I tore the dress over and over again, watching the ribbons of fabric cascade on the floor like pieces of my broken heart. I picked them up and threw them in the bin.

Feeling numb, I undressed and got into bed, trying not

to imagine what George and Lisa were doing. Were they laughing at me? Stupid Holly and her delusions? More likely they weren't thinking about me at all.

When I woke up, Lisa was lying asleep on the airbed beside me, a faint smile on her face. I had never hated anyone so much in my entire life.

Chapter 22

Tom, carrying a sleepy Jack, walks me back to my cottage after the bonfire but doesn't accept my offer to come inside. I push open the door, nearly stepping on a brown envelope which is waiting for me on the doormat. I shut the door quickly and make sure it is double locked before picking up the package and taking it into the living room. The house feels cold and unwelcoming. I place the envelope on the coffee table and set about lighting a fire, knowing that I am putting off the inevitable. The envelope has no return address and has been hand delivered. I wonder what my stalker has in store for me now.

I sit on the hearth rug, waiting for the flames to lick the screwed-up balls of newspaper and kindling and feel the fleeting warmth from the woodburning stove as the fire takes hold. I grab the blanket from the sofa and wrap myself in it as I open the envelope and take out the contents. A collection of newspaper cuttings falls onto the floor. George's face stares out at me from every one of them. The press used his Facebook profile in the early reports. It shows a fun-loving guy necking a bottle of beer on a hot, summer's day. Later, they replaced it with a graduation picture, obviously supplied by his parents. 'Tragedy on Paradise Island' reads one of the headlines. 'Did drink and drugs contribute to George's death?' asks another. I leaf through the cuttings; the paper is as soft and thin as tissue. There are tiny holes in the corners of the articles as if they have been pinned up on a noticeboard and they have yellowed from being exposed to the sun. My hands are shaking as I force myself to go through them, wondering who has kept them all this time only to send them to me now. Tears run down my face. I loved George more than I have ever loved anyone; more than I love Tom. I think people forget that. Just because we were young, and we hadn't been together that long, didn't mean our relationship wasn't serious.

My stalker wants me to confess, but that's impossible. We made a pact and I can't break it without getting Kristóf into trouble too. It would be my word against his; he could tell them anything. He could tell them I killed George. Besides, what difference would it make after all this time? George is dead and there is nothing we can do to change that. Telling the truth would ruin everything. I don't need to see these clippings to be reminded of what happened to him. It's something I am going to have to live with for the rest of my life.

I take the clippings and throw them into the fire. I wish I could cauterise my memories as easily. I sit watching the flames, flicking through flashbacks like photos in an album, wishing that things were different. But they aren't.

I sleep badly. Every time I close my eyes, I see Meg staring at me from that filthy mattress, begging me to save her. I don't know what to do. Whoever sent me that photo clearly got to Meg; but did he kill her? Is that what he plans to do to me if I don't do what he wants? Surely prison would be better than death? I can't imagine being incarcerated. Would they even let me serve my sentence in a British prison? Or would they ship me back to Thailand? Would I be allowed to see my family? I wake up in the night, dripping in sweat, wishing that I didn't live alone. I know I would feel safer with Tom by my side. He would never let anyone hurt me.

I wake up exhausted, shower and make myself a strong coffee. I knock over the milk and then put a ladder in my tights in my haste to get dressed. I set off late and miss Rhona who will have gone ahead without me. A mum, holding the hands of an adorable pair of twins wearing matching fluffy coats, walks ahead of me. They look like they are going to nursery and I wonder if they will be in my class next year.

Outside the school gates, parents are manoeuvring their oversized cars, ignoring the no parking signs and empty threats of a penalty. Angry words are exchanged between the parents which will, no doubt, be replaced by fake pleasantries when they see each other later. I keep my head down and walk quickly, hoping not to be pulled aside by an anxious parent. The last thing I need right now is another delay.

On the way in, I bump into Diane and casually ask about the flowers, but she's as little help as Samantha.

'I didn't take much notice, love. I thought he was a delivery man. Now I come to think of it, he didn't have a uniform on, but they don't always these days, do they?'

The best description I can get from her is that he looked like a young Robert Redford.

I am so tired. I set up my classroom, greet the children and my teaching assistant, and begin the lesson on autopilot but my mind is still whirring with who sent the flowers and how he managed to get hold of Meg's bracelet. I still can't believe that Meg is dead and that I will never see her again.

We are reading *George's Marvellous Medicine*, one of the children's favourites, but every time I say the character's name, I feel my eyes fill with tears and my voice breaks. I can't carry on like this. Through my blurred vision, I can see the kids staring at me in horror.

'Miss?' Bilal, the bravest kid in the class, asks me. 'Are you OK, miss?'

I can't speak. It's almost like I am watching the scene from above. The teaching assistant quietly takes the book from my hands and tells the children to go back to their chairs. She sends Bilal to fetch Rhona. I am glued to the chair. I'm afraid if I try to move, I am going to fall. Snot is seeping from my nostrils and I can feel the salty mix of tears and mucous on my lips. I must look a sight. I reach into my bag for a tissue, but I don't have the energy to complete the manoeuvre. All the stress and worries I've been bottling up over the past few weeks are flooding back in huge tidal waves and I can feel my shoulders shake as I hide my face in my sleeves.

'Miss Metcalfe?' Rhona's voice. She is crouching in front of me, pushing my arm away from my face. 'Holly,' she whispers urgently. I look into her concerned eyes, but I can't stop.

Rhona stands up. 'Right class, I want you all to get your books out and write me a story about a rabbit.'

'What kind of rabbit, miss?'

'It can be any kind you like. But no talking.'

I can hear the clatter of kids getting out their pens as Rhona kneels in front of me again. 'Holly, what on earth's the matter?'

I shake my head. 'I don't know.'

'Come on.'

Rhona helps me to stand and steers me towards the door. 'Everyone be very quiet please. Miss Metcalfe isn't feeling very well.'

We stand in the corridor and Rhona wipes my face down with a tissue. The tears are drying up and I can control my breathing again, but I am acutely embarrassed. I can't believe I broke down in front of my class. It's so humiliating.

'What's going on?'

I should tell her. Rhona is my friend; she wouldn't judge. I shake my head. 'It's nothing really. I've been getting these messages on my phone.'

'What kind of messages? Threatening ones?'

'I guess.'

'Oh my God, Holly. Why didn't you say anything? Let me see.'

'I've deleted them,' I lie.

'Well you need to report it. You can get help with this sort of stuff. Do you think it's a parent?'

'No, I don't think so. I don't know. It's all anonymous. Thing is, he knows where I work. I got these flowers. And I've had stuff posted through my door.'

'Holly, this is serious. He's stalking you. Why didn't you say anything? You must have been so scared.'

Rhona's the least judgmental person I know. I've always been able to tell her anything.

'I thought he might stop. He says that I ...'

'What does he want you to do Holly?'

I look into her eyes. Rhona looks really concerned and I know I should be able to trust her, but I can't find the words.

'I don't know. It doesn't matter.'

'It does matter. Holly, what aren't you telling me? What does he want you to do?'

'Nothing. It's fine. Look, I over-reacted, that's all.'

'Come on Holly, you can tell me. I'm your best friend. You can tell me anything.'

I want to tell her. I really do. She might even understand why we did what we did once she hears the full story. Can I trust her?

'I mean, it's not like you've killed someone,' she jokes. 'Whatever it is, it can't be that bad.'

I shut my mouth. Take a deep breath. Fake a smile. I can't believe how close I came to telling Rhona everything. How could she possibly understand? Besides, Rhona is married to a cop. I can't see her turning a blind eye to what we did. 'Honestly, I'm fine. It's been a tough week. PMT. Not enough sleep.'

'I'm worried about you.'

'I'm being a drama queen, forget about it.'

'But this guy ...'

'It was only a couple of text messages. It was probably a wrong number.'

'You said he'd been to your house.'

'Seriously, Rhona. I'm fine. Come on, you'd better get to class. 'Orrible Oliver will have staged a mutiny by the time you get back.'

She pauses but the moment has passed, and she can tell I am not going to carry on talking.

'You're sure you're OK to go back in?'

'Yes, I'm fine. Honestly.'

'And you don't want to talk to Rob about it?'

'I'm sure. I'm overreacting. It's nothing I can't handle. I need to get some sleep.'

'OK,' she says, still looking worried and I know she will

raise the subject again. But for the meantime I am off the hook. 'Well you know you can talk to me, any time day or night. My door is always open. And there's always a bed for you if you get spooked and want to stay over.'

'Thanks Rhona, I really appreciate it.'

I take a deep breath and walk back into the classroom, feeling like a complete idiot. I need to get my head together if I am going to deal with this. I nearly cracked and told my darkest secret and I can't let myself be that weak again.

Chapter 23

Nathan has been absent for eight days now without a word from his mother and I'm starting to get worried. All the kids have had some sort of sniffle – it's only to be expected at this time of year – but my calls to Emma's mobile and her landline have gone unanswered. Trevor calls me into his office to discuss the matter.

He keeps me waiting for several minutes while he finishes his paperwork, adding his signature with a flourish. I sit awkwardly as he demonstrates how much busier he is than anyone else in the building. Finally, he looks up, puts his hands together in front of him and meets my gaze in a way that I am sure he has picked up on one of his management away days.

'So, Nathan Whitaker. Unauthorised absence.'

'Yes, I'm sure it's nothing to worry about but I haven't managed to get hold of his mum, and he's not been to school for over a week now.'

Trevor outlines the next steps as if he is following an instruction manual.

'If he misses ten days then we will have to inform social services,' he says pompously in a tone which doesn't invite contradiction. But I don't want Emma to get in trouble.

'Maybe I should go and see them? See if something's wrong before we take it any further? There might be something we could do to help?'

'You don't want to compromise your position, Holly. These things can take a very nasty turn if you don't follow the rules.'

I swallow back a response. Sometimes I wonder if Trevor is actually human or a sophisticated piece of artificial intelligence. I wish for once he would fuck up. Arrive at school with a hangover, or spill ketchup down his fastidiously ironed shirts. I wonder what he's like at home; whether he maintains this regime in his domestic life or whether he's a complete slob the minute he walks through the door. I can't imagine Trevor ever wearing jogging bottoms or sitting in front of crap TV with a beer. I picture him every evening sitting at his laptop, salivating over statistics, perhaps eating the same nutritionally balanced meal and performing fifty press-ups before bed. He never mentions a wife, or even a partner. I can't imagine Trevor romantically involved. The thought of it makes me slightly queasy.

'We'll bookmark this discussion for another day and reconvene,' he says. 'How are you getting on with the photography for the school play?'

I stifle a groan. Trevor asked me ages ago to take some

publicity shots so that we can promote the annual theatrical debacle to the parents, but with everything else that has been going on recently, I haven't got around to it. Rhona has been appointed director this year, but Trevor has ruled out some of her more liberal additions to the script for fear of a backlash from the parents.

'I'll have them to you by the end of the week,' I rashly promise, wondering if I can get Rhona to help me. She says I need to be more assertive with Trevor but when I am sitting opposite him, I find it hard to come up with excuses. He can be very demanding but always makes his requests seem perfectly reasonable. He expects paperwork above and beyond what is usually required and puts far too much pressure on the staff to be 'innovative' and 'go the extra mile'. I still try to bring something fresh to every class but there is a limit on how much variety you can bring to teaching reception. I am relieved when Trevor finally dismisses me, reiterating his command that I leave the Nathan situation to him.

I know I should listen to Trevor; I know I should follow procedures; but something isn't right, and I can't wait for the system to kick into gear. I would never forgive myself if something happens to one of my pupils because I didn't act soon enough. In our safeguarding training we are told never to ignore the warning signs. Surely, it's better to act and be wrong, than allow a situation to escalate? I have been worried about Nathan since he started. He doesn't behave like the other children; he is withdrawn and cowers whenever anyone speaks to him. It's not unusual for children starting school to be shy, but this is different. It's as if he is permanently afraid. Surely it can't harm to go and find out what's the matter?

I drive up to Emma's house at lunchtime, navigating the narrow roads lined with unforgiving drystone walls and down the pot-holed track to the farm. The landscape around me is breath taking. Every so often I am caught off-guard by how beautiful the Yorkshire Dales is. I take my surroundings for granted but there's a reason why so many tourists flock to this area for a holiday. For once it isn't raining and the views are spectacular. The sun is low in the sky, making driving difficult but bathing the hills in a golden hue. The limestone pavements which have been here for thousands of years spread majestically across the moors as sheep quietly graze on the tufts of grass that peek out from the rock.

I park the car in the untidy farmyard and climb out, not bothering to lock it behind me. We are miles away from anywhere up here, a place often cut off in winter. I can hear a dog barking from one of the outbuildings and the sheep bleating in the fields but there is no other sign of life. I don't know if I would like to live up here; it must be pitch black at night and every sound would be magnified. I step over the piles of mud and manure, wishing I hadn't worn heels and feeling less and less confident by the minute. Trevor will kill me if he knows I have disobeyed his orders.

Emma's cottage has dirty mullion windows laced with huge cobwebs. I ring the doorbell, but I don't hear any sound. After a couple of minutes, I try the door knocker and then rap on the window. Eventually I hear movement from within.

Emma opens the door a couple of inches and eyes me suspiciously. 'Yes?'

'I'm Holly, Nathan's teacher?'

'Nathan's ill.' She starts to close the door again, but I push it back. I am stronger than she is, and the door opens wider to reveal a thin, pale woman dressed in dirty jeans and a fleece covered in dog hairs. Nathan's mother could pass for a teenager, but a closer inspection reveals a sprinkle of grey hair and bags under her eyes that betray her age.

With an assertiveness I don't feel, I carry on talking. 'Thing is, if he's missing school, you really need to call us, otherwise we have to report you. They could take you to court, Mrs Whitaker.'

This has the desired effect. 'No need for that,' she says. 'He'll be in tomorrow.'

Something's not right. From the way she holds the door and looks back over her shoulder, I can tell she doesn't want me here. Is someone else in the house? Someone she doesn't want me to see? Regardless, I ask, 'Can I come in?'

'It's not convenient right now.'

'Is everything OK?'

She looks into my eyes and I think I read fear, panic, anxiety cross them. 'Everything's fine.' She pushes the door to a close and I can hear her lock it behind her. I stand in the yard for a while biting my lip and wondering whether to knock again. She didn't look fine, but what can I do? She obviously doesn't want my help.

I look up and in one of the upstairs windows I can see a little face watching me through the dirty pane. It's Nathan. I wave but he disappears from view. I wonder whether I should call the police, but what would I say? Emma has every right not to let me into her house. I walk back to my car and manoeuvre out of the yard. I haven't achieved anything by coming here but at least I have established that Nathan is home and seems OK. I suppose the only thing I can do is wait until tomorrow and see if I can get some answers out of him.

Chapter 24

Does Holly have any idea what she put Mark's family through? The media were on their doorstep within hours of the police breaking the news. They barely had a chance to digest the information themselves before being thrust in front of the cameras like animals in a zoo, every movement analysed by the press and public.

Photographers, with long lenses, gathered outside the family home, making it impossible to leave the premises. His father offered to sort them out with his shot gun so, with his mother doped up on sympathy and tranquilisers, it was left to Mark to be the family spokesperson. He found some suitable photographs of George for the police press office to release and approved a statement pleading for privacy during this difficult time. He read the statement out at a press conference with lights flashing in his face and reporters pestering him for an exclusive. When he saw the coverage on the news that evening, he barely recognised himself.

The media lapped up the narrative of a young life wasted

through drugs and alcohol. They took pictures from George's Facebook account and spun a morality tale of the dangers of privilege and excess. The toxicology report gave credence to the comments from so-called friends about George's party lifestyle. They found amphetamines and large quantities of alcohol in his blood. His mother asked the Thai police to investigate whether his drink had been spiked, refusing to believe her little boy would dabble with drugs, but Mark knew his brother. The police and the Foreign Office were kind to her, but it was never going to be a serious line of inquiry. As far as they were concerned, it was a tragic accident, one they saw far too often in holiday resorts catering for young backpackers.

In the end, Mark called one of his old pals from Cambridge, now a reporter on *The Telegraph*, to set the record straight. He put together a sensitive obituary, outlining George's sporting achievements and huge potential. It appeased his father and comforted his mother, but this heavily sanitised version of George's life was no nearer the truth than the one the tabloids had painted. His little brother was impulsive, impetuous, infectious. He was no angel, but there was no malice in him either. He didn't deserve to die.

An appeal for information on social media brought about a barrage of photographs and anecdotes from the full moon party where George had died. People said they had seen him arguing with his friends and leaving with a dark-haired woman, but none of these claims could be substantiated. Pictures emerged of George drinking from a bucket of cocktail, surrounded by bikini-clad women; dancing on the beach with his arms in the air and sweat glistening on his forehead; and leaning backwards with a huge grin on his face as he limboed underneath a blazing fire rope. Nothing that gave them any reason to suspect that what happened hadn't been a tragic accident. There were no witnesses and the young woman, if she had even existed, had never been identified.

George's position in society and the circumstances surrounding his death held the media's interest for a little while, enough to put them through hell and back, but without a crime, without an investigation or criminal proceedings, they soon moved on. Fiona, who had disappeared to a clinic in Switzerland as soon as the story broke, re-emerged and came to pay her respects, the epitome of grace and elegance. She married a year later and hadn't been in touch since. To her credit, she never spoke to the press, not even to refute the many stories about George's infidelity. Mark still gets calls sometimes, usually freelancers trying their luck or TV documentary makers offering large sums of money for exclusive interviews, but he has always declined. It's not money he needs, it's the truth.

Chapter 25

Five years ago

I never asked Lisa what happened that night with George; I guess I was afraid of the answer. Neither of them mentioned it again and I put it down as a meaningless one-night stand. I hid my hurt under fake smiles, but I felt betrayed. Why was it always so easy for Lisa? She could have any man she wanted, why did she have to take George?

I didn't have much time to dwell on my broken heart. The last few weeks of term were intense with last-minute cramming, frayed tempers and sleepless nights. Real life was looming, and we had to make big decisions about what we were going to do with the rest of our lives. I had applied to teacher training college while Kristóf planned to make a living out of his poetry and thought teaching was 'selling out'. Meg was looking at graduate training schemes and George was thinking of joining his brother in Singapore for a few years. The thought of George being on the other side of the planet gnawed at my insides, but

I had resigned myself to the fact that we were never meant to be. I had had three years to tell him how I felt, and I hadn't. It wasn't going to happen now. At least we had the summer together to look forward to before we went our separate ways.

Lisa and my parents came over to help us clear out the house at the end of our third year. I looked around my empty room with a sense of sadness. The single bed had been stripped ready for the next occupant, there were tiny circles on the painted walls where my posters had been pinned and my stuff was crammed into cardboard boxes and black bin bags. For the past three years, Meg, Kristóf and George had been like my family. Everything was changing and I couldn't imagine a future without them in my life.

Kristóf had already left, carrying his possessions in a huge backpack. If I hadn't caught him sneaking out of the front door, then he probably wouldn't have even said goodbye. I wondered whether he would turn up at the airport. Three years on, and I still couldn't work out what was going on in that head. George's parents hadn't bothered to come but had sent a driver and a man to help him with his luggage. He didn't look thrilled to be going home but he knew better than to argue with his parents. I was kind of relieved. I really didn't want him spending any more time with Lisa.

Meg and I had booked a Chinese meal for a farewell treat and to say thank you to our families. The restaurant was noisy, busy and served great food. We ordered a banquet for eight and we were soon surrounded by steaming dishes of rice, noodles and meat in brightly coloured sauces. Meg's grandmother, a fierce looking Jamaican woman wearing a bright pink dress and matching shoes, was keeping us entertained. She had taken a shine to my dad and was making no attempt to hide it.

'You look a lot like him,' she commented.

Meg looked mortified and started to explain, but I cut her off.

'Thank you,' I said. By a twist of fate, I did look like my father, even though we weren't biologically related. It was a running joke in our family that I was such a daddy's girl, I was turning into him. Lisa took after Mum, a fact that she vehemently denied every time it was pointed out.

It was times like these, big changes in my life, when I didn't know how I was supposed to feel about being adopted. Should I be upset that my birth mother wasn't here to see me graduate? Or just pleased that my real family, the one that had loved me, cared for me and supported me, were here? How could I feel anything for someone I had never known? Throughout my childhood, even during my turbulent teenage years, I never doubted my parents loved me. They never treated me any differently to Lisa, but now doubts were creeping in. I wondered how they would feel if Lisa and I fell out, whether they would take sides. I didn't want to find out. For all our sakes, I decided to put her betrayal behind me and move on with my life.

Meg tactfully changed the subject and started chatting enthusiastically about our plans for backpacking; the countries we would be travelling to and the experiences we were anticipating over the next three months. We were going to start in Cambodia, travel through Vietnam and end up in Thailand before heading back to the UK in September. Since our exams, we had spent our time poring over guidebooks and travel websites planning our route.

'Aren't you worried?' Mum asked Naomi.

'About this one? Meg can get into scrapes in her own backyard. I can't see it being any different in Asia.'

'Mum! I'm twenty-one now, a grown woman. I don't get into scrapes!' Meg winked at me mischievously. We both knew different.

'You'll always be our little girl,' Dad said fondly. 'Wherever you are in the world.'

'Still, things are different in these countries. You can't trust the police for a start.'

Lisa rolled her eyes. 'Mum, what do you think they're going to do? She'll be fine. She can't spend her whole life in Morecambe.'

'Well, it was good enough for me and your father!' Mum sniffed.

'Stop worrying, Mum. I'll call you every few days. You can even track us on our phones if you're worried! Although I'd rather you didn't!'

'You have to let them go at some point,' Naomi said. 'And they've got each other; these two are joined at the hip.'

Meg squeezed my hand under the table. 'Don't worry Mrs Metcalfe, we'll take care of Holly for you.'

I felt vaguely patronised even though they meant well. When were they going to let me grow up? I was an adult now, more than capable of looking after myself. Maybe this adventure was what I needed to gain some independence.

The attention thankfully turned to Lisa and her latest round of auditions. She had got a part in a Finnish TV commercial and an unpaid role in a fringe theatre production, but she was optimistic that both would get her noticed by a big agent.

'You OK?' Meg asked me quietly.

'Yeah, of course.'

'It's going to be great, don't let them scare you.'

'I'm not.' And I wasn't. I had my best friend by my side, what could possibly go wrong?

*

The plane lurched from side to side as the seatbelt sign flashed on. Meg was struggling to walk in a straight line as she made her way back from the toilets, apologising as she bumped into people. She slid into the seat next to me and gripped my hand like a vice.

'What's happening?' she said, her voice trembling.

'Just a bit of turbulence, don't worry.'

The plane shuddered again and an announcement was

made asking people to return to their seats. You could feel the tension rising as people started to buckle up. Meg bit her lip. She had almost backed out of the whole trip at Manchester Airport and her fear of flying had not eased throughout the journey.

'Try not to think about it.'

She nodded and put her earphones in. From the adjacent set of seats, Kristóf lifted his head from out of his book and looked over.

'Is Meg OK?' he mouthed.

I nodded and smiled. It had been a bit of a surprise when Kristóf had shown up at Manchester Airport. He hadn't been in touch since we left university and I had started to think we would never see him again. He seemed relaxed and cheerful, putting up with George as he moaned about the size of the seats in economy class, not used to slumming it. George had been making full use of the drinks trolley for much of the flight and was now fast asleep with his mouth open.

'I am never doing this again,' Meg groaned. 'I'm coming back by boat.'

'I'm not sure that's going to be any more comfortable.' I tried to distract her by reading her passages out of my guidebook but she clearly wasn't in the mood to hear about the ancient temples of Angkor or the Royal Palace and Silver Pagoda in Phnom Penh. Eventually I heard her breathing steady and her head dropped onto my shoulder as she started to drift off.

I looked out the window with excitement but there was nothing to see except endless clouds. I couldn't believe it. After months of planning, we were finally on our way! The last-minute arrangements had fallen into place and all my belongings for the next three months had been crammed into a sixty-litre backpack. I hadn't been able to bring half the stuff I had bought for the trip, Lisa finally convincing me that I didn't need a dozen paperbacks or three tubes of toothpaste.

'I'm sure they sell toothpaste in Thailand,' she said. 'And you've got your kindle.'

She hadn't said so, but I thought Lisa might be a bit jealous about our trip. I had promised to send her lots of photos of our travels and in turn she would keep me updated about her new life in London. I still hadn't forgiven her for sleeping with George, but she seemed to have moved on, so I tried to push it to the back of my mind.

The plane tipped again, waking Meg up. She looked like she was going to throw up. I handed her the paper sick bag and prayed that the turbulence wouldn't last much longer. We still had several hours to go before we reached Bangkok and then we had to change planes to fly directly to Siem Reap in Cambodia.

It was going to be a very long journey ...

Chapter 26

We arrive at Rhona's house for dinner shortly after seven. It's the first time we have been invited anywhere as a couple and I'm delighted Tom agreed to come. Jack is having a sleep over with one of his friends, so we can relax and make a night of it.

Rhona and Rob live in a cottage in the centre of the village, subject to draconian conservation rules. There is a date stone above the door; but even without it, you can tell from the low beamed ceilings, the thick stone walls and the flagged floors, that the cottage is seventeenth century. Situated on the Main Street, their living room is the perfect vantage point for spying on people coming home from the pub or out for an evening stroll, and ideal for nipping to the Spar shop if you run out of milk. They have lived in this cottage all their married life. Rob grew up in the village and boasts about his unparalleled knowledge of the families that make up its community. He is a member of the local historical society and regularly gives talks at the library. In his spare time, he locks himself away in his study, poring over genealogical records and tracing his roots back across the centuries. He met Rhona on a night out in Bradford, brought her home to meet his mother, and she fell in love with the quiet charm of the Yorkshire Dales.

On paper, Rob and Rhona are very different, but they have a strong chemistry and a rock-solid bond. Their relationship went through the mill when they found out they couldn't have children; but they came out the other side stronger than ever. Rhona doesn't talk about it much, and I wonder how she must feel surrounded by other people's children all day, but I guess it's something she's learnt to live with.

I never feel completely relaxed around Rob. I don't know whether it's because he's my best friend's husband and I wonder how much she tells him, or whether it's because he's a policeman, but I always feel like I am under some sort of interrogation when he is asking me questions. He likes to tease me about my love life and I wonder whether he will act the fool in front of Tom. I'm not sure how much they will have in common. Rob has a directness that can be off-putting whereas Tom is the epitome of diplomacy. Rhona's husband also has pretty Conservative views while Tom is a staunch Labour supporter.

Rob greets us at the door and leads us into the living room. Usually when I go for dinner, we eat in the kitchen, but tonight I can see that the dining room has been laid formally and candles lit. I am touched. Rhona greets us both with a kiss and compliments me on my dress.

'What can I get you Tom? Beer? Wine?'

'Beer would be great.'

'Holly?'

'White wine would be lovely.' I don't normally drink on a school night, but the alcohol might relax me. Rhona hasn't mentioned the messages since I had my meltdown and I know I can trust her not to say anything in front of Tom, but I am still on edge in case she lets something slip after a few drinks.

'Who's the chef?' Tom asks.

'That would be Rob,' Rhona laughs. 'I can't boil an egg.'

She's lying. Rhona is a serviceable cook, but Rob is the one who likes to make an effort: trawling farmers' markets at the weekend and tracking down obscure ingredients in Manchester to transform his dishes. The smell of Thai food coming out of the kitchen brings back bitter memories. My stomach growls, but I'm not sure whether it's hunger or fear.

'I hope you like green curry,' Rob says to Tom.

'Love it.'

'You'll have to tell us whether it lives up to the real thing, Holly,' Rob suggests, and Tom looks at me, surprised.

'I didn't know you'd been to Thailand,' he says.

'A long time ago,' I say, quickly changing the subject before he can ask anything else.

Over dinner the conversation ranges from Brexit (Rob's in favour, Tom's vehemently opposed), a planning application for a new development on the edge of the village and proposed cuts to neighbourhood policing. The heat of the curry is making my nose stream and despite what I tell Rob, it's not a patch on the food we had in Asia. It was hard to find a bad meal in Thailand; even the cheapest street food was delicious and full of flavour. Rob's version is heavy on the chilli which overpowers the whole dish.

Rhona is unusually quiet and is drinking steadily. She doesn't even seem to be tasting the wine. Her cheeks are growing pink and her lips are stained dark purple. She is managing to make conversation but there is a harshness about her face that isn't usually there. Every time Rob makes a pronouncement, she rolls her eyes or makes a sarcastic remark and I wonder how much she has had to drink. She's always liked a tipple, and often jokes about getting to 'wine o'clock', but she seems to be drinking more and more these days.

Rob is talking about a joint enterprise case that hit the newspapers this week involving a group of young men in Birmingham. The mothers are appealing against the sentence.

'Well, I think that's right,' says Rhona, mindlessly topping up her glass. 'I mean being there isn't the same as actually killing someone, is it? And think of all those kids who are behind bars for being in the wrong place at the wrong time.'

'It's madness; another example of the courts caving in to pressure from parents who can't bear to think of their

precious sons getting involved in gangs,' Rob says pompously. 'It's hard enough to get a prosecution these days with
all the hoops we have to jump through.'

'Yes, but you wouldn't want someone to go to prison
for a crime they didn't commit?'

'When they're all in it together, when they cover for each
other afterwards, then it doesn't matter who pulls the
trigger. They're all culpable. What do you think Holly?'

'Err, I haven't really given it much thought,' I lie, desperately hoping for a change in subject matter. I can feel my
cheeks burning and I hope the others think I have just
had one too many.

Rhona won't let it go. 'Culpable, yes. But are they all
murderers? I mean if someone drives the getaway car, is
he as guilty as the man who holds a gun to someone's
head?'

'Yes, I think he is.' Rob sounds angry and his voice is
rising. Clearly, he thinks being a policeman makes him the
expert on the subject.

'But they're only kids. Some of them are still in their
teens. They're not old enough to make those kinds of
decisions.'

'Old enough to carry a gun, old enough to be in a gang,
old enough to face the consequences.'

There is an awkward silence as Rob makes his declaration. Tom hasn't said anything, but I can tell he wants to.
Rhona starts to clear the plates and I help her. In the
kitchen she takes a deep breath.

'Sorry about that. You know what he's like when he gets on his high horse. No-one else's opinion counts.'

'Are you two OK?'

'Yes, of course. He's just irritating me tonight, bloody know-it-all.'

I smile and go back to the dining room. Fortunately, the conversation has moved on now and the atmosphere is considerably lighter. I sip my drink, thinking about what Rob said about culpability. As teachers, we are always being dragged in to adjudicate the children's squabbles and quite frankly, we don't care who or what provoked the fight, we just want an end to it. Are the police the same? Do they care about the ins and outs of a crime, or do they just want a result? I wonder how many cases of joint enterprise Rob has actually dealt with. The Yorkshire Dales is not exactly overridden with gangs and, apart from a temporary secondment to Leeds, I don't think Rob has had much experience with gun crime.

Rob leaves the table to bring in dessert and Rhona asks us what our plans are for Christmas. Tom and I haven't really discussed Christmas yet; I was hoping we were going to spend it together, so I am disappointed when he tells Rhona he is planning to take Jack to see his parents in Suffolk. He could have at least discussed it with me first. It's hard to keep the disappointment creeping over my face and I can tell Rhona has picked up on it.

'What about you, Hol? Going back to your folks?' Rhona gives me a sympathetic smile.

'I guess so.'

'Maybe we can do something for New Year?' Tom suggests.

'That would be nice.'

Later, as we are leaving the house, Tom apologises. 'I'm sorry about Christmas, I was put on the spot. Do you want to spend it together?'

'I'd love to, but if you've already made plans ...'

He draws me close and puts his arms around me. 'Plans can be changed.'

'I really want you to meet my family. I want them to spend some time with Jack. To know that we're serious about each other. We are, aren't we?'

My heart is pounding so hard I am sure he must be able to hear it. I have never spoken to Tom about how I feel about him. I've always pretended to be fine about our relationship, but he must know that I want more. Most women of my age are settling down, getting married, having children. I don't want to be cast casually aside after he's had his fill of me. I'd rather know now how Tom feels than let my heart be broken again.

We are standing outside the row of shops in the village centre. The moon is full and bathing the cobbled street in silver light. It is so quiet that you can hear an owl hooting in the distance. We pass the stocks where they used to imprison thieves and liars and make our way to Tom's house. I shiver. The ghosts of the village, brought to mind from Rob's stories of local folklore, seem to be making their presence felt. I've had too much wine; I'm losing my grip on what is real and what is in my head, but Tom brings me back to the present.

'I love you, Holly.'

The ghosts swirl and then disappear. I have waited a long time to hear Tom say those words. 'I love you too.'

We walk to his house, hand in hand, stupid grins on our faces. Being with Tom makes me feel invincible, like nothing bad could ever happen. All my fears and worries fade away and I am filled with happiness. He loves me. Tom loves me. Finally, after all these years, I have found 'the one', someone I can spend the rest of my life with.

Chapter 27

Emma is true to her word and the next day Nathan is back at school. That hasn't stopped me being concerned; quite the opposite. He doesn't look up when I call out his name during registration and sits staring at his hands. His eyes are ringed with grey shadows and he isn't wearing any socks. When the kids start getting art stuff from the cupboard, he stays in his seat. Eventually he joins the other children at the table and pulls some red card towards him, but he doesn't interact with his classmates and barely responds when Phoebe snatches a pen out of his hand.

The kids are making poppies for Remembrance Sunday. They have been learning about World War One and bombarding me with questions about guns and death. Some of the boys display a morbid curiosity about the subject, with a complete lack of empathy. Phoebe wants to put glitter on her poppy, which I am not sure is entirely appropriate, but I am too distracted by Nathan's behaviour to object. We leave them on the radiator to dry and I notice that he has barely touched his.

Rhona comes in after lunch carrying a stack of costumes for the school play. She wants the kids to dress up so that we can take some preview pictures for the posters. I appear to have become the school's unofficial photographer since Rhona let slip that I have a half-decent camera and spend a lot of my time on the fells taking pictures. However, taking exactly the right shot of the sun rising over Pen-y-ghent and getting thirty children to look at the camera and smile at the same time are very different challenges.

Phoebe makes a fuss over her costume, which is too big, and I am helping her to adjust it when I glance over and notice two large yellow bruises at the top of Nathan's arms. He sees me looking and tries to cover himself up. Leaving Phoebe in the hands of the teaching assistant, I lead Nathan to the corner of the room away from the others and examine him. I can't see any other bruises, but he seems very underweight.

'How did you get these, Nathan?' I ask gently but he shakes his head and refuses to answer.

My camera is in my hand and I think about taking photographs for evidence, but before I do Nathan wriggles away from me. I let him go. I don't want to upset him any further or draw the attention of the other kids, but I'm really worried now. Has Emma, or Samantha, hurt him? Kids get bruises all the time, I know that, but these don't look like they have come from a fall or rough and tumble in the playground. It looks like someone has grabbed him. I need to report it.

Nathan lines up with the other children and smiles for the camera dutifully as Bilal, who can't resist a photo opportunity, ruins the shot by posing with his hand on his hips, Kardashian style. It takes me several attempts to get a half-decent shot.

'I don't know how you manage these lot, they're exhausting,' Rhona says as she gathers up the costumes. I quickly tell her about the bruises on Nathan's arms, keeping my voice down so that I won't be overheard.

'Holly, you have to tell Trevor.'

'I know, but what if I'm wrong?'

'What if you're right?'

I feel a pang of irrational fear. If Emma is hurting Nathan, then it's my responsibility to do something about it. But what will happen then? Will they take him away from her? Will I have to stand up in court and give evidence against Emma? Will Nathan spend the rest of his childhood being shipped around foster families? I went through the care system. I know it can be for the best sometimes, but not everyone is as lucky as I was. What if something happens to Nathan while in care and it's all my fault?

I wind myself up all afternoon weighing up the pros and cons of reporting Emma to the authorities, but in the end, I know that I can't live with myself if it turns out she is hurting Nathan and I did nothing to stop it. I go to find Trevor as soon as the school day finishes and barge into his office without knocking. He looks up from his computer, startled by the sudden invasion.

'It's about Nathan Whitaker. I found bruises on his arms and I really think we need to report it to the child protection team.'

Trevor's face falls as he gestures for me to take a seat. I take a deep breath, reminding myself I am doing the right thing, and relay my suspicions. As I do, I realise I don't have much evidence, just a gut feeling. Trevor calmly takes notes with his fountain pen, his face inscrutable, and I want to shake him into action.

'I'm scared that if we don't report this, something terrible is going to happen and we'll only have ourselves to blame.'

'Leave it with me,' he says.

'But you will do something, won't you?'

'I said, leave it with me. This is very serious, Holly, we need to tread carefully when it comes to safeguarding.'

'Don't you think I don't know that?' I can feel my temper rising and I struggle to keep a grip on it.

Trevor is silent as he re-reads his notes. Finally, he says 'To be honest Holly, I think we need more evidence before we go to the authorities.'

'We need to do something now!' I am almost shouting. 'There's something wrong, Trevor. When I went up to the farm yesterday, Emma wouldn't even speak to me ...' I trail off, realising I have dropped myself in it.

'You went up to their house? After I explicitly told you not to?'

'Yes, I'm sorry.' I take a deep breath and try to control my anger. 'I wanted to speak to her, find out what's going on.'

Trevor looks furious. 'How dare you flout my authority like that?'

I have never seen the head lose his cool before. I take a deep breath and try to maintain my own composure as he continues. 'Do you realise how this makes me look? It looks like I can't even control my own staff, let alone a school. I am the designated safeguarding lead, and I will decide what action should be taken, not you. It is absolutely imperative that we follow procedures.'

'This isn't about you. It's about a little boy who may be in trouble.'

He clenches his fist around the fountain pen. He looks like he would willingly stab me in the eye with it as he struggles to contain his fury. Finally, with a shaking voice, he says: 'Holly, I'm very disappointed. You're young, inexperienced. On this occasion, I will let you off with a verbal warning. But if you ever do anything like this again, I will be forced to take disciplinary action.'

How has this ended up being about me? I want him to take action, but not against me. Realising I am in danger of losing my job if I carry on pushing him, I leave the room, slamming the door behind me. Diane looks up from her desk, but I storm past her before she can ask me any questions. I will be the talk of the staff room tomorrow, but I don't care. I have never displayed my temper at work before and it feels good to let it out once in a while. I'm sick of letting people walk all over me. I will be keeping a very close eye on Nathan from now on and I'll report it to social services myself if I have to. I won't let anything happen to him because Trevor hasn't got the guts to rock the boat.

My head is full of all the clever retorts I would have said to Trevor if I had thought of them earlier, when my phone pings with a message. It's anonymous, again. Where does this guy get all these different numbers from? I'm not in the mood to deal with more cryptic nonsense, but I open it anyway. It's a link to a YouTube channel. My stalker has chosen to go public. There is nothing to identify the owner of the channel, but the account promises that this is the first video in a series. It's already had ten views.

I press play. I know the film well. The camera work is shaky because Meg was laughing as she filmed it. My hair is scraped back into a high ponytail, and I am wearing a vest top with spaghetti straps. My face is tanned and free of make-up. I am sitting at a table in front of a huge steel tray filled with raw meat and vegetables. In the centre of the tray is a raised dome and meat is gently cooking. A pile of yellow noodles sits at one side of the tray alongside broccoli and pak choi. A Cambodian barbeque looks and operates a bit like the fondue set my parents bring out every time they have a dinner party. I remember the meat came in small piles and included snake. I don't remember what the other meat was, but I remember George joking that it might be dog and daring me to eat it. In the video I am laughing and shaking my head. George grabs some chopsticks and moves the meat towards me. He drops the meat onto the tray and it sizzles for a while before he picks it up again and lifts it to my lips. Reluctantly I take it, swallow it down with a gulp of beer and then lift my arms in a celebratory cheer.

My phone beeps with another message: *I'm getting sick of waiting, Holly. You have 72 hours.*

Seventy-two hours and then, what? Another video. Or something much worse?

I put my phone away, feeling sick. I can't put this off much longer. I am going to have to speak to Kristóf.

Chapter 28

Cambodia, five years ago

Stepping out of the artificial coolness of Siem Reap Airport and into the overwhelming heat of the mid-afternoon sun, we were immediately besieged by a dozen tuk-tuk drivers offering us their services. I could almost feel myself wilt in the humidity, a reminder that we were on the other side of the world and far away from the mild summer we had left behind. It had been a long flight, broken up by transfers at Dubai and Bangkok, but it wasn't until we left the airport, that it really felt like we were on the other side of the world. The drivers clamoured around us, speaking broken English, German, French, Spanish, trying to guess our nationality. George took control, negotiating a fare with a driver dressed in beige chinos and a pale blue shirt, who spoke good enough English to barter his price. The driver – who introduced himself as 'Mister Kim' – led us towards a rickety carriage attached to an ancient motorbike.

We threw our heavy backpacks in and climbed inside, grabbing on to the handrails as Mr Kim started his engine and the tuk-tuk picked up speed. From the open back of the vehicle, we watched the countryside fly past and tried not to breathe in the toxic fumes from the chugging exhaust. There seemed to be no order to the roads; I wasn't even sure which side we were supposed to be driving on. We passed fields full of wandering water buffalo and ponds covered in lotus flowers, tiny children selling petrol out of plastic coke bottles by the roadside, farmers towing trailers piled high with sacks of rice and school children in uniforms hitching a lift. Whole families were precariously balanced on scooters as they weaved around trucks. You could feel every bump in the road.

'Why don't we have these at home?' Meg asked. 'They're so cool.'

'Err because it's always bloody raining?' George replied with a smile, as the tuk-tuk turned a corner at breakneck speed almost throwing me on to his lap.

It suddenly hit me that we were actually doing this. We were backpackers. Until this point it had felt like a fantasy. The sort of thing you talk about with your friends after a few drinks. Even when I boarded the plane, it didn't feel very real. It felt like we were just going on holiday for a couple of weeks. Now we were on our own, far away from the safety blanket of our parents or university, all our possessions crammed into backpacks.

I felt a mixture of nerves and excitement as we arrived

at the three-storey guesthouse advertising rooms for $8 a night. What kind of place charged $8 a night for rooms? I had visions of cockroaches and dirty bedding, so I was pleasantly surprised to discover the accommodation was lovely. The receptionist greeted us with a warm smile and took us on a tour of the premises. The hostel had a small pool and a garden area with stone statues, bright pink flowers and palm trees creating shade. An Australian couple greeted us as we walked past. They had tanned skin and top knots and looked perfectly at ease in these surroundings. Would we look like that in three months' time? I tried to picture Kristóf with his hair tied back in a ponytail and a bushy beard, but it was impossible.

There were two dormitories: one for girls and one for boys and a shared bathroom area. Everything was basic, but clean. A window had been left wide open in the dormitory and a large ceiling fan circulated air noisily, creating a welcome breeze. The room was deserted apart from a young woman in the corner who was fast asleep amid a pile of clothes. The set-up reminded me of going on school trips as a teenager. I wondered what the other guests would be like and where they were now. Probably exploring the temples or ziplining through the jungle. Excitement replaced the nausea. Meg and I couldn't stop grinning at each other.

The receptionist handed us our keys, reminding us not to leave valuables in the room and to use the lockers; but it didn't look like anyone had taken much notice. There were piles of belongings everywhere and chargers for mobile phones and tablets stuck into every electric socket. Meg and I had been given a bunk bed to share and she quickly claimed the top bunk by swinging herself up the ladder. The bed creaked ominously and for a moment I thought it was going to collapse. Without warning, a pair of Converse fell to the floor, narrowly missing my head, and the smell of Meg's sweaty feet reached my nostrils.

'I'm going to get some sleep,' Meg yawned. 'Night, night.'

I shoved my backpack underneath the bed and laid down, looking up at the crossed wire mesh that separated me from Meg. I closed my eyes, but I was too excited to sleep. I wondered if I was brave enough to go for a walk and explore the town by myself but decided that I wasn't. What if I got lost and couldn't find the hostel again? I contemplated going for a swim to cool down, but I didn't have the energy. Instead, I reached into my bag and took out a packet of Hobnobs and my *Lonely Planet* guide. The book was full of highlighted sections, turned down pages and pencil notes. Reading all about the sights we were going to see and the amazing experiences we were going to have made me feel better. I was on the trip of a lifetime with my best friends, one that I would probably remember for the rest of my life. I had nothing to worry about.

Darkness fell early on our first night in Cambodia. By the time we had met the boys and left the hostel, the streets of Siem Reap were already lit up by neon signs. The different sights, sounds and smells were overwhelming. Wafts of incense spiralled into the air from the tiny temples interspersed between the guest houses, bars and stalls selling everything you could possibly think of. Huge twists of thick electricity cables hung dangerously low and crackled just above our heads. Stray dogs wandered the streets, their ribs protruding from their scrawny bodies. Young monks with shaved heads and saffron robes walked serenely through the crowds, ignoring the attention they were attracting from tourists. Bare-footed children with wide chestnut eyes ran alongside us, holding out their hands and every two minutes we were offered a tuk-tuk.

We wandered to the night market, browsing stall after stall of cheap goods and fake designer handbags. George wanted to find a food stall selling fried tarantulas. He had seen it on a travel programme and was desperate to try one, but fortunately he was disappointed. The smell of fish sauce permeated everything, making my stomach recoil even though George reassured me it didn't taste as bad as it smelt. It was noisy, sweaty and frenetic. Everywhere we went, we were set upon by traders promising 'good price for you, lady' until it got irritating and we moved away from the busy market to find some food.

We sat down outside a cafe at a rickety table with plastic chairs and ordered beer. The waiter didn't ask for ID, which made a pleasant change from the UK. The beers arrived accompanied by glasses of iced water. I pushed my glass to one side – all the guidebooks said to only drink bottled water – and savoured the chilled beer which went some way to cooling me down. I picked up the laminated menu, relieved to find everything was translated into English, and picked the most familiar option: chicken fried rice.

'Oh my God, this is delicious,' Meg enthused, holding out a spoonful of the Amok fish curry she had ordered. 'You have to try it.'

I took a tiny sip and immediately wished I had been braver with my food choices. The curry was sweet and creamy, nothing like I was expecting. 'That's heavenly.'

Meg grinned at me. My dish arrived, hot and fresh, with a type of herb that tasted like aniseed. I hadn't eaten much in the last twenty-four hours, so I wolfed it down, relieved that it didn't taste much different to the fried rice we had at home. All around us were backpackers, making the most of the cheap food and beer. I could hear American and Australian accents intermingle with Dutch and French. Everyone spoke English, which was a relief, because my Khmer was patchy at best and I had been too frightened of accidentally giving offence to use it.

Over dinner we planned our excursions for the next few days. We had chosen to come to Siem Reap because of its proximity to Angkor Wat, one of the largest temples in the world and one of the most photographed. We had hired a driver for the day to take us around the extensive complex. I had spent hours looking at images on the internet of the majestic sandstone buildings, fascinated by images of the ancient banyan trees wrapping their tendrils around intricate carvings that dated back to the twelfth century.

While Kristóf delivered one of his many lectures about

the dangers of landmines in Cambodia, my attention was drawn to a man sitting on the street, opposite the restaurant. He had no legs and he had to manoeuvre himself around using his hands. He had a small rug next to him on which he was selling friendship bracelets made out of thin cotton. I wondered what had happened to him; whether his disability was due to war or disease and what he thought about all these carefree tourists, frivolously spending their money on meals out and alcohol. As we left the restaurant, I dragged Meg across to buy one. She chose a bright blue one to match her hair and to accompany the charm bracelet from her father. The disabled man handed me my change with a toothless smile and I thought about all the things I had worried about earlier, and how clueless I was about the real world. I had told my dad that travelling was going to open my eyes and force me to grow up, and I already felt that was the case.

By the time we reached the hostel, I was dizzy with exhaustion. I took the bottle of water I had bought from a stall on the way home and placed it on the floor beside my bed. Meg climbed up on to the top bunk and turned on her reading light to write her journal. The dorm was now full of people speaking a mix of languages and heavily accented English. There were girls that looked like they had been travelling a long time: their hair braided with colourful strands and spiritual tattoos on their arms and neck; and girls who looked like we did: terrified, away from home for the first time, and clutching on to their possessions. Most were in their early twenties but there were a few older ones as well, including a tiny French woman who could have been in her fifties. House music was playing from one of the portable speakers at the other side of the room, but I was too tired to care. I closed my eyes and fell fast asleep.

I woke up disorientated, desperate for a drink, my head thumping with dehydration. There was a strong smell of BO in the room and I thought I could hear a buzzing sound which I prayed wasn't a mosquito. My skin was itching, and I wasn't sure whether that was from the bed sheets or the heat in the dormitory. Even at night it didn't seem to get much cooler. I checked my phone and was surprised to see it was nearly 6am. I drank some water, which was now warm and musty, and ventured to the shower blocks, wearing my flip-flops to protect me from whatever water borne diseases might be lurking in the bathroom. I passed a cleaner, sweeping the floors, wearing a cloth mask over his mouth, and tried out one of the few phrases I had learned from my guidebooks to greet him.

'Suostei'. I felt self-conscious, hoping I had pronounced it right. He bowed his head, but I couldn't tell whether that was a greeting or whether he was just avoiding a painful conversation with a mad English woman first thing in the morning.

The water dribbled out of the shower head stone cold but that was refreshing after such a hot night. I washed myself quickly, wanting to avoid any interaction with the other guests while half-naked. I crept back into the dormitory wearing my towel and got dressed behind the thin curtains that offered each bed a little privacy. By the time Meg woke up, I was ready to face the day.

None of the pictures I had seen on the internet prepared me for the majesty of Angkor Wat. The tuk-tuk dropped us off at the entrance and Meg and I gazed up at the grand temple complex with its serene moat and long corridors lined with pillars while the boys sorted out admission. I grabbed my camera and snapped away, trying to capture the perfect image of the monument reflected in the water. Inside the temple, it was cool and dark, the shade a welcome relief from the sun which had emerged maliciously from the cloud cover to burn my pasty skin. The heat in Asia was nothing like the burning heat of the Mediterranean or the benign warmth of an English summer; it was intense and suffocating, making my t-shirt drip with sweat in a few minutes. It zapped my energy, forcing me to walk slowly and take frequent stops. The temple was crowded, thousands of visitors snapping away and posing for selfies.

I took photographs of everything: the intricate bas-reliefs along the corridors, the vertigo-inducing steps leading to the upper levels, the offerings of cakes and bottled water laid before statues of the Buddha. George laughed at me and told me to calm down with all the assurance of someone who could come back to Asia whenever he felt like it. A group of young girls, dressed in traditional Khmer outfits, posed with a family of overweight Americans and

I imagined their faces, trapped in a silver frame, on a mantelpiece, thousands of miles away for years to come.

Eventually George pulled us away, complaining that he needed a beer, and we climbed back into the tuk-tuk.

'I don't feel so good,' Meg groaned as we set off. There was a thin sheen of sweat on her face and she was shivering. I handed her my bottle of water and she gulped it down but as we got closer to the city centre, she started to squirm in her seat.

'I don't think I'm going to make it,' she whispered.

'Shall I stop the driver?'

She shook her head. We were nearly there and, as we rounded the corner, she jumped out and legged it to the hostel. It was hardly a surprise – Meg and George had been daring each other to eat dried chillies from the market the night before – but she looked dreadful. I was glad that I had declined.

A few hours later she was laid in her bunk, clutching her stomach. The boys were waiting for me downstairs, wanting to go out, but I didn't want to leave her. We had promised our parents that we would look out for each other.

'Go,' she said. 'I'm just going to sleep it off.'

I hesitated. I knew she wouldn't leave me if the situation was reversed. I wrapped the thin sheet around her and checked she had enough water. 'Message me if you get any worse.'

'I'll be fine. You worry too much, Hol. Go and enjoy yourself.'

Chapter 29

Kristóf teaches Romantic Poetry at a prestigious university in the Midlands. I call in sick for the first time in my career and set off early the next day. Trevor will think I'm avoiding him, but I don't care. The roads are quiet as I zip along the country roads with the car lights on full beam. Dawn arrives: a pale peach hue smudged with silky grey clouds and the traffic starts to build as I reach the M65. According to the sat nav I should arrive around 10am, all being well. I hit Manchester at rush hour and swear as the traffic grinds to a halt and then crawls along the M60. I'm used to rural driving, which has its disadvantages, but at least I don't have to put up with this every morning.

I know that Kristóf is working today. I called yesterday pretending to be a student and checked that his lecture was going ahead. I haven't spoken to Kristóf for five years. The last time I saw him we were in the middle of the turmoil that followed George's death. He was calm and authoritative, keeping the whole thing together while Meg and I tried not to fall apart. He was the one who spoke to the Thai police and the Foreign Office, who told us what to say and who made us promise never to reveal what really happened that night. Once we got home, I didn't want to see him again. I still don't, but he's the only one who can help me now.

The journey takes longer than I expected and Kristóf is half-way through his lecture by the time I find the right room. I sneak in the back and sit with the students, watching my former friend deliver his thoughts on Coleridge's *Kubla Khan*. Listening to Kristóf talk about the hallucinogenic quality of the poem brings back all our discussions at university. I look around the hall. Some of the students are listening intently; others are playing with their phones underneath the desk. Kristóf seems quite oblivious of his audience. I try to imagine him dealing with students; I can't picture him taking much of an interest in their welfare. But perhaps I have misjudged him. I've grown up, so he must have done too.

He doesn't look much different; his hair has receded a little and he has put on some weight but otherwise he is the same man I knew at university. He is wearing blue jeans and a cord green blazer. Underneath his jacket, I catch glimpses of a faded black t-shirt which I am sure I recognise from our university days. He is sporting a scruffy black beard and his hair is unruly as ever. I wonder what his students make of him; perhaps some of the girls fancy him.

The lecture finishes and there is a clamour as students gather their possessions and leave the hall. Against the tide, I walk down to the front of the room where Kristóf is talking to a pretty brunette and I hover, waiting to get his attention. Finally, he looks up and meets my eye. He looks like he has seen a ghost.

'Hi Kristóf.'

'Holly? What on earth are you doing here?'

The student gives me a dirty look and retreats. Kristóf stares at me, running his hand through his hair. I can't tell if he is angry or pleased to see me.

'I'm sorry to turn up unannounced like this. I should have called first.'

'No, it's fine. Sorry, it's a surprise, that's all.' He looks away and gathers up his books into a battered leather satchel.

'Can we talk?'

'Yes, of course. But not here.'

I follow him as he leads me out of the lecture theatre, down a corridor and into an untidy office. Kristóf looks so out of place in this environment, surrounded by young people glued to their mobile phones. But then again, Kristóf had always looked out of place. He was a man born in the wrong era. It's no wonder that he buries himself in the words of long dead poets.

I sit down on one of the chairs he must use for tutorials as he goes to the small kitchen area and switches on the kettle. 'Coffee?'

'Please.'

'Sorry, I don't have any milk.' He hands me a cup of black coffee in a chipped mug. His hands are shaking a little as he gulps down his drink.

'That's fine.'

He sits down opposite me and gives me an intense stare. 'It is good to see you again.'

'Is it?'

'Of course.'

I take a gulp of black coffee but it's too hot and burns the top of my mouth.

'How are you?'

'Oh, you know. I'm doing OK.'

'I read your book. I'm glad you're still writing.'

'I write more than I publish, put it that way,' he says with a wry smile. 'You were right, there's not much money in poetry.'

It feels so false, this 'how are you' exchange, so wrong. It's the type of conversation you have in the supermarket with someone you barely know, not someone you have been to hell and back with. Kristóf and I spent almost every day together at uni and yet here we are struggling to manage the most facile conversation. Back then, we were never lost for things to talk about: philosophy, politics, art, culture, current affairs, everything came under the scrutiny of our youthful observation. Looking back, that time in my life seems like a halcyon period: a time before responsibility, before regret, and I wonder if that's why Kristóf has chosen to cocoon himself here, trying to capture something that we have lost.

'I didn't come for a social visit. I came about Meg.'

'I thought that might be it. Bit of a shock.'

'Do you think it was an accident?'

'What do you mean?' He looks genuinely surprised, as if the idea had never occurred to him.

'Meg wasn't a drug addict.'

'People change, Holly. It's been a while.'

'Had you been in touch with her?'

'No, not since ...'

'Thailand.'

I take out my phone and show him the picture of Meg lying on the filthy mattress. He scrutinises it, his expression unreadable. I need to know whether he has seen it before. He hands me back the phone and our fingers touch for a fleeting moment. He pulls back as if I have burned him.

'So?' he says eventually.

'So? Someone sent me this, and Meg's bracelet. The silver one? The one her father gave her. He's threatening me, sending me messages, telling me I need to confess. I think he killed Meg. And if we don't do something, it will be us next.'

'Don't be so dramatic. That picture doesn't prove anything.' Kristóf sounds cross now, staring into his empty coffee cup like he wishes it were whisky.

'It proves he was there when she died.'

'Not necessarily. It's just someone trying to scare you.'

I look again at the picture. Photographs can be deceiving; I know that better than anyone. I pocket the phone. 'Well, it's working.' I take a deep breath, knowing that he's not going to like what I say next. 'I think we need to break the pact, go to the police and tell them what really happened.'

Kristóf pushes back his hair again, a nervous gesture that I am starting to find irritating.

'No,' he says simply.

'If we go together, it might not be so bad. It's been, what, five years? Can they even prosecute you after all that time?'

'Don't be stupid, Holly. Of course they can.'

'Well, maybe they'll look on us more favourably for coming forward.'

'I can't believe you're even considering this. You made a promise, Holly. Don't you remember?'

'Yes, I remember, but this guy knows ...'

'No-one knows. No-one else was there, Holly.'

'Perhaps someone saw us? There were hundreds of people at that party, any one of them could have been passing by.'

'If they had, they would have reported it at the time. We've been through this, Holly. No-one saw us. No-one knew we were there. I know you feel guilty about George, and I do too, but this isn't going to bring him back.' He sits back on his chair, his face resolute. I had forgotten this side of him; his arrogance and belief that everyone needs to listen to what he has to say. It was this sanctimonious attitude that got us into this mess in the first place. But I am not as naïve as I once was. I don't have to do as he says.

'Well, I'll go on my own then.'

'If you go to the police they will have to investigate. Think about what that will do to George's family. You weren't at the funeral, Holly, you don't know what it was like. His parents, his brother, his whole family, were devastated. Do you really want to bring that all up again? And for what? To assuage your guilt? And what about your family? And mine? This isn't only about you, Holly. My mum isn't well, this will kill her.'

I feel a fresh wave of regret as I think about my no-show at George's funeral. Meg, Kristóf and I had agreed to go together, but I couldn't face it. I couldn't stand to see Fiona playing the grieving fiancée after everything George and I had meant to each other. Besides, I was certain they would see guilt written all over my face. In the end, I told them I was ill, promised to visit George's parents soon; a promise I didn't keep.

'Do you have any idea who might be sending these messages?' Kristóf asks. 'What makes you so sure it's a man?'

'They sent me flowers. The florist remembered him but there was no CCTV, no evidence, just a scrappy description that could have been anyone. It must be someone we know.'

'How can it be? The only other people who were there were Meg and George. Unless you think I'm sending these messages?'

'It crossed my mind.'

'Is that why you're here? Because you think I'm stalking you? Look, I know it must be scary getting these messages, but what can this person do to you anyway? Surely if they had any evidence, then they would have already gone to the police? They only want you to confess because they can't prove anything.'

I bite my lip; I daren't tell him about the photo I took that night at the beach. He would be furious.

'We don't know what he's capable of. What if he wants to hurt us?'

'Have they actually done anything to you? Other than make a few empty threats?' Kristóf's imperious attitude is really starting to piss me off.

'You don't know what it's like.'

Kristóf leans over to his filing cabinet and brings out a manila folder. 'I keep them in here, just in case.' He hands the file over to me.

It is like something from an Agatha Christie novel: words cut out of newspapers and a letter typed on to cream writing paper. I go through them; the messages may be in a different format but they're more or less the same as the ones I have received.

'Who uses a typewriter these days?'

'I do. For my poetry. They wrote it on my machine, in my house.'

There are photographs of the four of us, printed on photographic paper. They look like they have been developed professionally.

'We should take this to the police. Maybe they can trace something. All my correspondence has been digital, but they can check IP addresses, can't they?'

I don't really know what an IP address is, but I'm sure I've heard them mentioned when we did some cyber security training. Now that I know I'm not the only one receiving the messages, I feel strangely emboldened. If both Kristóf and I report it, then surely, the police will have to do something?

'You need to go home, forget about it. They'll get bored soon.'

'And what if he doesn't? What if Meg was ignoring his messages? Look what happened to her.'

'I highly doubt this person had anything to do with Meg's death. It's not really in the same league, is it? Sending the odd poison pen letter and murdering someone in cold blood.'

I'm not convinced.

'Besides, if they were going to kill us, wouldn't they have done so by now?' Kristóf continues. 'I've been ignoring these letters for months. Clearly, they realised they weren't getting anywhere with me, so they moved on to you. What happened to Meg was terrible, but there's no reason to think it was anything other than an overdose. Go to the police now Holly and you're throwing everything away for nothing.'

I hesitate. Every time I think that I need to report it, I think about going to jail. I don't think I would last two minutes in prison.

'I won't back you up. If you do this, I'll tell them you're lying. That you're attention seeking. There's no proof that we were anywhere near George when he died. It'll be my word against yours.'

Only I do have proof. But I can't go to the police on my own, I'm not brave enough. Besides, the photo only proves that I was there; Kristóf could still deny any involvement and then the whole thing could be pinned on me. And what about Tom and Jack? He says he loves me, but would Tom wait for me if I went to prison? I doubt it. I think about the impact on all my family and friends and realise I can't put them through it. Maybe Kristóf is right. Either way, I can't do it without him.

'Fine.'

'You're doing the right thing. This is someone playing with our heads. They're not going to attack us.'

'I hope you're right Kristóf,' I gather my things and stand up.

'I've missed you, Holly. Stay in touch.'

Social convention tells me I should agree, but we're long past that now. I wish I had never come. He's been no use whatsoever. He's as stubborn and arrogant as he ever was.

'Stay strong, Holly. Keep your promise.'

Kristóf looks as if he is about to hug me, but I draw away. I can't wait to get out of his office. For all his talk about the impact on everyone else, I know that he is only interested in looking after himself.

Chapter 30

Meg had only told him half the story. After she died, Mark had turned to Kristóf for answers. He was sure that the academic knew something about his brother's death. Had he been there? Was he protecting someone, or was he to blame? Had George's death been an accident or murder? All Mark wanted was the truth.

Kristóf wasn't a difficult person to keep track of. Every day he rode to classes on his rickety old bicycle, ate the same lunch at the same campus cafeteria, and took the same route home down winding country roads. Evenings were spent at his desk writing or reading a book with a glass of wine in his hand. Mark couldn't believe this guy was in his twenties. He led the life of a pensioner.

He had seemed lost in the summer holidays when his classes stopped, and his work commitments dwindled. Mark had followed him for a miserable week in Snowdonia in which Kristóf had taken long hikes in the mountains and spent his evenings eating in traditional pubs and reading obscure tomes from the second-hand bookshops he frequented wherever he went. His poetry was melancholic, dwelling on death and the futility of life. Mark had read it, hoping for signs of repentance and remorse, but it was self-indulgent introspection, nothing more.

Kristóf was occasionally booked as a speaker for summer schools run by the university and Mark had spotted his name on a list of delegates for several literature festivals, but for the most part he seemed to eschew social engagements. He certainly didn't appear to have many friends. He had no social media accounts to look through and very little in the way of a digital footprint. His university email account had been easy to hack into but, judging by the plethora of unopened messages, it wasn't something he checked very often.

Had Kristóf killed his brother? And if so, why? They were friends. George could be a dick sometimes, Mark knew that, but he couldn't believe someone might actually want to kill him. From all the evidence he had gathered, Kristóf was a skinny man, unaccustomed to physical activity. He didn't look remotely capable of hurting someone like George; let alone killing him and leaving him for dead.

Mark bought newspapers from a supermarket, using the self-service till as an added precaution, and wore latex gloves to cut out the letters. It was unlikely that Kristóf would take the messages to the police, and even more unlikely that they would use precious resources tracking down the author of a poison pen letter, but Mark couldn't take any chances. He knew that the tiniest skin cell or a shaft of hair could leave his DNA. He couldn't risk getting caught before he knew the truth.

It hadn't been difficult to break into Kristóf's house. The lock on the rented property was low quality and not difficult to break. The house was sparsely furnished with little in the way of personal adornments. A dining room, long abandoned for its original purpose, housed piles and piles of books. There was no television. The kitchen was stocked with several cases of quality red wine and just the basics for subsistence. The bed had been made neatly and his clothes hung orderly in the wardrobe. Mark looked through his bank statements, filed neatly in a concertina file, placed on the bottom shelf of the bookcase. Kristóf earned a good wage from the university and received quarterly royalties from his published works but gave most of it away in significant and regular donations to an overseas charity helping Cambodian street children to access education and training. This unexpected philanthropy surprised Mark. No wonder Kristóf never seemed to have any money.

There were no personal photographs, although there were stacks of notebooks lying beside an old typewriter. Mark flipped through them. More poetry, written in pencil and scored through hundreds of times. Whole pages of synonyms and metaphors. A few odd lines scattered here and there, but nothing about his brother. Mark made a thorough search but couldn't find a journal. He suspected that if Kristóf had one, it would be in the battered leather satchel he carried around with him.

Mark copied out some of his personal poems, the ones that hadn't been published, to freak him out a little. He wrote a note on his typewriter to prove he could access his life whenever he wanted to. He sent letters to his university address, his home address and his parents' house to demonstrate his reach, but he never got a response. He waited for the call from his mother, telling him that the police were reopening the case, that someone had come forward with information, but it never came.

Kristóf was an intelligent man but he wasn't responding to Mark's threats. Mark had been planning his next move to get Kristóf to talk when he got the Google Alert about Holly's river rescue. Meg had been an emotional car crash, incapable of reason; Kristóf was a loner with a complete lack of conscience; but Holly was an entirely different prospect. Holly wouldn't ignore him. She had too much to lose.

Chapter 31

Cambodia, five years ago

Meg was poorly for three days and missed most of the temples. George, Kristóf and I ended up exploring without her and by the time our last day in Siem Reap came around, I was desperate to chill out. Kristóf headed off to a museum with his guidebook and a ridiculous Panama hat that made him look about sixty, while Meg and I doused our bodies in sun cream and headed to the pool. I lay face down in the sunshine, idly watching a scarlet dragonfly hovering over the water, and felt my body relax. Relentless sightseeing in the intense heat had taken its toll and I felt myself nodding off.

George joined us after half an hour. He dived into the pool, swimming underwater and then emerged, shaking water from his curly hair, looking like he should be in a Diet Coke ad. As he pulled himself out of the water, his sculpted torso glittering in the sunshine, I could see the other girls around the pool watching him and felt a sense of pride when he plonked himself on the lounger next to mine.

'What are you reading?' he asked, grabbing the paperback that was face down beside me. 'Anything juicy?'

It wasn't. I had picked it up from the airport. It was a piece of literary fiction that had won multiple awards and which I was trying very hard to like. I was planning on ditching it pretty soon for something lighter.

'Thought it might be *Fifty Shades of Grey*.' I flushed. I had read the book – who hadn't? – but I wasn't planning to discuss its contents with George. I had never seen George with a novel. I didn't even know if he liked reading.

'We should go out tonight. I mean out, out. To a club or something.'

With Meg poorly and Kristóf disinclined, we hadn't really made the most of the nightlife in Siem Reap, sticking to drinking beer at the makeshift pavement cafes and heading back to the hostel before midnight. The bars and clubs of Pub Street were full of noisy backpackers and touts trying to entice you with drinks promotions and offers of a 'good time'.

'Sure.'

'Count me out,' Meg said, clutching her stomach. 'I'm sticking to water for the foreseeable future.'

I didn't blame her. We had a six-hour bus journey to Phnom Penh the next day but I didn't want to miss up on the chance to spend time alone with George.

'Well, I can't see Mr Tedious wanting to boogie on down,'

he said. 'It looks like it's going to be just you and me, kiddo.'

'OK, but don't pull some hot backpacker and leave me on my tod.'

'Hey, I have all the hot backpackers I would ever need, right here, right now,' he said. 'I promise I won't leave your side.'

George was as good as his word. We soon discovered that cocktails in Siem Reap were strong and cheap. After a few mojitos I started to relax and enjoy myself. George was good company, making me laugh with his pithy observations of the people around us and mocking Kristóf for his need to educate us on Cambodian history at every opportunity.

'The guy is so boring!'

'He's alright. He means well.'

'You're only saying that because he worships the arse off you.'

'Don't be daft.'

I was grateful we were sitting in the dark, so George couldn't see me blush. He had dragged me into a club which advertised unlimited drinks and a ping pong show. It was nothing like the clubs back at home – it was more of a bar really – with the girls performing on a platform hidden behind red curtains at the back of the premises. George said it would be a laugh, but I think even he was shocked. I had never seen anything like it in my life, and I never wanted to repeat the experience.

'Oh, come on, Holly. You know he's got a crush on you. That's the only reason, I haven't …'

'Haven't what?' I could feel my heart thumping against my chest.

'Nothing, forget I said anything.' George looked away.

'Haven't what, George?' I leant towards him, hardly breathing, praying that I had read the situation correctly. A vision of George seducing my sister flashed across my memory, but I put it to one side.

He looked at me and our faces were so close that I could see flecks of amber in his beautiful brown eyes. 'Oh, fuck it,' he said and kissed me.

I had been waiting for this moment for three years and it was everything I thought it would be. George slipped his hands underneath my top as I pulled him closer. I knew neither of us wanted to stop at kissing, but we couldn't go back to the hostel. I don't know whether it was the sexually charged atmosphere of the club or my desperate need to feel him inside me, but I nodded towards the toilets. Giggling, we made our way through the dancers and slipped into a cubicle. Like all night clubs, it was disgusting and dirty with toilet paper all around the seat, grey water on the floor and a sharp smell of urine. But we didn't care. George pushed me up against the wall, staring into my eyes and kissing me passionately as we fumbled around with zips and underwear. I was so turned on at that point I didn't care about our surroundings. I couldn't believe this was finally happening.

It was over in minutes. As we sneaked back out of the toilets, wondering if anyone had spotted us, I couldn't stop grinning. I had to pinch myself to check that I hadn't just hallucinated.

We went to the bar and ordered a round of shots and the hit of alcohol went someway to bringing my heart rate down to a normal level. I was buzzing from the sex and the alcohol and I was desperate to talk to George about what this meant for us. Was it a one-off? Or the start of something? If we were going to be in a relationship, then we would have to tell the others, and how would they react? Had George planned this when he asked me to the club? So many questions but they could be answered another time. I had to be content with the knowledge that, for at least one night, I had been the sole focus of George's attention. There was no way we could go back to being just friends after this.

Chapter 32

The rain has been relentless all day, hammering at the windows. The sky is a dull white and the view from my classroom is washed in tones of grey. It's too wet for the kids to play outdoors and they are fractious and demanding. The ancient radiators in the corner of the room are pumping out heat with ruthless efficiency and making my head ache. I'm relieved when the clock finally gets to half past three and the kids can go home.

All weekend I have been dwelling on my conversation with Kristóf. Tom kept asking me what was wrong, but how could I explain? I blamed my mood on PMT, the same excuse I gave Trevor when he questioned my absence from work on Friday. I still don't know what to do. Kristóf thinks I'm overreacting, that this will all blow over, but I trusted his judgement before, I would be a fool to do so again.

It has now been seventy-two hours since the video went online. I am itching to check the YouTube channel to see if anything has been posted but I stupidly left my phone at home this morning. It's probably no bad thing. My nerves are frayed and paranoia jangles my veins constantly. I can't carry on like this, living in fear all of the time. I want, I need, this to end. I want to get on with my life without looking over my shoulder, wondering who's watching me. I want to switch on my phone without worrying about what messages I might receive. The only time I feel safe is when I'm with Tom and then I worry that I am putting him, and Jack, in danger too. I can't imagine walking into the village police station and handing myself in, but what choice do I have?

I try to imagine what the investigation would be like. Would they send me back to Thailand to face justice? The media would have a field day; my face would be plastered across the papers, they would doorstep my family and friends, Tom and Jack. Going to the police means losing everything I have worked for, my freedom. It means losing Tom. It would devastate my parents. And if Kristóf lies, if he tells them he wasn't there, that he knew nothing about George's death, then I would take all the blame. There's no evidence, no-one to speak on my behalf now that Meg is dead. It would be my word against his. I would be putting everything and everyone I care about at risk.

I say goodnight to the teaching assistant and I am just about to leave when I hear a soft tap on the classroom door and a young woman enters the room. In school uniform, Samantha looks younger than she did when she was working. She's still just a kid really, a fact accentuated by the heavy foundation she doesn't need and her thick, black and perfectly formed eyebrows.

'Holly?' She sounds uncomfortable using my first name, not yet accustomed to addressing teachers informally.

'Hi Samantha, come in.' I keep my tone light and encouraging. I don't want to frighten her away.

She glances around the classroom. 'It looks much smaller than I remember.'

'Well, I imagine you were a lot smaller then too.'

She perches on a table, watching me for a while. The silence is disconcerting.

'Is everything OK?'

'You came to the farm.'

'Yes, I went to see your mother.'

'What about?'

I hesitate. This is my opportunity to find out what's happening, but will I only make things worse by involving Samantha? What would Trevor want me to do? Fill out a form probably. I have to say something. 'I was worried about your brother.'

'Did she talk to you?'

'Not really.'

Samantha chews her lip. She's clearly got something to tell me, otherwise why would she be here? Does she know about the bruises?

'Mum says you're trying to get Nathan taken away from us.'

'That's the last thing I want to do. But I am worried

227

about him.' I move towards her, but she takes a step back.

'Nathan's fine. I'm old enough to look after him.' She sticks out her chin defiantly.

No, you're not. I need to tread carefully; I don't want to lose her confidence. 'Does your mum know you're here?'

She shakes her head. 'She's not very well. Why can't you leave us alone?'

'I want to help. Has your mum been to see a doctor?'

'He just gives her pills and stuff, but she won't take them. Says they turn her into a zombie.' Samantha hesitates. 'It was different when Dad was here. He always used to look after us.'

'It's not your job to take his place,' I say softly. This time she lets me put my hand on her shoulder. 'Please, let me help.'

'You can't do nothing. Just leave us alone. It will kill her if they take Nathan away.'

I flinch at the word. It's the same phrase Kristóf used about his mother: is it just hyperbole or is it really that serious? I can't be responsible for another person's death. I have to remind myself that Samantha is a teenager, she is bound to be dramatic. But what if reporting her does push Emma over the edge?

'I'm sorry Samantha, but I can't let this go. I wouldn't be doing my job.'

She shrugs me off. 'I knew this would be a waste of time. None of you give a shit, not really. I thought if I came to see you, I could make you understand but you're all the same.'

'If your mum is this bad then maybe she does need help. I'm sure you're doing a great job at home, but sometimes people in your mum's situation need a bit more support. Maybe social services can help her cope better while your dad's away.'

'You won't tell her I've been here, will you?'

I hesitate. 'Not if you don't want me to.'

I give Samantha my mobile phone number – a move I'm sure Trevor would disapprove of – and she leaves, promising to text me if she needs my help.

As soon as she closes the door, I sit down. My head is pounding with all the pressure that has been building up over the last few weeks. I don't know how much more I can take before I crack. I replay the conversation with Samantha in my head. Have I done the right thing? What right do I have to interfere with someone else's family life? I feel completely out of my depth. I have been trained to deal with safeguarding issues, but I'm not a parent. I don't know what it's like to try to look after a teenager and a little boy. How can I be trusted to handle someone else's problems? I can't even handle my own.

'Hey, you ready to set off?'

Rhona comes into the room and looks concerned as she sees my face.

'You OK?'

'Yeah, just a bit of a headache.'

'Do you think you're coming down with something? There's a nasty flu bug going around.'

I tell her about the conversation with Samantha.

'Do you want me to go with you to see Trevor?'

I shake my head. I'm not sure I should tell Trevor anything; he's cross enough with me as it is. What if he thinks I went behind his back and instigated Samantha's visit?

'You're doing the right thing,' Rhona reassures me. 'Besides, they don't just take kids away like that. There are all sorts of interventions they do first. God, I can't believe it's got this bad. Poor Emma.'

'Do you know her?'

'Only vaguely. Samantha was in my class, but it was mostly Liam I dealt with. He was a nice guy; I couldn't believe it when he went to prison. Goes to show really. It's always the quiet ones. Don't worry about it, Holly, you've made the right call. You can't turn a blind eye to these things and hope they go away. Talking of which, have you had any more messages from that creep recently?'

Should I tell her what's going on and see how she reacts? If I tell her what really happened that night then maybe she would come with me to the police, tell me what to say and do. But even if they believe it wasn't my fault, I still kept quiet about George's death all those years and I'm pretty sure that's a crime. No, I can't get Rhona involved. The fewer people that know my secrets, the better.

'I think he may have got bored and moved on to someone else.'

'Oh well, that's something at least. Listen, you need to

take your mind off things. Why don't we go Christmas shopping this weekend in Leeds? Inflict some serious damage on our credit cards?'

I haven't even started thinking about Christmas shopping yet and it's always fun with Rhona, so I smile and agree. The moment's gone. I'm not going to confess ... to Rhona, or to the police. I'm just going to have to live with the consequences.

Chapter 33

I don't want to go home after school. I can't stand another evening sitting in by myself, dwelling on the past. Instead, I drop my bags off, grab my walking boots and my phone, and head for the hills. The sun is starting to set, and it will be dark soon, but I can squeeze in a short walk to clear my head. The sky is full of colour and I draw comfort from the inevitability of the sun setting and rising irrespective of my problems. Being surrounded by nature gives me space and perspective. I don't know if it's a good idea to head out on my own, but if this guy's going to hurt me, he's had plenty of opportunity to do so before now. Besides, the hills are my territory. I know them better than most. I'm probably safer out here than trapped in my own home.

There's no-one around as I make my way up the path leading from the cottages to the fells. The stone walls are shoulder height here and create an alleyway. The mud, slick from the recent rainfall, sucks at my boots, coating them like cement and releasing a satisfying squelch with every step. Uneven rocks prod the arches of my feet through my boots and threaten to twist my ankle. I leave the village behind me and cross a field, passing sheep huddled underneath a denuded oak tree, their fleeces offering enviable protection from the gusts of icy wind that are now picking up strength as the sun sinks behind the hills. Everything out here is simple and peaceful, the way it should be. It's only humans that make life complicated.

I should turn back before it gets dark, but the walk is doing me good. Every step is a step further away from my troubles. I wish I could stay up here forever and not return to the real world. Maybe I should leave? Get on a plane and head somewhere in the sun. It's not a practical plan; I don't have any savings and I wouldn't get any work without a visa, not legitimate work anyway. And I can't just leave everything behind. I've got too much to lose. No, I need to face this head on.

A couple of walkers returning to the village bid me good evening, looking surprised to see anyone heading up the hillside at this time of day. I don't even have a torch with me and I know that I am being reckless. I may know these hills like the back of my hand but that won't help me if the clouds descend and I lose my bearings. However, there is something magical about being alone on the hillside at night. The stars are just starting to emerge, and the silence is something I have been craving all day. I can feel my surroundings soothe my anxiety and calm my mind. I may even sleep tonight.

Still, as darkness rapidly spreads over the countryside,

I force myself to be sensible and turn around. It is already freezing cold and I don't fancy being exposed to the elements all night. These hills may be beautiful, but they can also be deadly.

At first, I think the grey smoke spiralling from one of the houses in the village must be coming from a wood burning stove or someone taking advantage of the darkness to burn their garden rubbish. Then I realise the orange glow that accompanies it is far larger than it would be for a domestic fire. One of the cottages in my row is ablaze.

I run towards them, slipping on the uneven footpath. As I get closer, the acrid smoke makes my eyes smart but even through my blurred vision I can see that the ground floor of my house is alight. The flames have broken through the windows and are now licking the side of the building. Sparks pirouette in the sky and I can hear crashes and bangs coming from inside the house as the fire consumes its contents. My heart is pounding in my chest and my lungs feel like they are going to burst. I feel powerless in the face of the blaze as it rampages through my home.

A man is standing outside the house with his back towards me, watching it burn. My brain switches to auto-pilot as I force myself to stop running. It's him; it's got to be. Who else would just stand there as my life goes up in flames?

I dig around for my mobile phone and call 999, keeping my voice low to make sure he doesn't hear me above the roar of the fire. I hope the holiday cottages either side of me are empty. I answer their questions, give them my address and phone number, and beg them to hurry. I am reassured that the fire service is on its way and I hang up, still maintaining my distance from the man who clearly thinks he is watching me burn to death.

Our fire station is retained, so I imagine firefighters right now being disturbed from their favourite television programmes by their pagers, shrugging on their protective gear, and promising their loved ones that they will be back home soon. The smoke from the fire is making my eyes water as I pray for the fire service to hurry up. Will they be able to save anything? The fire looks like it is spreading to the second storey and I think about all my books and photographs; my clothes and possessions being destroyed. Everything will be lost if they don't get here soon. At least I am not trapped in there. At least I am alive. Who is doing this to me? What kind of sadist stands there thinking someone is burning to death?

I crouch behind the stone wall, ignoring the thistles which are pressing through my thin walking trousers, take out my mobile phone and film him. My heart is thundering in my chest and I'm sure he must be able to hear it. This is the first time I have seen the man who wants to kill me. He is tall and muscular, wearing dark clothes that emphasise his build. Could it be Kristóf? I don't think so, but I can't be sure. His hair is hidden by a black woollen hat and he is wearing an expensive brand of trainers. There is nothing distinctive about him whatsoever. I need him to turn around so that I can see his face.

Finally, above the roar of the fire comes the wail of a siren. In the distance I can see the flashing lights of two fire engines snaking their way through the village. The man runs towards a car which has been parked some way down the track. I emerge from my hiding place and manage to zoom in on the number plate. As he fumbles with the car door, he turns around and looks me straight in the face.

The horror on his face is only matched by my own as everything slots into place. He looks for a minute as if he is going to stick around, finish the job off, but the sound of the sirens is getting louder, and he jumps into his car and turns on the engine. I am still in shock as I watch him drive away. It can't be him. It just can't.

Chapter 34

Mark has reached the end of his patience. He is fed up of appealing to Holly's better nature. He isn't sure she has one. He knows that she has gone to see Kristóf, presumably to discuss going to the police, and he has waited to hear that the case has been reopened, that new evidence has come to light, but the bastard must have persuaded her to keep quiet.

His rental of the holiday cottage has come to an end. He has packed up his things and is heading back to London but first he needs to scare Holly into submission. He needs to keep the pressure on, scare her into going to the police. A life in prison can't compensate for George's death but at least he will have the satisfaction of seeing her lose everything.

He breaks into Holly's house using the key he stole from Rhona on Saturday night. For a policewoman's wife, she is extremely careless with her handbag after she's had a few drinks in the Black Swan. It had been easy to slip his hand into her open bag and steal her keys, slip off the one marked with Holly's name and slide them back without her even noticing.

The house is a mess. There are still breakfast things left out in the kitchen: a bowl encrusted with congealed Weetabix, half a cup of cold coffee, the empty milk carton placed on the floor next to an overflowing bin that smells of decay. There are books everywhere and a pile of dirty washing next to the machine. Mark wrinkles his nose in disgust. How can anyone live like this?

At least there is some sense of décor in the living room. A blanket thrown over the sofa with matching cushions, black and white photographs on the walls, and a stack of magazines on the coffee table. Mark flicks through them but there's nothing of interest. He recognises Holly's sister on the front page of one of them, promoting some big storyline, and moves it to the top of the pile.

Holly has left her mobile phone on the table in the hallway. It only takes a few minutes to unlock the phone and download the app that will give him full access to its contents. She really shouldn't leave these things lying around.

He has only just put the phone back when he hears Holly's key in the front door. He darts back into the living room and hides behind the door as he hears her come in, put down her bags and scrabble around in the hallway. He holds his breath, scanning the room for something to attack her with. Then he hears the front door closing again. He creeps to the window of the living room and watches her walk back down the path, noting that she has changed into her walking boots. He releases his breath. That was close; too close.

He figures he has about half an hour before she comes back.

On the mantelpiece in the living room is a tall advent candle with numbers marked along the side to indicate the days left until Christmas. He glances around and finds a felt box full of craft materials in the corner of the room. Perfect. He drags it across the room and places it underneath the candle. It will look like it has been lit and then fallen into the box. Only he and Holly will know that it is no accident. A fire will show her that he means business, that he is prepared to do anything to get to the truth. He won't kill her, not yet anyway, but maybe this will be enough to push her into a confession?

Mark lights the candle and drops it into the box. It smoulders for a while, releasing toxic fumes, but then goes out. Cursing, he rearranges the materials in the box, adds some firelighters that he found next to the wood burning stove, relights the candle and makes sure it is properly alight before stepping back. There is a draft coming from the fireplace, enough to waft the flames from the box to the rug. The fire starts to spread and black smoke fills the room.

Sweat drips from his forehead and his breath comes out in rasps as he fumbles with the back-door key and finally falls out of the cottage. The cold wind whips his face and momentarily leaves him winded as he stumbles to the front of the building. He lifts his phone and starts filming as the fire takes hold. The orange flames against the black moonlit sky is a beautiful and devastating sight.

He can't risk hanging around. It won't take very long in this village for someone to call the emergency services and he needs to be as far away as possible when they arrive. As he turns to get into the hire car, he sees Holly filming him. Shit. Has she recognised him? They've never met, but she must have seen his face in the newspapers. Has she caught him on camera? That would be the end of everything.

He could go back, fight her and grab her phone but it's too much of a risk. Instead, he gets into the car and with trembling hands starts the engine. He has to get out of there before the fire brigade arrives. He had been planning to go back to London, beg Mia for forgiveness and carry on his investigations from there, but it's too late now; he can't involve Mia in this, he can't ask her to lie for him. Mia is pure and sweet, and he doesn't want her tainted by Holly's evil. It isn't fair if he ends up going down instead of her. He isn't a bad person. He has only ever wanted the truth; her lies have forced him into this position.

Mark feels his panic diminish the further he drives away from Yorkshire. He starts to think more rationally, put things back into order. The cottage and the car were rented on a stolen credit card and can't be traced back to him. Any evidence he has been in Holly's house will be destroyed in the blaze. He can access her phone remotely, wipe the video, and it will be her word against his. He just needs to stay off the grid a bit longer.

He drives through the night, with no particular destination in mind, his only plan to get as far away from Yorkshire as he can. In the early hours of the morning, he finds himself a few miles away from Kristóf's workplace. He pulls over and rests his head on the steering wheel, half-expecting to hear sirens following him but it is completely silent.

He gets out his phone and opens the app that gives him access to Holly's device. He reviews the video she took of him. Although it is dark, his face is clearly visible. He deletes it, hoping it's not too late. What can the police do without any evidence? If Holly reports him, then everything will come out. Will she risk that? Will she finally admit what they did to his brother? If she does, if the truth finally comes out, then it might be worth going to prison for.

But in the meantime, he has unfinished business with Kristóf.

Chapter 35

Once the fire crews arrive, there's not much I can do. The guy in charge leads me to a safe distance as they cordon off the road, asking me all sorts of questions about the contents of the house, if I have any gas canisters, how to switch the utilities off. My brain is whirling as I try to take in what I've seen. I can't think straight.

'There was someone there,' I tell him. 'Someone was watching the house. I think he started it deliberately.'

The fire officer tells me that he will pass on the information to the police, but their priority is getting the fire under control before it spreads to any other building.

'Is there somewhere you can stay tonight, love? I can give you the number for the emergency housing team but to be honest, you're going to be lucky if they can find you somewhere decent at this time of night.'

I tell him I will be fine, and ring Tom. My throat hurts from the smoke and I can barely get the words out as I tell him what's happened. He offers to collect me, but that would mean disturbing Jack and it's only a short walk.

Besides, I need time to think. George is alive! It must have been him all this time, sending me the messages. He must have survived his injuries, been hiding out somewhere. Maybe he lost his memory? I still can't work out why he left it so long to come and find me or why he would want me to confess to a murder I clearly didn't commit. But it was him. I'm sure of it.

Knowing that George didn't die has thrown me completely. He was my first love and I have mourned him for five years. I thought I had watched him die. No-one could have survived those injuries, could they? But he must have done. He must know that we left him for dead, that we lied to the police, to his family and friends. He must have been lying in wait all this time waiting to get his revenge. The thought sends a shiver down my spine. He killed Meg, I'm sure of it. It will be me or Kristóf next.

As I walk through the village, I can see people peeking through the curtains, watching the grey smoke spiralling from my house. They will all think the fire was an accident, that I was careless, but that's better than the truth. That's better than them knowing that someone hates me so much they would destroy everything I have. I know I should be thankful just to be alive, but I've lost everything. And George did that to me. Did he think I was in the house? Did he think he was watching me die?

Tom is standing at the doorway when I arrive and hugs me tightly. My tears soak into his shirt. I never want him to let me go. He means everything to me. How do I even start to tell him what I've done?

'Thank God, you're OK,' he says, pulling me inside.

'Can I stay here for a few days? Just until they sort my house out?'

'Of course, you don't need to ask.'

I am overwhelmed with exhaustion and just want to sleep but I am smelly and dirty and need a shower. I scrub myself raw trying to get rid of the smell of the fire, letting the hot water cascade down my face and wash away my tears. Am I putting Tom and Jack at risk just by being here? Would George hurt them too? He's proved tonight that he is capable of anything.

It's only when I get out, wrap myself in a towel and walk into Tom's bedroom that I realise I don't have anything to wear. The clothes that I arrived in are covered in soot and mud and stink of smoke. I've got nothing suitable for work tomorrow. I look at the wardrobe and hesitate. Could I borrow some of Rebecca's clothes? I open the wardrobe door and stare at the rail full of expensive dresses, pressed trousers and silk blouses.

'Help yourself, you're about the same size, I think.'

I jump, startled, and feel guilty about being caught prying. 'Sorry, I don't have any clothes.'

It dawns on me then that everything's gone. I have nothing left. The books I have been collecting since I was a teenager reduced to ashes, the photographs of my childhood, the worthless sentimental things that make up a life.

Tears well up and I am overwhelmed by fatigue. I don't think I can take any more.

Tom wraps his arms around me. 'It's fine. That's what I came up to say. Help yourself, if it isn't too weird.'

It is weird. I don't want to bring back bad memories. I take out a pair of black trousers and a burgundy silk shirt and hang them on the wardrobe door for tomorrow. In the meantime, I borrow one of Tom's t-shirts to sleep in.

'You poor thing,' he says, kissing my forehead. 'Do you want to talk about it?'

I shake my head. 'I just want to go to bed.'

*

The next day, Rob comes to the school to take my statement. Tom tried to persuade me to take the day off sick, but I wanted to keep busy, distract myself from the thoughts that kept me awake all night. What does George want? Why has he come back after all this time? And what does he intend to do next? Now he knows I'm alive, he will come back to finish the job, I'm sure of that. I'm not safe anywhere.

We sit in an empty classroom and Rob takes out his notebook.

'How are you doing, Holly?'

'I'm fine. It's all a bit of a shock.'

'Aye, it will be. Well, they've secured the building but you're going to need to arrange for a structural engineer to assess the damage. I trust you've got insurance.'

'Yes, I've let them know.'

'The fire service will be doing a full investigation, but they've asked me to come along and get a bit of information from you. It says here you saw someone outside your house last night?'

'Yes, that's right. I think the fire was started deliberately.'

Rob looks sceptical. 'We haven't had the official report yet, but the fire crew think it was started by a candle in the living room.'

'That wasn't me. I didn't go into the house after work, I went straight out for a walk.'

'Are you sure? Your bags were in the hallway.'

'Well, that is, I did go in but only for a few minutes, and just to drop off my bags and grab my phone.'

Rob makes a note of this. 'And you're sure you didn't light a candle?'

'No, why would I do that? They must have been inside my house.'

'Did you notice any signs of a break in?'

'No, but then again I wasn't looking. I told you, I was only in there a couple of minutes. I'm telling you Rob, the fire was started deliberately and made to look like an accident.' Like Meg's death, I remind myself.

Rob leans back on his chair. 'Why would anyone want to do that?'

I bite my lip. If I tell Rob about George, then I will have to tell him what we did. But if George is still alive, then we didn't kill him. But what if he disappears again? My confession could put me in prison for the rest of my life; it could even mean the death penalty if they take me back to Thailand.

'I've been getting these messages on my phone. Someone from my past.'

Rob looks up at me. 'What kind of messages?'

I get out my phone to show him, scroll through the saved messages but there are none there. It's as if the phone has been wiped. What the hell?

'They were there yesterday, I swear. Look, I took a video.'

But that's gone too.

'Listen Holly, it's been a long night.'

'I'm not lying. I told Rhona about them.'

'You showed them to Rhona?'

'Well, no, she didn't see them, but they were there.'

'This person from your past. Can you give me his name?'

'It's George. George Bolton. Only he's dead.'

Rob looks confused. 'You're saying a dead person is trying to contact you?'

'No, everyone thought he was dead. But he wasn't. Don't you see, he must have been alive all this time?'

Rob sets down his pen.

'Holly, you need to get some rest, you're not thinking straight. This all sounds ... well ...'

'Crazy?'

'A little far-fetched maybe. I mean people don't just come back from the dead.'

'It's not unheard of.'

'It's a lot less common than you think. I mean, when did this person die?'

'Five years ago. In Thailand. They found his body on the beach. Only it can't have been him, could it?'

'But presumably the family identified the body?'

'Yeah, but ... listen, I know it sounds ridiculous but there must have been a mistake.'

Rob puts down his notebook. 'Look, maybe we should leave this for another day? When you've had a bit of time to think things through?'

I take a deep breath. Maybe I am going mad, seeing things that aren't there. Maybe George's ghost is coming back to haunt me? A ghost with access to technology that can wipe my phone remotely and retrieve photos that I destroyed five years ago? A ghost that can send me parcels of press cuttings and videos of my past? None of it makes any sense. If George is still alive, and I'm convinced he is, then he's going to be impossible to track down. He must be using a different name and travelling under someone else's passport. If the police try to trace George Bolton, they will only trace him back to a dead body in Thailand. If only I still had the video, I could double check what I saw last night, but George is always one step ahead of me. He must have planned this for years.

Rob puts away his notebook. 'Holly, I hate to ask you this, but I know you wanted to take your relationship with Tom to the next stage. You didn't think you might hurry things on a bit?'

I am genuinely shocked that Rob could think that of me and curse Rhona for talking behind my back. 'Of course not!'

'Only, you have to admit, it's a bit odd that you were out of the house at the time. Are you in a habit of taking walks in the dark?'

'No, but ... listen, why would I burn down my own house? That's ridiculous.'

I realise I need to talk to Kristóf. Once he realises George is still alive, that we can't be prosecuted for murder, then he will back me up. Maybe we can go to the police together, tell them everything. Get them to re-open the case. Find out once and for all what happened to George.

'Get some rest, Holly. We'll pick this up another time.'

'Can I go back into my house? Get some clothes?'

'I'm afraid not. Not until they say it's safe.'

'How long will that be?'

'I don't know, Holly. It was some fire. The house is badly damaged.' He stands up. 'I'd offer you our spare room, but under the circumstances ...'

'It's OK, I'll stay with Tom.'

After Rob leaves, I stay in the classroom to ring Kristóf. We can break the pact now. They can't arrest us for a murder we didn't commit. All these years of feeling guilty and George is still alive. He must have been biding his time, waiting to take his revenge.

'I'd like to speak to Kristóf please.'

'I'm afraid, Dr Szabó isn't in today,' his secretary answers, her voice wary.

'This is Holly Metcalfe, an old friend of his. I visited him last week. Could you give me his home number? It is an emergency.'

'I'm afraid I can't do that, Miss Metcalfe.'

'Oh God, I know. Data protection and all that. He won't mind, I promise.'

'No, I'm afraid you don't understand. Dr Szabó passed away this morning.'

I can't speak. I feel like I am going to fall down. I sit down on a chair and try to breathe.

'Are you there?'

'Yes, yes, I'm here.'

'I'm sorry to break it to you like that, we've only just found out ourselves. It's a big shock as you can imagine.'

'What happened?'

'He was knocked off his bike on the way to work. Hit and run driver, they said. A terrible accident.'

Chapter 36

Vietnam, five years ago

Ho Chi Minh City was a complete contrast to the relative sleepiness of Cambodia. We arrived early evening in the backpacker area of Bui Vien but the neon-lit bars were already full of drunk Westerners. Scooters came at us from every direction as we crossed the road amid a cacophony of motorbike engines and tooting horns. I felt the familiar thrill of arriving in a new place and trying to figure it all out.

This time we were staying in a guesthouse rather than a hostel. Meg was in the process of asking the receptionist for two twin rooms when George interrupted.

'Holly and I are going to share. And we'll be wanting a double bed.'

He winked at me and I felt myself going red. I hadn't planned to tell the others quite like that, but I was glad it was out in the open. I was fed up of sneaking around, finding excuses to spend time alone with George, and I didn't like constantly lying to Meg. She had nearly caught us snogging once or twice; it was only a matter of time before our relationship was out in the open.

Meg looked up, confused, but I could tell from the expression on Kristóf's face that he had seen this coming.

'We've been seeing each other,' I explained.

'I thought as much,' Kristóf said sourly.

Meg's expression was unreadable. 'Well, you kept that quiet,' she said finally, but I could tell by the tone of her voice that she wasn't happy.

'You still wan' two rooms?' the receptionist asked.

'I'm not sharing with him,' Meg said, looking at Kristóf.

'Three rooms. I'll pay the extra,' George offered before either of them could protest.

Meg and Kristóf didn't say a word as we followed the lady up the steep winding stairs, but the atmosphere was heavy with unspoken opinions. I had been so wrapped up in George over the past few weeks that I had never really stopped to think about what impact our relationship might have on the dynamics of the group. I wished that George had spoken to me first; perhaps we could have thought of a more sensitive way to share our news.

'So, shall we meet up for a beer in about an hour?' I asked, my voice squeaking and false, as the receptionist handed out keys and explained the no smoking policy.

'Whatever.' Meg let herself in to her room and slammed the door behind her.

Kristóf shrugged his shoulders and walked off down

the corridor, leaving us alone. George wrapped his arms around me. 'Don't worry about Meg, she's just jealous.'

I didn't think jealousy had anything to do with it. I wanted to talk to Meg, apologise for keeping secrets from her, but I knew there was no point when she was in this mood. It was better to let her calm down.

'I thought she would be happy for us,' I said as we let ourselves into the poky double room with no window. A threadbare sheet with dubious stains covered the bed and the electricity sockets were hanging off the wall at dangerous angles. It wasn't exactly the romantic set up I had in mind.

'She'll get used to the idea. The heart wants what the heart wants, Holly.' George sounded so cheesy that I had to laugh. 'Anyway, we couldn't carry on sneaking around like that forever, could we?'

My heart leapt at his casual use of the word 'forever'. I still didn't really know how George felt about me. We had only been seeing each other for a few weeks but everything felt accelerated when you were travelling and constantly in each other's company. We'd only managed to have sex once since the night in the club and we were both desperate to get our hands on each other. But was I just a holiday fling or was he serious about me? Would he break off his engagement to Fiona? I already knew how I felt about George. I had loved him for years. I couldn't believe it was finally happening.

Ho Chi Minh City was busy and frenetic. It was difficult

to walk down the street without being pestered by hawkers selling sunglasses or touts trying to pull you into their shop or café. The noise from the traffic was relentless. Motorbikes regularly mounted the pavement and there was a pervading smell of diesel in the stifling air. We were continually getting lost as we tried to navigate our way around the city using Google maps and common sense. We bickered constantly. None of us were getting much sleep; the beds in the guesthouse were rock hard and we were all much more irritable than usual. Meg and Kristóf made a big show of not acknowledging our relationship and our efforts to lighten the mood were met with icy indifference. I hated being the cause of all this conflict between us but George told me I was worrying too much, that they would get over it soon enough.

A week in Ho Chi Minh City was long enough to take in the sights and it was a relief to climb on board the sleeper train which would take us to Da Nang. We were heading to Hoi An, one of the most romantic cities in Vietnam and had booked a cabin for the seventeen-hour journey. We all had separate bunks so at least there was no awkwardness about the sleeping arrangements. The sun was setting as the Reunification Express train trundled through the countryside. Women wearing conical hats waved at us from the rice paddy fields. The others played cards as I snuggled into my blanket with a book, but I soon found myself drifting off with the motion of the train.

The Beach

It was the middle of the night when I woke up. I peeked out of the curtains and could see mountains silhouetted against the inky sky. The countryside was still and serene, the only noise from the train as it passed sleepy villages and deserted railway stations. The others were fast asleep. I stared at George for a while, drinking in his features in repose. I couldn't believe that someone so handsome, so perfect, would be interested in me.

*

Hoi An was by far the prettiest place we had visited on our travels so far. The old town was lit by hundreds of paper lanterns laced across the street. George and I had sneaked off to spend some rare time together, promising to meet the others for a drink later, and were walking hand in hand down the quaint streets lined with tiny shops and restaurants. My backpack was already stuffed with souvenirs of our travels, but I wished that I could buy some of the art on offer. We crossed the wooden Japanese bridge and made our way down to the river where people were lighting candles and floating them downstream.

'Come on, let's get a boat ride!' George suggested, grabbing my hand and pulling me towards the bank of the river where wooden canoes were lined up, waiting to take passengers. He negotiated the fare and held my hand as I stepped cautiously into the boat. He sat behind me and I relaxed into his arms, feeling like the luckiest girl on the planet, as the woman gracefully steered us away from the crowds of tourists taking pictures from the bridge.

George kissed my ear. 'Happy?'

'Perfectly.'

'Good.'

I should have left it there, I shouldn't have said anything, I just wanted the moment to be perfect, but I pushed it too far.

'George?'

'Hmm?'

'I love you.'

It was the first time I had ever said it to anyone and I desperately wanted him to say it back. I felt his arms tense and I turned my head to look at him. His face told me everything I needed to know.

'Where did that come from?' he said, finally.

I turned away so that he couldn't see me; my cheeks burning with humiliation. 'Nothing, it doesn't matter.'

'We've only been seeing each other a few weeks.'

'I know, it's just that we've known each other for ages.'

'I like you, Hol. I like you a lot. But things are more complicated than that. There's Fiona to think about.'

Ah the F word. I was wondering when she would be mentioned. We had managed to avoid the subject so far but it was always on my mind. Was he really going to go back to her after all this? She didn't love him like I did, no-one could. Their relationship was a joke.

'Let's just enjoy what we've got for now, shall we?' he suggested. 'Have some fun.'

'Of course,' I said, trying to sound like I meant it. George was right; it was too early to talk about love. There was plenty of time for our feelings to develop and in the meantime, I could just enjoy spending time with him, making memories. 'Forget I said anything.'

Chapter 37

I thought living with Tom would be perfect, but now I'm here, things aren't quite what I pictured. I'm just a guest. Everything around me belongs to Tom and Jack, even down to the toothpaste I use and the margarine in the fridge. I still don't have access to most of my possessions. Some of them have been taken as evidence until the police decide whether to treat the fire as arson. Most of my clothes and books have been ruined. The contractors assigned by the insurance company say it could be months before I can move back home.

The fire has set everyone's tongues wagging – it even made the local newspaper, with a warning from a fire service 'spokesman' about the dangers of leaving lit candles unsupervised. They've made me look like a fool, although I suppose it's better than being suspected of arson. I haven't heard anything from the police since I spoke to Rob and I just need to know what's happening. Am I being investigated? Are they trying to trace George? Every time the phone goes, my heart skips a beat.

I haven't heard from George since the fire. Maybe he is lying low, planning his next move. I wonder where he has been living: Thailand or the UK? Does his family know that he's alive? Why has it taken him so long to wreak his revenge? I'm sure he killed both Kristóf and Meg and that means there's only me left. Is he out there now, planning his next attack? Is he watching me at this very moment? I can't just sit around waiting to be his next victim. I have to talk to him, tell him my side of the story, hope that he can forgive me and that we can both move on with our lives.

At least Tom seems happy to have me here and Jack has adapted very quickly. Spending all day and all evening with a five-year-old is tiring though. Going from a single person in a part-time relationship to a full-time mother is a bit of a culture shock. The only time we get any peace and quiet is when he goes to bed and then I'm too knackered to do anything apart from watch crap telly while Tom plays computer games on his tablet.

We both agreed, after my one disastrous attempt to make coq au vin, that Tom will do all the cooking. We have already settled into a routine. I keep an eye on Jack while he is in the kitchen and then we all eat together. Jack is usually quite happy entertaining himself with the contents of his capacious toy box while I catch up on my lesson planning.

'Mummy,' he says, making me jump. For a second, I wonder if he is referring to me, but he isn't looking in my direction. He is sitting on the rug in the middle of the living room chattering into a toy phone. I don't know the best way to handle this.

'Is she on the phone?'

'She lives in America,' he tells me, over emphasising every syllable of the country.

'Yes, she does.'

'Is America far away?'

'Yes, it's a long, long way.'

'Do you have to go on an aeroplane?'

'Yes.'

'Or a rocket?'

'Well, not quite a rocket.'

'You go to the moon on a rocket.' He loses interest in the phone and grabs a rocket instead and I breathe a sigh of relief. I don't know what Tom has told him about his mother and the last thing I want to do is put my foot in it. I grab the TV remote and put on some kids' channel to entertain Jack while I work.

The television is already full of Christmas adverts, relentlessly promoting images of families sitting around the dinner table, exchanging perfectly wrapped presents and enjoying wonderful food. I know it's only marketing but I'm finding it increasingly irritating. Christmas is only a few weeks' away now and I'm still waiting to find out from Tom what he is doing. At this rate, I am going to end up going on my own to Mum and Dad's, like a pathetic loser. Even Lisa is talking about bringing her new boyfriend up to meet them.

I haven't got a clue what to buy Jack. He's into the same things all five-year-olds love: trains, cars, superheroes, but I want it to be something special, something that signifies what I will mean to him in the future. I want him to look back at our first Christmas together with happy memories. I know I am being sentimental, and I need to be careful around Tom. He's really sensitive when it comes to Jack's feelings. If I push things too far, he might back off.

I go Christmas shopping with Rhona on Saturday. Experience tells me that going shopping with Rhona means drinking plenty of wine, so we leave the cars behind and take the bus into Skipton and the train to Leeds. On the journey there, we chat about mundane things: work, the school play, life with Tom. She doesn't mention the investigation and I don't ask.

The sky is grey and the rain persistent. Leeds is crowded and noisy. Being in a city centre again after weeks in the quiet countryside feels quite bewildering. We make our way briskly to the shopping centre to get out of the rain. Around us the brightly lit signs are reflected on the wet pavement like light cast through stained glass windows. Being back in Leeds brings back memories of my time here as a student and I think about Meg. How can someone go from being a bright, ambitious student to a drug addict in a couple of years? But I already know the answer to that. Guilt does that to you. George must have tracked her down first, before going after Kristóf.

Rhona is an indiscriminate shopper who casually throws

items into her basket without checking either price or quality. I dither, trying to pick the perfect present for Jack and Tom. Eventually I settle on a racing car for Jack; it is expensive and garish enough to win over his heart, but it doesn't look like I am trying to make a statement or usurp Rebecca. I buy cufflinks and a bottle of Scotch for Tom. I pick up some gifts for Mum and Dad and spend ages debating what to buy for my sister: what do you get the girl who has everything? Nothing I could pick up in Leeds could match what she can get from the designer stores in London. I settle for some champagne flutes. Should I get something for her boyfriend too? But I don't know anything about him, apart from his name is Alex and he is away on business a lot. Their relationship will probably be over by Christmas anyway. Lisa's love affairs tend to be intense and short-lived.

'You OK? You seem miles away.'

'Yeah, just ready for lunch.' We are standing in a long queue in Debenhams and shuffling towards the tills. Rhona is laden down with bags and has to keep putting them down and picking them back up every time the queue moves forward. The store is over-heated and full of women with to do lists and sharp elbows. It's making me feel claustrophobic.

'Ready for wine, more like. I think we've got enough for today, don't you? Shall we go and get tiddly?'

Sometimes I think Rhona has a problem with her drinking, but neither of us ever mentions it. I know that she alternates buying wine from the corner shop and the more anonymous supermarket in town to avoid people talking about her. I can sometimes smell alcohol on her breath in the morning. Knowing I should suggest a coffee, but not wanting to ruin our day, I nod my head and we pile into a wine bar, banging against tables with our collection of shopping bags. Rhona gets us a bottle of red wine to share.

'Cheaper than by the glass,' she says, even though I will only have one, so she will end up drinking the rest.

We settle at a table near the window so that we can watch all the Christmas shoppers emerging from the stores. I take a sip of the ruby red wine and the alcohol hits me immediately. Rhona gulps hers. 'Ah that's better. So, how are you? How's living with Tom?'

'Fine, yeah, great.'

'Quite a shock though living with someone full-time isn't it? Discovering their nasty habits?'

'I didn't realise anyone could snore so loudly!' I chuckle.

'Oh God I know, Rob wears one of those snore guards.'

'Do they work?'

'Not really. A sharp elbow in the ribs usually works better. Failing that, perhaps a pillow over the head?'

I can't suppress my curiosity any longer. 'Has Rob said anything about the fire investigation?'

'Rob isn't a detective,' Rhona reminds me. 'He doesn't get involved with investigations.'

'Yeah, but he would know what was happening, wouldn't he?'

Her face sharpens. 'Even if he did, he wouldn't tell me. He could lose his job.'

I don't know whether she's lying to me or not. I wonder whether Rob has passed on the information I gave him about George. He didn't seem to believe me. Besides, how do you even start tracing a person everyone thinks is dead? I can't imagine the Thai authorities would be too helpful after all this time.

'He thinks I started the fire deliberately to move in with Tom.'

'What? That's crazy. It was just an accident, wasn't it? I thought you'd left a candle burning.'

'No, that's what I keep telling them. I didn't light that candle.'

I tell Rhona what I told Rob. She listens carefully but I can't tell from her expression whether she believes me or not. It does sound far-fetched when I tell her my theory that George is still alive.

She pours another glass of wine. 'And you really think he's behind the messages and the fire?'

'I saw him.'

'But it was dark, and you must have been in a terrible shock.'

'I saw him, Rhona, I'm sure of it.'

'It all just sounds a bit ...'

'Unbelievable?'

'But why would he want to kill you?'

It's a question I can't really answer. 'He blames me for

something that happened to him in the past. When we were in Thailand together.'

'It must be something pretty bad to set fire to your house.'

I pause. How much should I tell her? 'I just need to talk to him, explain what really happened.'

Rhona takes a sip of wine, choosing her words carefully. 'Leave it to the police, Holly. They know what they're doing, and they take stalking very seriously these days. I'm sure they will track down whoever is behind all this. And at least you'll be safe living with Tom in the meantime.'

I suppose I am just going to have to trust the police to do their job. Rhona's right. Tom may look harmless but he's a black belt in ju-jitsu, and George wouldn't know what hit him if he tried to attack me.

Rhona hesitates. 'Listen, I know I shouldn't tell you this, but they may have found something that corroborates your story. There was a car driving erratically away from the village a few minutes after you called 999.'

'Did they get its registration?'

'It was a hire car apparently. But if the guy used his ID to rent the car, then they'll be able to track him down.'

My heart sinks. There's no way George would be stupid enough to use his own ID to rent a car.

'And in the meantime, we will all keep an eye on you. We'll make sure you're never alone and he won't harm you.'

I don't know if it is the wine or Rhona's kind words, but I start to feel better. George can't evade the police forever. Sooner or later he is going to make a mistake, and they'll catch him.

'Now, it's your turn to help me. I need to sort out this bloody nativity before 'Orrible Oliver ruins the whole thing,' she says, sloshing more wine into my glass and calling the waiter over to order another bottle.

Chapter 38

Mark doesn't feel any guilt about killing Kristóf. The guy was without compassion or feeling. He had stood at his brother's funeral, even shaken Mark's hand, all the time knowing that he could have alleviated their suffering by telling the truth. The bastard deserved to die. His family deserve to suffer as Mark's family have. Mark is only sorry that there are so few people to mourn his death.

With Kristóf dispensed of, Mark can turn his attention back to Holly. He wonders if he dares go back to the village so soon. Will they be looking for him? He imagines detectives poring over CCTV images, tracing his car, searching for footprints and DNA. He was careful, wasn't he? But Holly saw him. They could be tracking him right now.

He will go back to London for a while, melt into the crowds. There is business there that he needs to attend to. He won't go home. It's too much of a risk and he doesn't want to get Mia involved. Maybe he will go to her work, watch her from afar, check that she's OK without him. He won't try to contact her. There would be too many questions and she wouldn't understand. She would tell him to go to the police, to go through the proper channels, but he has trusted the authorities before, and they let him down. He will return when it's all over, beg forgiveness for abandoning her and hope that they can pick up where they left off. Perhaps they could even get married, start a family of their own.

He just wants this to be over now.

Chapter 39

Vietnam, five years ago

Arriving in the Old Quarter of Hanoi was like stepping back in time. As we navigated our way to our next hostel, we passed men having their hair cut by street barbers, their small mirrors propped up against the city's crumbling walls; women selling fruit from heavy panniers; and old men pedalling tourists around on wobbly rickshaws. The narrow houses looked like they might topple over on you at any minute and the pavement was blocked by people crouched on plastic stools around boiling pots of noodle soup.

Food made me miss home: fish and chips doused in salt and vinegar and served in newspaper, Sunday roasts at my parents' house, spaghetti bolognese with garlic bread and cheese. I had got braver with my food choices, and the fruit in South-East Asia was amazing, but I missed the convenience of grabbing a packet of crisps or a pre-packed sandwich. I had been calling Mum and Dad over Skype every couple of days, but it felt like they were living in a different world. They were worried about my sister, struggling to scrape a living in London, but proud that she had managed to land a small part in a West End production.

I hadn't told them about George; I wanted to see if it was going somewhere first. He had asked me not to tell my family and friends, or put anything on Facebook, in case Fiona saw it. I wondered what my sister would make of our relationship. Would she be jealous? Did she even think about the night they spent together?

George and I hadn't discussed our relationship since I dropped the L-bomb but it seemed as if Meg and Kristóf were starting to get used to us being together. So, when George announced that he had splashed out on a trip to Halong Bay for us all, I thought they would be grateful. Instead, Meg and Kristóf spent the whole journey scowling out of the window of the cramped minibus like a couple of teenagers.

Half-way there we stopped at a huge complex geared up for coach parties. It was full of souvenirs, over-priced textiles and smiling shop assistants on commission. Meg and I rushed to the loo. Standing in line she pulled out her phone and pretended to check her messages so that she didn't have to talk to me.

By the time it was my turn, there was only a squat toilet left, something I had managed to avoid so far on the trip. I was desperate for a wee though and couldn't wait. There was no light so when I closed the door behind me, I could barely see my surroundings, which was probably no bad thing. There was a distinctive smell of shit and I could hear flies buzzing. I pulled down my shorts and knickers and perched, praying that I wouldn't lose my balance. Eventually I managed to pee. There was no loo roll but fortunately I had some tissues in my bag. There didn't seem to be a flush but there was a bucket of water in the corner and a plastic scoop, so I splashed some around hoping that it would get rid of the urine. I scrubbed my hands with antibacterial hand gel as I pushed open the door and breathed in the fresh air, feeling a sense of pride that I had got through it.

Meg was waiting for me outside, washing her hands in the sink. 'You should have waited,' she said. 'There were plenty of Western ones.'

'It was fine,' I lied.

'Really? You've got piss all over your shorts.'

I looked behind me in horror as she burst into laughter. 'God, you're so gullible.' There was an edge of cruelty about her mirth though, and I realised she wasn't referring to my shorts.

'What is your problem?'

'Forget about it, Holly. You're not going to listen to me anyway.'

'No, go on. I really want to know. If it's about me and George ...'

'He's not right for you. There, I've said it. He's going to break your heart.'

'You don't know that.'

'He's engaged, Holly. You're just a bit of fun to him.'

'You don't know what you're talking about. George and I ...'

'Oh, forget about it, you're impossible.'

She turned and stomped off in the direction of the shuttle bus. Tears pricked my eyes as I tried to steady my breath. Meg was my best friend in the whole world, closer than a sister, and I didn't want to lose her over my relationship with George. Why was she making things so difficult for us? She could have at least listened to what I had to say. Maybe she wouldn't be so down on us if she knew how we felt about each other. But by the time I got back to the bus, she was already deep in conversation with Kristóf and the opportunity to talk had passed.

Eventually we reached the jetty and climbed on board the converted Chinese junk boat that would take us around the scenic bay. There were about thirty guests in total, a mix of age and nationalities. Our cabin had a wooden bed fixed to the floor and a tiny en suite bathroom. From the window we could see limestone cliffs rising out of the glittering teal water. It was gorgeous. We dumped our bags and returned to the deck to take pictures as the boat started to chug around the bay. The breeze was a welcome relief after the stifling heat of the city.

As I leant over the deck to take photographs of the fishing boats crisscrossing the bay, George settled on one of the sun loungers and ordered a beer. I stood there taking in the scenery, feeling like I had found paradise. It really was one of the most beautiful places I had ever been. A couple who had been arguing about insect repellent were now kissing, silhouetted against an apricot sky. I watched the sun set and the sky darken, the water reflecting the green lights from fishing boats dotted along the horizon.

Dinner was served in small bowls in the middle of the table for everyone to dip in to and included fresh seafood in a range of aromatic sauces. I had never tried seafood before, put off by the smell and the look of it, and helped myself to chicken in a pineapple sauce instead.

George rolled his eyes and held out a piece of calamari with his chopsticks. 'Go on, be adventurous for a change. You might like it.'

The squid wobbled menacingly as if it were still alive, but I didn't want George to think I was a coward. I leaned towards him and took the piece between my teeth, chewing tentatively and then swallowing it as fast as I could before it hit my taste buds. I took a big gulp of Sprite to wash it down. It had the consistency of rubber and all I could taste was the ginger and lemongrass that it had been marinated in. I pulled a face.

'How can you not like it? They've just caught it, grilled it and served it. It's as fresh as you can get,' George enthused.

'Yeah, lovely. I'll stick to chips.'

'You can take the girl out of the North ...'

'What's that supposed to mean?' Meg snapped.

'I was joking. Chill out, will you?' George turned to my best friend with an angry look which was returned.

'I'm sick of you lording it over us all the time, like you're some sort of philanthropist taking pity on the poor.'

'I didn't notice you complaining when I paid for this trip.'

'You never even bloody asked. I can pay for my own ticket thanks.'

'Meg, he was only being nice.' I looked around; people were staring at us. It was a small dining area, and they could hear every word. We were ruining the romantic atmosphere with our argument.

'Oh yeah, trust you to stick up for him.'

'Meg, calm down, you're making a scene.'

She threw her napkin onto her plate and got up to leave, pushing past the polite waiter who was about to clear our plates. Compared to the natural reserve of the Vietnamese people we had met so far, Meg's outburst seemed doubly rude.

'I am so sorry,' I said to him. I glanced at the others. 'I'd better go after her, see if she's OK.'

'Leave her to calm down,' Kristóf advised. 'But maybe you two should take it down a notch.'

'We're not doing anything wrong.'

We finished the rest of the meal in silence. I pleaded a headache and went to bed early leaving the two men to stay up drinking. Tears rolled down my eyes and soaked my pillow. Why couldn't Meg just be happy for us? When

George crept in, climbing into bed and holding me close, I pretended to be asleep. I could smell whisky on his breath as his breathing deepened into a steady rhythm. From the bed, I could see the stars twinkling in the dark sky like hundreds of fireflies and I thought how romantic tonight would have been if Meg hadn't spoiled everything.

By morning, the tension had cleared a little. We had a polite breakfast, pretending nothing had happened, and managed some stilted conversation about the scenery around us. I made a special effort to spend more time with Meg, sitting next to her on the bus on the way back to Hanoi and ignoring George, who was making no effort to disguise the fact that he was bored senseless in Kristóf's company. He thought I was wasting my time and called Meg a moody bitch behind her back, but I was desperate for things to go back to normal. For the first time, I wondered if George and I had done the right thing getting together on this trip. It wasn't like we planned it, but perhaps we should have waited until we got home?

*

Back in Hanoi, Kristóf and George made plans to go to the Military History Museum and I snatched the opportunity to clear the air with Meg. The serene pools and quiet courtyards of the Temple of Literature carried an atmosphere of peace and meditation and seemed a good place to repair a friendship. We walked in silence for a while until we found a shady spot to sit and take in the view.

'We can't carry on like this, Meg. You're going to have to talk to me at some point.'

'You've changed since you two got together,' Meg grumbled. 'You run after him like a besotted puppy.'

'That's not true. I'm still the same person. I really like him, I always have.'

'I'm worried about you, that's all,' she said in a softer voice. 'He's going to hurt you.'

I tried not to let her words get to me. She didn't know George; not like I did. 'Don't say that.'

'You know what he's like. He can't keep it in his trousers.'

I could feel my temper rising. 'It's different with me. He wouldn't do that.' I desperately wanted to believe it.

'He slept with your sister.'

'You don't know that.'

'Oh, come on, Holly. Don't be so naïve.'

'He told me nothing happened. They just talked and cuddled.'

'And you believe him? You know what he's like, Holly. He sees women as playthings. You're his latest bit of fun. When we go home, he'll go back to his rich boy life and marry that Fiona woman and you'll be heartbroken.'

'You don't know what you're talking about. He really likes me. Please be happy for us, Meg. I don't want to fall out. You're my best friend.'

'That's why I'm looking out for you. Why couldn't you have fallen for Kristóf?'

'Kristóf?' I laughed. 'You hate Kristóf!'

'No, I don't. He just does my head in. But at least he would look after you, be nice to you.'

'I don't see him like that. Kristóf's just a friend. You can't help who you fall in love with.'

'You think it's love?'

'Yeah, maybe. In time.'

'Well, I hope you know what you're doing.'

'I do,' I said, with more confidence than I felt. 'Friends again?'

'We never stopped being friends. I'm trying to look out for you.'

'I know, and I appreciate it.'

That night Meg made more of an effort to speak to George, listening politely as he described in great detail the airplanes and military craft they had seen. We ordered spring rolls and duck fried rice and shared it harmoniously. She didn't argue when George picked up the bill and linked her arm with mine as we walked back to the hostel. I was glad we had managed to talk. I had a feeling that things were going to be alright again.

Chapter 40

Under normal circumstances, I probably wouldn't have gone to Kristóf's funeral. Too many memories, too many questions. But if, as I suspect, George is behind the hit and run, then he might be there too. I need to talk to him before he goes too far; before he kills me too.

I get to the crematorium early and walk around the grounds for a while, until more people arrive and I can blend in with the crowd. The gardens are peaceful and well kept, a place of solace and reflection. It is a cold, wet day and I wish I had worn thicker tights. I watch from a distance as people arrive and greet each other with kisses on the cheeks and careful hugs. I recognise Kristóf's mother and father from their visits to university and there is a woman with a baby that I assume is his elder sister. The number of people attending is pitifully small. I scan the mourners, trying to spot George. Surely, he wouldn't miss this opportunity to observe the misery he has caused?

I wait until most people have gone inside and then sneak into the back row. The service is mercifully short. The registrar talks about Kristóf's academic achievements and his writing, that he was a much-loved uncle, brother and son with a passion for literature. His father reads out one of his poems in a strong Hungarian accent, so different from Kristóf's. His voice breaks as he comes to the end and he struggles to finish it. Music plays as the curtain closes on the coffin and we all file out into the driving rain.

I am about to return to my car when I am engulfed in a warm hug by Kristóf's mother, a small woman in a black wool coat.

'Holly, I am so pleased you could come.'

'I'm very sorry for your loss,' I say, as I move out of her embrace and shake hands with Kristóf's father, a handsome man in his late fifties. He looks like Kristóf: the same dark eyebrows and brooding eyes.

'You will join us for the wake, won't you dear?'

I hesitate, trying to think of an excuse but don't manage to come up with one quickly enough, so I dutifully nod, wondering how long I need to stay. I am a fraud, a hypocrite. I am not here to mourn. I am here to save myself from Kristóf's fate.

The wake is held in the function room of a riverside pub. Through the windows I can see ducks squabbling, dipping in and out of the water, shaking their feathers. From the amount of catering laid on, his parents clearly expected a bigger turn out. A group of academics from the university huddle together, balancing platefuls of sandwiches with cups of tea. Kristóf's sister tries to pacify her crying baby by jiggling him on her hip. There is no-one here that I recognise and there's no sign of George. It was a waste of time coming.

'Looks like it might snow,' Kristóf's mother creeps up behind me. 'Do you have a long drive?'

I nod. 'Are you staying here tonight?'

'Yes, just for the night, but then we go back. We have our dogs to see to.'

I ask politely about them and feign interest in her response, glad that we are sticking to a safe subject. I zone out her conversation as I look around the pub, wondering if I can spot George.

'Can you imagine who would do such a thing?' Kristóf's mother's question brings me back to reality.

'Sorry, what thing?'

'To knock someone over and not even stop?'

I shake my head, wondering if I should tell her my suspicions that Kristóf's death was no accident, but what would it achieve? I have no proof and it would only make her grief worse. I've been wondering about the folder full of messages that Kristóf kept. Surely the university will be going through his things by now, clearing out his office for someone else to occupy? Will they go through every file or stack it all in boxes and shove it in a cellar somewhere? Should I try to retrieve the folder before it's too late and hand it over to Rob? Would it be enough to convince him that I'm not going mad?

'I really don't know. Have the police said anything?'

'They're appealing for witnesses, but no-one's come forward yet. They must have been driving at some speed.'

'It's terrible. It must be awful for you.'

I look at this kind, lovely woman and feel another surge of guilt. I should never have come to the funeral. This is all my fault. If I had said something before, if I had only spoken up at the time, Kristóf might be alive.

'I'm so pleased to see you. I thought you and Kristóf had lost touch after what happened to that poor boy in Thailand.'

'We did for a while.'

'It was so upsetting for you all. And now this.'

I don't deserve her sympathy, but I can feel tears welling up. I blink them away. I feel like an imposter, a ghoul. I shouldn't have come. I should be back with Tom and Jack, cuddled up in front of a DVD and far away from all this grief and sadness.

'He was very fond of you. I always hoped one day you might ...'

'We were only ever friends,' I correct her.

'Of course, I'm sorry. Are you married? Do you have children?'

'I have a son. A stepson actually. He's five.'

I pull out my mobile and show her a picture of Jack. It's the first time I have done this, and I wonder how Tom would react if he could see me, but it feels nice to play the part of a proud parent for a change. Besides, we are living together now so we're a family. It's only a matter of time before Jack starts calling me 'mum'.

'I'm glad you're happy, love,' she pats my arm and moves away. I put my phone away, feeling a pang of guilt. I shouldn't be showing off my family when she has just lost her son.

As soon as I get a chance, I make my excuses and slip away. I only came here to find George and he's not here. Maybe he's running scared now that I've seen him? Or is he is hiding in the shadows, letting the dust settle, before making his next move?

Chapter 41

It snows overnight. The first flakes started to fall, dancing in the amber glow of the streetlights, as we went to bed. By morning, a thick blanket has covered the estate and Jack is beside himself with excitement, begging to go out in his pyjamas and make a snowman. Tom looks like he might relent but I can't afford to be late. I have already had a text from Trevor saying the school will stay open, even though the outlying farms will be cut off, so half the kids will be missing. As a compromise, Tom goes into the garage and returns with a bright red sledge under his arm and we pull Jack to school. He sits regally on his plastic carriage as we drag him over the bridge. The surrounding landscape looks like a painting, the drystone walls providing a picturesque contrast to the white hills and the swollen river. I wish I had brought my camera.

A few heads turn as we arrive at the school gate, but a couple of the mothers smile at me in tacit approval. In the playground, the kids are busy making snowmen and flouting the ban on snowball fights. The path leading up to the main entrance has already been turned into a skid patch by the boys in year six. I don't tell them off. After weeks of grey clouds and persistent rain, the snow provides welcome entertainment. Even as an adult, I share their thrill of waking up in the morning to find snow covering the ground; the simple pleasure of being the first to step on to the pristine pathway with a satisfying crunch; shivering in to the cocoon of my warm winter coat and feeling the comfort of thick woollen socks protecting my toes. The world seems cleaner, more magical, and more beautiful.

Inside the classroom, the radiators are pumping out intense heat. The children trot in, red cheeked and giddy with soaked mittens and slushy boots. They take a while to settle as I take the register, noting that Nathan is one of the missing students and hoping that Emma has informed the school this time.

This morning we are rehearsing for the school nativity. The children in my class don't have big roles to play, most of them are stars or sheep, but they do have a few carols, so we need to practise the words every day in the hope that they sink in. Mostly I am worried that the kids won't be able to keep still for that long. Rhona is despairing of 'Orrible Oliver who has somehow managed to bully himself into the role of Joseph. *Might as well put that gob to good use*, Rhona said under her breath when Trevor made the announcement.

We are halfway through *Away in a Manger*, when the

fire alarm goes off. The children jump up and run around screaming.

'Everyone stand still,' I shout and remarkably they do. 'Now line up, quietly.'

The children form a disorderly line with the teaching assistant at the back. It's against the rules, and will no doubt earn me another reprimand, but I stop to grab as many coats as I can otherwise the poor things will freeze to death. We are one of the last classes to arrive in the playground, earning me a look of disapproval from Trevor, who is pacing up and down on his mobile phone, shivering in his shirt sleeves. Until that moment, it never occurred to me that the fire alarm would be anything other than a drill and that we would receive an email this afternoon outlining key messages and performance stats. I look back at the building, but I can't see any smoke.

I am counting heads when I notice someone standing by the school railings. From this distance, I can't see their face, but they are holding up a mobile phone and it looks like they are filming the kids.

'Hey,' I shout, walking towards them. The figure looks up, turns and runs. Trevor has heard me shouting and is already in pursuit. He sprints across the playground with unexpected athleticism, but the figure has already disappeared down one of the alleyways that lead onto the fells. I exchange glances with Rhona and Diane, wondering if we should call the police or wait until Trevor returns. The kids carry on playing, oblivious to the drama.

Finally, Trevor comes back, holding his stomach and wheezing for breath. Sweat glistens on his forehead and I can see wet patches underneath his pristine white shirt.

'Did you get a good look at him?'

'No, not really.' From this distance, I couldn't even tell if they were a man or a woman, but the height and build made me think that the figure was male. He was wearing jeans and a grey hooded top. There was nothing distinctive about him, but he could well have been the same person who was standing outside my house watching it burn.

'We'll have to report it to the police. Bloody pervert.'

'Do you think that's what it was?'

'What else?'

What else indeed? Am I being paranoid or was the figure filming me? Was it George? This is getting too much. The George I knew would never hurt a child; but then again, I never thought he would be capable of killing Meg and Kristóf either.

Trevor tells us we can return to the classroom. I round up the kids, my mind spinning. Am I being paranoid? What was he doing here? Was he going to abduct one of the kids, or was he just trying to scare me, remind me that he can enter my life anytime, anywhere? If so, he's taken a huge risk by returning to the village. He must know the police will be looking for him. He is getting reckless ... or desperate. I'm not sure if this is a good thing or a bad thing.

Sure enough, ten minutes later my phone beeps with a

notification. I open it, not even caring that the kids and the teaching assistant can see me using my phone in class. The video shows me with the children, and then zooms in on Jack's face. There's no message but the intention is clear. I'm not only putting myself in danger, but Jack too. I tremble at the thought of anyone hurting Jack. Tom would never forgive me if something happens and I could have stopped it. I need to tell the police.

Rob arrives an hour later to take a statement. I wait for ten minutes and then make my way to Trevor's office to intercept him as he comes out.

'Keep an eye out,' Rob is saying to Trevor, who appears to have changed his shirt. He must keep a spare one in the office. 'If you see anyone hanging around again, ring us straight away.'

'Of course.'

'Might be nothing, just a coincidence. But you can't be too careful when it comes to kiddies.' He puts away his notebook and shakes Trevor's hand before he notices me.

'I need to talk to you, Rob.'

Rob looks annoyed. 'Can't it wait Holly? I've got a lot on today.'

Trevor walks back into his office and closes the door.

'I know who set off the alarm, the man at the school gates. It was George.'

He looks at me sceptically and then leads me outside. The snow is already melting and has turned to grey sludge. 'Look Holly, you've got to let this go. George Bolton is dead. My mate in CID checked the files and there's no way there's been a mistake. His parents identified him in person.'

'Look.' I show him the video on my phone. 'He's after Jack. Please Rob, you have to believe me. I know he's alive.'

Rob sighs but takes a closer look. 'Can I take this? Maybe someone from the station can trace the number.'

I feel apprehensive at handing over my phone to the police to root through, but I am desperate enough to let them. 'I know it's George. Who else would it be?'

'I don't know, a parent with a grudge? Someone who fancies you? An ex-boyfriend?'

'It's not. It's George, I'm telling you.'

Rob pockets my phone and puts his hand on my shoulder like a concerned father. 'Holly, get some rest, please. You're driving yourself nuts with this.'

Chapter 42

Mark had lost count of how often he had bailed his brother out. There was the time George ran up a huge debt on his credit card playing on online casinos; or when he was caught with cocaine at boarding school and threatened with expulsion; and they had both agreed never to mention that embarrassing night with the hookers on George's twenty-first. There were memories he couldn't share with anyone.

Other memories: long summers spent in Italy at their parents' villa, learning to ski in the French alps, that trip to Florida when their father threatened to feed them to the alligators if they didn't stop squabbling. One time, they sneaked away from the nanny and went out on the lake in the old wooden rowing boat. They had been expressly forbidden from going on to the water by themselves, but Mark had persuaded George that they wouldn't get into trouble. George had only been young, maybe five or six, and couldn't swim.

They stole into the kitchen and filled their rucksacks

with apples and biscuits for their expedition into unchartered territory. Mark took the lead, and scared George half to death with stories of snakes lurking in the bushes and bears hidden behind the trees. When they got to the lake, George had cried and wanted to go back, but Mark took his hand and told him it would be fine.

They had not gone too far from the jetty when Mark lost the first oar. He had pushed against the water too hard, lost his balance and dropped the oar in the water. He tried to reach for it, but it floated away and no matter how hard he tried to paddle, it remained beyond his grasp. Mark tried to get back to the jetty, but it was too difficult with just one oar and George was too little to make a difference.

It started to get cold and dark. They ate their biscuits miserably, contemplating how much trouble they were going to be in when they were finally rescued. Eventually, just as the stars started to make their presence felt, he heard voices calling their names and distant figures silhouetted against the light coming from the lake house.

Robinson, their gamekeeper, was the one who swam out to rescue them. He appeared at the side of the boat like an otter and pulled himself in, uttering swear words under his breath as the vessel tipped. He rowed the intrepid explorers to shore where they were greeted by the rescue party, carrying warm blankets. His mother carried George up the woodland path into the house while he trailed behind. Later, when they were warm and dry, and had been fed bowls of tomato soup with big chunks of bread, they were called into his father's study to account for themselves.

'I expected better of you, Marcus,' his father scolded. 'You're the eldest. You're supposed to be the leader. Your brother can't swim; he could have drowned.'

George, to his credit, took his share of the blame and the punishment. You could rely on George not to blab, to always have your back. The two boys looked alike: the same sandy curls, the same brown eyes they had inherited from their father, but they had very different temperaments. George was naturally sunny and the baby of the family. Everyone doted on him and he accepted their love without questioning it. George looked up to his elder brother, expected him to have all the answers, and sometimes Mark resented him for it.

He had secured George a job at his firm for when he graduated and offered him a room in his flat until he was settled. He had been looking forward to showing George the nightlife in Singapore and introducing him to Mia. George never got to meet her, thanks to Holly.

He misses Mia, the warmth of her body, the softness of her gaze, the constant reassurance that he is a good person, that he is loved. He told her he was going on a business trip, but he hasn't called her since he arrived in Yorkshire. She will have contacted his mother by now, trying to find him. He regrets that, he doesn't want them to worry.

Mark's guilt turns to anger: this is Holly's fault, again. If she would just admit what she's done, this could all be over. He could go home, have his life back.

Chapter 43

Thailand, five years ago

Our relationship started to rot as quickly as it had ripened. George was like a butterfly in Bangkok, his eyes constantly roving from one beautiful flower to the next, clearly regretting saddling himself with a girlfriend when he could be exploring other possibilities. The girls in the red-light district area of the city were pushy and playful, not caring that he was attached and I grew increasingly irritated by their approaches. I had bought George a ring in the night market and wanted him to wear it on his wedding finger to show he was unavailable but he had just laughed at the idea. For the first time I felt a twinge of sympathy for Fiona; she'd put up with this for years. But I thought things would be different with me.

We had started to argue. George resented me for spending time with Meg, and Meg complained of being ignored when I spent time with George. It got to the point where I couldn't please anyone. Kristóf was taciturn, finding excuses to go off on his own as much as possible. He had wanted to spend more time in the North of the country, go further afield than Chiang Mai, but the rest of us were keen to enjoy the hedonistic pleasures of the islands in the South. Perhaps a bit of rest and relaxation was what we needed to repair some bridges? The four of us had been the best of friends for three years and I didn't want our relationship to destroy that.

Our first few days on the island were idyllic. We sunbathed on the white sandy beach, drinking in the view of the traditional longboats bobbing in the water. The resort was full of bars and restaurants and it felt more like being on holiday than travelling. We had been lucky with the weather up to that point. Apart from the occasional downpour, we had enjoyed long days of sunshine in Cambodia and Vietnam. But on the fourth day, the weather turned and it rained solidly for the next week. Every day I looked out of the window, hoping to see sunshine but was greeted by heavy rain and grey clouds in the sky like smudges of charcoal. The sea turned the colour of dirty dishwater and plastic bottles re-emerged from its depths, covered in barnacles that looked like flowers. Mangy dogs traversed the beach, picking at the discarded litter left by thoughtless backpackers who had come here to drink and party.

We were stuck in the hostel most days, playing cards or grumbling about the weather. The boat trips we had planned were cancelled and there wasn't much else to do.

The Beach

We sat at the beach front bars drinking half-price cocktails and ignoring touts offering cheap massages and tuk-tuks. Old men whizzed past on their scooters with their significantly younger Thai girlfriends. Kristóf was going stir-crazy and retreated into his books. George was trying to make the best of it but even he was failing to find anything positive to say about the experience. We bickered constantly.

'Would it be totally wrong to have a burger and chips?' I suggested, as we took our seats at a beachside café, which had been protected from the rain by tarpaulin sheets. I was sick of rice and noodles and craving English food.

'Totally,' George said, ordering Thai green curry for us both.

There was a heavy silence and I glanced over to where Meg was clearly resisting the urge to confront him. I prayed that she wouldn't but my prayers went unanswered.

'No-one ever says no to you, do they George?' Her words were thick with contempt. Why couldn't she just leave things alone?

'Not usually, no,' George replied cheerfully, deliberately misinterpreting her tone of voice. I held his hand under the table.

'It's fine, I like green curry.'

Meg raised her eyebrows at my conciliatory efforts. The curry arrived with pieces of chicken, aubergine and cour-gette floating in a coconut milk soup. Small circles of bright red chilli and yellow strips of ginger rested on top and I stirred it suspiciously. I really would have preferred a burger.

George watched as I used the spoon to lift the smallest amount to my lips. I let it fall on my tongue and waited for the spices to hit me.

'Good, yeah?'

I coughed as the chilli hit the back of my throat and took a huge gulp of Chang beer. The food in Thailand was much spicier than in the other countries we had visited. I nodded as he handed me a dish of vegetables which looked like a cross between broccoli and spinach.

'Morning glory,' he explained. It sounded like a sex act and I giggled. Meg rolled her eyes and made a point of ignoring us. Instead she asked Kristóf about the book he was reading; an obscure tome about the Khmer Empire.

The curry might not have been to my taste, but the dessert was delicious. The mango was sweet and rubbery, the sticky rice warm and infused with coconut milk, and fried mung beans were scattered on top to add an extra crunch. So far on this trip, desserts hadn't been much to get excited about, but this was something else. I moaned appreciatively as I gulped it down and contemplated a second helping. George laughed at me.

'Careful, Holly. You'll be getting fat.'

I dropped my spoon immediately. It was a flippant remark, but it cut me to the core. Did George think I was overweight?

'You are such a dick, George,' Meg scolded. 'There's not a scrap of fat on her.'

'I didn't say there was!'

'Please guys, stop arguing. I know he didn't mean it like that.' But I wasn't sure. Was George going off me already? I had put on some weight on this trip, but we all had. I didn't think it mattered to George what I looked like but maybe he preferred slimmer girls. It wouldn't harm me to cut down a bit.

Kristóf changed the subject, pointing out yet another temple that he wanted to visit. We spent the rest of the meal discussing the pros and cons of renting out scooters. It was easy and cheap enough to do but we were slightly wary given the number of backpackers we had seen with bandages around their knees and elbows. I had passed my driving test at university, but I wasn't the most confident of drivers. George was really keen but Kristóf thought it might be better to look into hiring a driver or joining a tour group. We left the café still arguing about the best course of action.

We were half-way back to the hostel when the wind suddenly whipped up the litter on the street giving us a few minutes' warning of a downpour. A low rumble of thunder and a crack of lightning heralded a storm. It suddenly went dark and rain started to fall in huge pellets, splashing the dark stone as people ran for shelter, holding plastic carrier bags over their heads for protection.

George grabbed my hand and we sprinted towards a shop where people were gathering under the awning. The rain became torrential, forming rivulets of dirty brown water along the street. My hair was plastered to my face and my trouser legs were soaked wet through. I was slipping and sliding on my flip-flops, struggling to keep up with George as he pulled me along. I was wearing a white t-shirt and looking down I could see that it had already turned see-through and the outline of my bra was visible. We huddled together in the tiny space that was left and shouted at Kristóf and Meg to hurry up.

Meg stopped running. Standing in the middle of the street she turned her head to the sky and let the rain wash her face. She laughed, moving her arms upwards. Everyone was looking at her, but she didn't care. She danced in the puddles, kicking up water so it splashed her bare legs. People were cheering and clapping and some even joined in. I looked up at George, expecting him to be laughing at her too, but he was staring, captivated by her.

Chapter 44

It's too wet to go to the park on Saturday so I take Jack for a walk around the village instead. It takes forever as he insists on jumping in every puddle we come across, muddy water splashing up his bright yellow boots. He is in a chatty mood, telling me all about the different planets in the solar system and how he wants to be an astronaut one day.

'You'll have to work hard at school if you want to be an astronaut,' I say. 'They're very clever.'

'More clever than you?'

'Much more.'

Jack looks momentarily perturbed by this nugget of information but doesn't let it bother him. I have long admired the unbridled ambition of five-year-olds. When does it get knocked out of us, I wonder? When do we stop believing that we can achieve anything we put our mind to? For me it was probably secondary school. I used to spend hours working on photography projects, taking hundreds of pictures until I got the right shot, learning about lighting and composition, visiting galleries for inspiration. When did I decide that photography was just a hobby, not something I should pursue?

As we walk into the Spar shop to pick up vegetables for dinner, I feel someone watching me. I turn my head sharply and see a figure move quickly behind a stand. Was it George? Grabbing Jack's hand, I march up the aisle determined to confront him. But it isn't George, it's Emma. She's standing at the bread aisle, pretending to choose a loaf, wearing skinny jeans, biker boots and a parka coat with a faux fur lined hood. Her hair is greasy and tied back, her eyes red and ringed with purple shadows. She looks at me defiantly.

'Are you following me?' I demand, wondering for a minute whether she is behind the messages, but that's impossible. There's no way she could possibly know what happened in Thailand.

'Having a nice time, are we?' she spits out sarcastically. 'With someone else's child?'

I push Jack behind me but keep hold of his hand.

'That's none of your business.'

'Nathan's none of your business, but that didn't stop you interfering, did it?' Her face is twisted with anger as she shouts. The other shoppers are staring at us and I can see them drinking in every detail of the drama.

'Look, we can talk about this, but not now, not here. Why don't you come to the school on Monday? We can talk about it properly.'

'You told them I was a bad mother.'

'No, I didn't. I didn't say that.'

'That's what you think. That's what you all think. That I can't look after him. Well, he's my son and you can't take him from me.'

'No-one wants to take him from you. I just think you need some help. It must be difficult with Liam being away.'

'What the fuck do you know about anything? You're a jumped-up little cow sticking your nose in where it's not wanted.'

I feel like bursting into tears, but Jack is watching me. I need to be the adult here. 'Let's talk about this another time.'

The store manager approaches us. He puts his hand on Emma's shoulder, but she shrugs him off. 'Don't touch me,' she snarls.

She moves towards me, her face less than an inch from mine. 'I'm warning you, stay away from my son, bitch.' And then she spits in my face before the shopkeeper drags her off and throws her out, telling her she's barred.

He returns, shaking his head in disgust. 'Are you alright, love?'

'I'm fine, honestly,' I say, wiping my face with a tissue, but I'm not fine. I am shaking and still clinging on to Jack's hand, who looks visibly upset by the whole encounter.

'We all saw what happened, love. You need to report that.'

'There's no need.'

'Well if you don't, I will. I'm not having behaviour like that in my shop. We don't need her sort around here.'

Everyone is looking at me now. I grab a few more items from the shelves, barely aware of what I am putting in the basket and pay for them. The woman at the till asks me if I am OK and I nod dutifully. This is going to go around the village like wildfire. Jack is still holding my hand but has gone very quiet. She gives him a lollipop.

I keep looking over my shoulder as we walk home but there is no sign of Emma. I don't want to report the incident and run the risk of Rob thinking I'm attention seeking again but too many people witnessed the altercation for me to keep quiet. Fortunately, the police station is closed on Saturdays. The front desk is manned by volunteers and is only open for a couple of hours each day, so I will have to leave it until Monday. Hopefully, by that time, the village gossips will have something else to talk about.

I'm sure that Rob still thinks I started the fire myself so that I could move in with Tom and that I made up the story about the messages. Unsurprisingly, the police haven't managed to track down the person who sent the video of Jack. George must have used a pay-as-you-go SIM card. At least they've given me my phone back. I haven't heard anything from George since the video; I'm guessing he's keeping a low profile, but I have a nagging feeling he hasn't finished with me yet.

While Jack gets out his toys, I light a fire in the woodburning stove. I tear up sheets of the local newspaper, noting that there is a Christmas fair in Skipton next weekend. It might be fun to take Jack to see Santa and drink mulled wine. I really need to make plans for Christmas Day now: my parents have been asking.

By the time Tom gets in from his ju-jitsu tournament, the house is a picture of domestic bliss. A casserole is bubbling away in the slow cooker and Jack and I are playing Junior Monopoly in the warm lounge. I stand up, kiss him and ask him how he got on.

'Not bad, came third, but I'm out of shape,' he says, picking up Jack and swinging him around. 'What have you two been up to today?'

'A lady shouted at Holly,' he says, in between squeals of delight.

Tom looks at me with concern.

'Nathan's mother,' I say. 'It was nothing.'

'She shouted at you?'

'She was upset. Honestly, I'm fine.'

'In front of Jack? What was she thinking?'

'It's par for the course when you're a teacher.'

'Are you going to report it?'

'Maybe.'

'You shouldn't be so soft, Holly. You can't let people treat you like that.' Tom's condescension is ruining the atmosphere. I change the subject instead, telling him about Jack's plans to be an astronaut.

Once Jack has gone to bed, we settle down on the sofa

with a bottle of red wine. We have turned off the lights and relax in the glow of the fire. Shadows flicker up the walls and the rain patters against the windows.

'I have something to tell you,' he says. 'And I don't think you're going to like it.'

I take a deep breath. Is he going to ask me to move back home? Has he had enough of my drama? We've had such a lovely day, why has he waited until now to spoil it?

'Go on.'

'Rebecca rang me today.'

'What?'

'Completely out of the blue. Wanted to speak to Jack.'

'Will you let her?'

'I don't know. Jack's got used to her not being around, this is going to completely throw him. But she's his mother. I can't keep them apart forever, it's not fair.'

'She walked out on him.'

'She walked out on me. Jack was ... collateral damage, I guess.'

I bite my lip. I know I need to put Jack first, but all I can think is what if Rebecca wants Tom back? How can I compete with the love of his life, the mother of his child? Why do I always end up the other woman, the second choice?

'Well, it's your decision.'

'I'm going to leave it a while, give it some more thought. But I thought I should tell you.'

'Thank you.'

I excuse myself to do the washing up. I turn on the taps and look at myself in the reflection of the window. I'm going to lose Tom to Rebecca, I know it. He was never mine in the first place, he always belonged to her deep down. She's going to take him from me and there's nothing I can do to stop it.

I grab a glass and smash it against the tap. It feels good to release my frustration. I hold up the broken glass to the light and watch the streaks of red wine glimmer. It looks like blood. I turn the glass and run it across the top of my hand, breaking the skin.

'Oh shit!' I call out and Tom comes running.

'Oh my God, what have you done?' He grabs a clean tea towel and wraps it around my hand. The blood soaks into the cloth immediately. The cut is sore but not too painful. I made sure it wasn't deep.

'Stupid glass jumped out of my hand.'

Tom sits me down in a chair and kneels in front of me to examine the wound. 'Ouch,' he says.

'Do you think I need to go to hospital?' It will mean getting Jack out of bed and getting a taxi as we've been drinking.

'No, I think you'll be OK. Look, it's stopped bleeding now.' He goes upstairs and fetches down the first aid box. It is well stocked; Jack is always falling over and injuring himself. He applies some gauze and wraps my hand in a bandage.

'Keep it upright.'

I lean over and kiss him. 'Thank you for looking after me.'

'Always,' he says, kissing me back.

Chapter 45

Waking up next to Tom on Sunday morning, I berate myself for my foolishness. Tom loves me; he would never go back to Rebecca. I need to stop being so paranoid. Just because George was unfaithful, it doesn't mean every man will be the same.

Falling in love with Tom was completely different from how I felt about George. With George everything was high-octane; like being swept away by rapids. Being with Tom on the other hand makes me feel secure, anchored. But if I love Tom, if I truly love Tom, then surely, I should be able to confide all my secrets? My love for him is unconditional so why can't I trust him to feel the same? He has been so kind and attentive to me recently, but would he still love me if he knew what I'd done?

It's only 7am so I slip out of bed quietly to make a cup of tea without disturbing Tom. I tiptoe along the corridor to Jack's room to see if he's awake. He often is by this time although the dark mornings mean he has started to sleep in longer. He is fast asleep underneath his Thomas the

Tank Engine duvet, a little hand dangling from the bed. I tuck him back in and he stirs but doesn't wake. I go downstairs, put the kettle on and switch on my mobile phone. It vibrates as I pop a teabag into a mug. There seems to be a lot of notifications, mostly from my sister. Seven missed calls and three messages asking me to ring her back. They started around 11.30 last night and went on until the early hours of the morning. My sister has never rung me so many times before; not even when she's drunk.

I try to call her, but she doesn't answer, so I leave a message and carry on making the tea. Almost immediately my phone vibrates again. I snatch it back up.

'Lisa? Are you OK?'

Lisa is in bits, sobbing down the phone. I can't make out what she's saying, only that it has something to do with a video.

'Hang on, Lisa. Breathe. Tell me what's wrong.'

'It's going viral. Oh my God, it's had 200,000 views already. The media's bound to get hold of it. I can't, I can't. What if Mum and Dad see it? They'll be so ashamed.'

'Ashamed? Of what? You're not making any sense.'

'It's Alex, he's posted a video of me online.'

'What kind of video?' But I already know the answer by the tone of her voice.

'It was just a bit of fun. It was only ever meant to be between us. He didn't even have a copy.'

'So how did he get hold of it?'

'I don't know, do I?' she shrieks. 'He must have gone through my laptop, the bastard. I trusted him.'

'Can't you report it? Get it taken down?'

'The police said it wouldn't do much good,' Lisa sobs. 'It's already out there. There'll be copies of it all over the internet by now. The PR woman said I just need to keep my head down, not give any interviews.'

'Do you want to come and stay with me?'

'I can't. I'm in the middle of a big storyline. Oh God, what am I going to do? This is a complete nightmare; it could ruin me.'

I don't know what to say. She's right of course. The media will pull her to pieces. Alex, whoever he is, must have planned this. I try to remember what Lisa has told me about him, but she has been so secretive. I don't think I have even seen his picture.

'Listen, Lisa. Will you do me a favour? Can you send me the link?'

'Oh God, surely you don't want to watch it?'

'Of course not,' I lie. 'But maybe Tom will know what to do. He's good at IT. He might be able to find something in the source code or whatever they do.'

'If you want, I don't know what difference it'll make. I'll send it over when I come off the phone.'

'Thanks. Are you sure you don't want to come up, even for a couple of days?'

'No, I'm fine, thanks though.'

'It'll die down soon, I promise. They'll find someone

else to gawp at. Try not to get too upset. Might be best to tell Mum and Dad though, so they don't hear it from anyone else. I'm sure they'll understand.'

'I hope so. Urgh. The thought of those vile men perving at me on the internet makes me feel sick.'

'Switch off your phone and laptop for a few days and let it blow over,' I say. 'They'll move on to someone else soon enough.'

'Yeah, maybe.' I can tell from the tone of her voice that she isn't planning to take my advice. 'I suppose I'd better call Mum and Dad.'

'Good luck. I'm sure they'll understand.'

Lisa rings off. I hear movement above my head followed by the sound of Jack thumping down the stairs on his backside. His head appears at the kitchen door.

'Who were you talking to?'

'My sister.'

'The one on TV?' Jack is very impressed that my sister is an actress even though we don't let him watch the programme. He perches on the kitchen stool and looks at me expectantly.

'That's right. Would you like some breakfast?'

'Can I have pancakes?' I hesitate – normally Jack has Weetabix with honey for his breakfast – I'm not sure I even know how to make pancakes. I suppose I can always Google the recipe.

'Sure. How about we make them together?'

I am just cleaning up our mess, and the mixture is

resting in the fridge, when my mobile beeps with a message from Lisa. Washing my hands quickly and making sure Jack can't see what I'm looking at, I press on the link.

It's pretty grotesque watching my sister shagging, but the video is mild; an ordinary couple having ordinary sex. She's done nothing to be ashamed of. It's been filmed on a webcam and you can see Lisa's face clearly. Alex's face is obscured but at one point he lifts his head up and you get a good look at him. I freeze it. I would recognise those features anywhere: those eyes, that sandy hair; but the nose isn't the same and the jawline is different. I know that face. The man in the photos has George's features but it isn't him. Checking that Jack is preoccupied with his tablet, I grab my laptop and run upstairs.

I lock myself in the bathroom and, balancing the laptop on my knees, I put George's name into the search engine and scroll down the results. The headlines are all familiar to me; I know which one I need. The one from *The Telegraph*, when the family speaks out. There is a group photograph from a family holiday in Switzerland. I enlarge the picture and look to the left of George where his older, taller brother is standing, his arm wrapped casually around a beautiful Asian woman. I compare it to the photo on my phone. There is no question that it's the same man. Lisa's boyfriend is George's brother, Mark.

I close the laptop, trying to quell my rising nausea. It must have been Mark behind the messages all along. Which means George is dead after all. My brain is like a pinball, bouncing off all the consequences and I feel sick to my stomach. Mark's already killed Meg and Kristóf and ruined my sister's reputation. He's threatened Jack and burned down my house. I thought I could handle this, but I can't. Too many people are getting hurt and it's all my fault.

Chapter 46

Mark had no desire to be unfaithful to Mia, but the ends justified the means. And Lisa had been so willing to fall into his arms, so trusting. All it took was a bit of flattery.

He loves Mia. Has loved her since the moment they met at a corporate dinner in Singapore. She worked for one of the city's investment banks and was more intelligent and more beautiful than anyone he had ever met. Compared to Mia, Lisa was a painted doll. Mia had let him do all the running, but it was worth it. When she finally let him into her bed, it felt like coming home.

They had only been together just over a year when George died. Having lost her father the year before, Mia understood his grief. She comforted him when he cried, supported him when he had to be strong, came back to England with him when his family needed him. When it was clear that he couldn't go back to Singapore and leave his mother, she agreed to stay. He didn't deserve her.

And now this. He has cheated on her, lied to her, left

her. Will she forgive him? Will she understand? Why should she? The desire to contact her is overwhelming, but Mark resists. He is nearly there. Holly is cracking, he can feel it. He has ruined her sister's reputation; she knows now that he can, and will, hurt everyone she loves in pursuit of the truth.

Chapter 47

Thailand, five years ago

Looking back, I have gone over and over the hours that led up to George's death, wondering if there had been any signs that our lives were about to change forever, but we were just four kids on a backpacking trip going to a beach party like thousands before us and thousands more to come.

We were coming to the end of our trip and had bought tickets to a full moon party to celebrate. Meg and I got ready in the shared dormitory which reeked of cheap perfume and incense. It felt like being back at uni again. We helped each other with our make-up while swigging from the half-bottle of vodka we had bought in the 7-11. Meg was in a good mood and it was nice to see her smiling and having fun. There was a mix of nationalities in the dorm – German, American, Australian, French and Russian – but everyone was about our age and up for a party. We borrowed some neon paint and a paintbrush from a couple of French girls and painted flowers and patterns on our arms and legs. We decorated our hair with the garlands we had bought earlier in the day.

There were hundreds of people at the party, ready to drink and dance all night. Stalls had been set up selling 'buckets' of cheap booze. They were the type of colourful plastic buckets you used to make sandcastles as a kid filled with cheap spirits and mixers. Each stall had a different name and vendors were shouting at us to get our attention as we walked past, offering free shots and hugs. A fire dancer had drawn the attention of a group of partygoers who stood mesmerised as he twirled a flaming baton around his body and high into the air. The balls of fire illuminated his chest, slick with protective oil, his tattoos dull against the glistening skin.

The sand was already covered in glass bottles, cigarette butts and discarded plastic trays full of half-eaten kebabs and slices of pizza. A row of men stood with their backs to the crowd pissing into the sea. A DJ was playing dance music while lasers lit up the sky. You could tell it was the sort of party where anything could happen. We exchanged excited grins as we headed to one of the bars. All around us people were dancing, shouting and laughing, pumping their hands in the air. It was going to be a good night.

George bought a round of beers. I knew I needed to take it steady otherwise I wouldn't last the night. The vodka from earlier was already making my head swim. It had stopped raining for once and the air was balmy. Above us a bright yellow moon dominated the night sky, reflected in the calm water. I looked around for George, but his attention was on a group of young, beautiful girls standing to the side of us. I turned away, trying not to read too much into it.

Meg grabbed my hand and pulled me onto a free space on the beach to dance. Kristóf stood with George, sipping his beer and trying to look relaxed. The atmosphere was electric. With the music, the setting and the crowds of excited people, it was impossible not to feel happy. Our trip might be coming to an end, but it had been a fantastic experience, one we would remember for the rest of our lives. I imagined us in twenty years' time, fondly recalling our trip to Thailand when we were twenty-one. George and I would be married by then, we would have children. Whatever happened, I knew that we would all stay friends for the rest of our lives, meeting up for birthdays, weddings, christenings and all the other rites of passage yet to come.

George and Kristóf had been joined by the group of girls who were laughing and flirting with them. Kristóf was looking distinctly uncomfortable, but George was clearly loving the attention.

'Are you going to put up with that?' Meg demanded, shouting over the music.

'They're only talking, he's not doing anything.'

'You're such a doormat, Holly.' She stormed off in the direction of the bar. I didn't want to go after her, but I didn't want to join the boys, and I definitely didn't want to be left dancing alone, so I followed.

Meg bought two more beers and handed me one as a peace offering. 'Sorry, it's your life. I shouldn't interfere.'

'I know you mean well, but I trust him.'

'I don't know if you should.'

I sipped my beer and didn't answer, watching everyone dancing around me. Bits of coral, like discarded bones, prodded my feet as lasers slashed through the sky. Why couldn't Meg just enjoy tonight and stop analysing my life? What did she know anyway? She had never even been in a serious relationship.

'I wish I could prove to you once and for all that George and I love each other. Yes, he may be a flirt, but he wouldn't cheat on me.'

'You're so sure about that, are you?'

'One hundred percent,' I lied. 'Try it. Go on.'

'What are you talking about?'

'I've seen him watching you. Try it on with him.' Even as I spoke, I doubted my own wisdom. He wouldn't do that to me, would he?

'Don't be ridiculous.'

'I want you to. I want you to hit on him and when he turns you down, which he will, we'll know for sure won't we?'

She looked at me defiantly. I was fully expecting her to refuse. 'OK, I will.'

'You will?'

'Yeah, you're so sure of him, why not? I mean nothing is going to happen, is it?'

'No, it won't. I trust him.'

'Right then.'

We headed back. I was relieved that there was no sign of the women; they must have moved on when they realised the boys weren't interested in them. I felt vindicated.

George greeted me with a kiss and a big hug. 'There you are! We were getting worried. Listen, I managed to score some E's off those girls.'

'Are you joking?'

'Of course not, come on, Hol. Look around you, everyone's high.'

I had heard all about the dangers of doing drugs in Thailand. There was no way I was going to risk it. I looked at Meg for support, but she looked tempted.

'Do what you like,' I said huffily.

George passed a pill discreetly to Meg and I watched them swill them down with beer. It wasn't long before they were both dancing like maniacs to the music, jumping up and down, crashing into other people. On drugs, George was even more tactile and flirtatious than usual, and I noticed he was dancing very close to Meg, who didn't seem to object to his attention. If anything, she looked to be encouraging him. I was fed up with the pair of them. Was she really going to try it on with him? And what was I going to do if she succeeded? I couldn't bear the thought of losing George.

'Having a good night?' Kristóf asked. He looked as miserable as I felt.

'Not really.'

'Want to go back?'

It was tempting but I shook my head. I was watching George and Meg and wondering whether I should go and dance with them, separate them, persuade Meg to call it off.

'He's such a dick,' Kristóf muttered under his breath.

'Who is?'

'George. Your so-called boyfriend.'

I turned my head, scrutinising his face. 'What do you mean by that?'

'Oh, come on Holly, he treats you like dirt. Look at him, he's all over Meg.'

'Don't be ridiculous. They're only dancing together. They're friends.'

Kristóf gave me a look of utter contempt. 'I don't think George knows how to be friends with the fairer sex.'

'You're just jealous.'

A look of hurt and anger flashed across his face. 'You know what, Holly. You're right. I am jealous. Because he doesn't deserve you. And you throw yourself at him thinking he's some sort of saviour who's going to whisk you away to his mansion and treat you like a princess for the rest of your life.'

'Are you calling me a gold digger?'

'You don't love him, not really.'

I was furious. First Meg, and now Kristóf. Why couldn't they leave me and George alone? Why did everyone have to have an opinion about our relationship?

'What do you know about love anyway?'

As soon as the words were out of my mouth, I regretted saying them. There was an awkward silence as Kristóf struggled to repress what he was about to say, but he couldn't. I knew what was coming and I willed him not to say it.

'I love you, Holly. I've loved you from the moment I first met you. But you're too wrapped up in that piece of shit to notice.'

He stormed away before I could reply. I didn't know whether to follow him or not but what could I say to make it better? I didn't love him, not like that, and I knew I never could. We were friends, nothing more. Why did he have to spoil it?

By the time I looked back at the dancers, Meg and George had disappeared too. I started to panic. I was in the middle of nowhere, surrounded by strangers and I had lost all my friends. I wanted to go home, desperately. The evening had begun with such promise but now it was ruined by jealousy and declarations. I moved through the crowds, pushing past a group of women posing for selfies, until I spotted George and Meg standing next to one of the food stands. George was leaning over, whispering into Meg's ear. She looked up at him, surprised, and then nodded. George took her hand and pulled her away from the party.

A few seconds later I saw Kristóf go after them. He looked back at me, but I was rooted to the spot, my brain two steps behind my eyes. What was happening? Why had they left me? Were they coming back? Eventually, I realised I didn't have much choice. I had to follow them.

Chapter 48

Thailand, five years ago

As soon as I left the party, I knew I had made a mistake. Away from the bright lights and the music, the beach felt deserted. The moon was hidden by clouds and it was pitch black, the only light coming from the beachfront villas and closed restaurants behind me. In the darkness, sounds were accentuated, and I could hear the wind whispering through the trees behind me. I used the light on my mobile phone to pick my way through the discarded rubbish and broken glass along the shore, a mixture of paranoia and adrenaline coursing through my veins.

Had my friends even come this way? Perhaps they had never left the party? I should go back and wait for them. I was only putting myself at risk. I was a young woman, alone in the darkness. Anything could happen. I clutched my bag close to my chest and picked up my pace. Further down the beach I could see lights coming from a late-night bar or hotel. I could go there and get a taxi back to the hostel. Confront them in the morning.

A lone dog scratching for food amid the plastic bottles and abandoned fast food trays looked up at me with disinterested yellow eyes as I walked on. The waves crested and crashed against the shore with a rhythmic roar, taking no heed of my racing heart. I looked behind me, but everything was in darkness. Where was Kristóf? Surely, he couldn't be that far away. He had left just before me.

A few seconds later, the moon emerged, casting a silvery light over the dark grey ocean, and I could make out a couple of figures at the water's edge. Even though their faces were in shadow, I could tell it was Meg and George. I was about to call out, in relief more than anything, when I saw George raise his hand towards Meg's face, cup her cheek and lean in to kiss her. My heart was in my mouth and my brain was whirring as I lifted my phone and took a photo. I couldn't believe George would betray me like this. Meg had been right all along.

Meg pulled away and slapped George across the cheek. They started arguing, which restored my faith in Meg a little, if not George. I was too far away to hear what they were saying but I watched as he grabbed her arm and they tussled, falling onto the sand. Meg tried to get away, but George pinned her down. She screamed, like an animal in pain, the noise piercing through the night until he put his hand over her mouth. I was frozen to the spot, torn between running for help and trying to assist her, as George held her down in the surf. What was happening? This was George. My George. He wouldn't do something like this. Meg was writhing against him, trying to get away. I heard a movement behind me and turned to see Kristóf running towards them with a large rock in his hand. Almost in slow motion, I saw him hit George on the back of the head and he fell to the ground.

I stood immobile as I watched the scene unfold as if in slow motion. Finally, I regained the use of my legs and ran towards them. Meg was crouched next to George's body, her face streaked with tears, her lipstick smudged and her top torn at the shoulder. Her hair was coated in sand. Kristóf had the look of a wild animal as he raised his arm to hit George again, who lay face down, not moving. I put myself between them and Kristóf lowered his arm.

'What did you do?' I bent down and put my fingers on George's neck. I couldn't feel a pulse. There was blood everywhere, mixing in with the sand and the sea like a tie dye t-shirt.

Kristóf dropped the rock, fell to his knees and whimpered like a beaten puppy. Meg put her arms around him, and he buried his head in her neck.

'It's OK, everything's going to be OK,' she said in a soothing voice, although I wasn't sure whether she was trying to reassure Kristóf or herself.

'We need to get help.' I took out my phone, but I didn't even know what number to call. It never occurred to me that I might need the emergency services in Thailand. But there must be medics at the party. 'We need to go and get someone.'

'Wait.'

Meg crouched next to George's head and used the light on her mobile phone to examine the wound. It was worse than I imagined. She didn't have to say anything; no-one could survive a wound like that.

'Oh God, Kristóf, what have you done?'

Kristóf was still crying, sitting on the sand, rocking back and forth. Meg slapped him hard across the face.

'Get a grip,' she hissed, looking around. 'We need to decide what to do. It's only a matter of time before someone walks past and then we're fucked.' She looked at me. 'Help me turn him over.'

'What? Why?'

'Just do it.' Meg grabbed the rock from where Kristóf had dropped it. Between us we managed to roll George onto his back, and she placed the rock carefully underneath the wound. Seeing George staring up at me was unnerving. I turned away. I thought I was going to be sick. I moved to close his eyes, but Meg stopped me.

'It will look like an accident. The sea will destroy any evidence we were even here. With any luck it might even move the body.'

'Are you mad?'

'Do you want Kristóf to go to prison? Or worse? You know they have the death sentence here for murder?'

I didn't know how to answer that. They had killed my boyfriend and now they wanted me to lie about it?

'We'll tell them it was an accident.'

'We won't say anything,' Kristóf said, quietly. 'No-one knows we're here. We'll say George went off with a woman. We'll go back to the hostel and report him missing tomorrow.'

'We can't leave him here.'

Meg stood up. 'Yes, we can.' She looked down at her clothes which were stained with George's blood. 'Fuck. I can't go back looking like this.'

'Wash them in the sea,' Kristóf said, his voice cool and rational as if he were solving a mathematical equation, not trying to get away with murder. Everything was happening so quickly, and I couldn't think straight.

Meg nodded, pulled off her t-shirt and walked into the sea. Kristóf went to help her and I was left at the water's edge with George. I looked around. The hotel was only a few hundred metres away. We could go there and ask for help. I didn't have to go along with this. I looked down at George, the man I loved, the man I wanted to spend the rest of my life with. How could he do this to me? How could he betray me like that? I never for one second thought he was capable of hurting Meg. Was this all my fault? I should never have suggested she went after George.

A few minutes later, Kristóf returned, followed closely by Meg, her wet t-shirt clinging to her curves.

'Come on, Holly, we need to get out of here,' she said,

looking around. The beach was deserted but it was only a matter of time before someone came along, returning to the hotel or looking for a secluded spot to cop off. I looked down at George's dead body, gently bobbing with the waves. Could we really get away with this? Lie to the authorities, lie to our families and friends?

'He's dead Holly and we're in serious shit,' Kristóf said. 'Do you want to spend the rest of your life rotting in a Thai prison?'

'Me? What have I done? This has nothing to do with me.'

'It's your word against ours,' Kristóf said quietly.

I couldn't speak. My two best friends in the whole world had turned against me. And the man that I loved was dead.

Everything was spinning out of control. The moonlight was giving George's skin a luminous glow which made him already look like a ghost. The whole thing felt like something out of a horror film.

'There's no time for you two to argue,' Kristóf commanded. 'We can't risk being found here.'

'Should we take his wallet?' Meg suggested. 'It'll look like a robbery.'

'No, leave it. It's best that it looks like an accident, then hopefully they won't investigate it too closely.'

'But what about his family? And the Foreign Office, won't they get involved? This is madness,' I said.

Kristóf took control. 'We'll report him missing tomorrow, OK? We saw him leaving with a girl and we thought he'd got lucky.'

'But what about me?' I asked.

'What about you?'

'Won't they think it's odd that he's gone off with some girl when he's in a relationship?'

'I'd hardly call it a "relationship", Holly. You were just shagging each other.'

'Don't tell them anything,' Kristóf said, ignoring Meg's remark. 'They'll only ask more questions. We're all friends, that's it. No-one at the hostel knew you were together. George went off with some girl and we stayed at the party. It will be easier this way, I promise.'

I don't know why I believed him, but my brain wasn't functioning properly, and I couldn't think of any alternative.

'We say nothing. Swear to me, Holly.'

I looked to Meg, but she was standing by Kristóf; they both looked so resolute. They were right, if it came to my word against theirs, I wouldn't stand a chance.

'OK, I swear.'

'We stick together, and we say nothing. Not now, not in a few weeks' time, not in a few years' time, not when we're lying on our deathbeds making our last confession. OK?'

'OK.'

'It's the only way we're going to get through this.'

I had no choice. I did what I was told and followed them back to the party. None of us looked back. We'd only been away for ten minutes but it felt like hours. People were still dancing and drinking, like nothing had happened, like we hadn't just killed my boyfriend. Meg bought us a round of drinks and we merged into the crowd like we had never been away. We were just friends, enjoying a night out. One of our group got lucky and left with a strange girl.

If I told myself that story enough times, maybe I would start to believe it.

Chapter 49

If this is a game of cat and mouse, then it's time to turn the tables. According to Mark's LinkedIn profile he is employed by an investment bank in London but when I rang their head office, they said he no longer worked there. Still, it didn't take much digging to find Mark's home address. He has a flat in London and a holiday home in the Cotswolds, so he must be doing alright for himself. I remember his family were always bragging about their elder son and his flash job in Singapore. They were constantly holding him up as an example to George of what he should be achieving in life. I book a train ticket to London and tell Tom I am going down to spend the day with my sister.

I get up early on Saturday morning to drive to Skipton train station. It has been raining heavily all week, and today is no exception. The drains, blocked by autumn leaves, can't take the deluge and the pavements are like rivers. Yesterday, the village was hit by the tail end of a storm. Gale force winds caused rubbish to hurtle across the road, bins were disembowelled, litter spilt like entrails across the path. As I made my way to school, I could see children leaning against the wind to stay upright.

I am packing up the car when I see someone watching me from the end of the driveway. It's Emma. I jump, wondering whether I should go back in the house or get in the car quickly and pretend I haven't seen her, but she holds up her hand.

'I'm not here to hurt you.'

The rain is lashing down and she must be soaked to the skin. I wonder how long she has been waiting out here.

'I can't talk. I need to catch a train.'

'It won't take long. I wanted to thank you.'

'Thank me? The last time you saw me you spat in my face.'

'I wasn't myself. I haven't been for a while. I needed help.'

Emma does look better, like someone who has had a long sleep after a bout of insomnia. She is less frightening when calm, but I haven't forgotten her aggression. If it was intimidating for me, it must have been terrifying for poor Jack. And how many times has she lost her temper with Nathan?

'Well, I'm glad things are improving.'

'Social services have actually been pretty good. They've got me a support worker and the doctors put me on some anti-depressants. They've not really kicked in yet but I'm feeling better.'

'That's great.'

'I just wasn't coping ... Nathan can be a handful, and well, I'm not proud, but sometimes I lost my temper. Samantha did her best but she's still only a kid herself.'

'I understand,' I say, although I don't really. Why didn't she ask for help if she was struggling?

'I would never have hurt him, you know. I love that child to bits.'

'I never thought otherwise.'

'And Liam'll be out soon.'

I don't know if this is wishful thinking, but I play along. 'That's good.'

'Anyway, like I said, thank you. I wish I was brave like you.'

'Me? Brave?'

'You stuck up for Nathan. I won't forget that. You're a good teacher.'

Despite myself I feel warmed by her words. No-one will ever know how close I came to turning a blind eye.

'Thank you. I hope things work out for you.'

'Yeah, you too. Bye.'

I watch Emma walk away before getting into the car. I sit for a while before putting the key in the ignition and think about what she said. Brave is the last thing I would call myself. I think about how scared I've been over the last few weeks and now I am finally going to confront my tormentor. Is that brave, or stupid? But I don't have any choice; I have to put a stop to this. I can't let Mark ruin my life.

341

I drive to Skipton and catch the early train to Leeds. It is still dark and rain streaks down the dirty windows as the countryside flies past. I haven't really thought about what I am going to do when I get to London. Mark lives with a partner. Does she know what he has been up to for the last few months? Does she know he's a killer? What if he isn't prepared to talk to me? What if he tries to hurt me? Despite my self-defence classes with Tom, I don't know if I could actually fight anyone if they physically attacked me. I won't go inside the house. I'll make him come with me to a nearby café, somewhere public.

By the time I get to the capital, it is almost noon and the weather has started to improve. I didn't tell Lisa I was coming but I am sure she will give me a bed for the night if I don't go back tonight. Things have gone alright for her since the exposure. The sex tape story was all over the tabloids but far from damaging her career, it only served to boost it. She has become the poster girl for revenge porn, invited onto *This Morning* and *Loose Women* to talk about the objectification of women and sexual double standards. Even Mum and Dad have been understanding.

Kings Cross station is crowded and suffocating. Tourists, young and old, are queuing up to have their picture taken at the Platform 9 ¾ sign; businesswomen walk briskly, wearing pumps with their designer suits; and a couple of bored police officers with high visibility jackets and dogs scan the crowds for suspicious behaviour. I make my way down the steps to the underground and manage to navigate the tube to Bayswater where Mark and his partner live. It dawns on me that this could be a complete waste of time. They are probably not going to be there. Mark could be following me right now or he could be in Yorkshire, planning more revenge attacks. At least I know Jack will be safe with Tom.

I wonder how Mark will feel about me entering his territory; the hunted becoming the hunter. My stomach is churning, and I want to turn around and run away as I hesitate outside the three-storey townhouse which Google Maps has directed me to. The house has been divided into apartments and I am just looking at the names next to each of the buzzers when a woman comes out of the front door.

She is in her mid-thirties and very smartly dressed. She is wearing high heels and her black sleek bob emphasises her elfin features. I recognise her from the photo in the paper.

'Can I help you?' she says.

'I'm looking for Mark Bolton?'

She scrutinises my face. 'What do you want him for?'

'My name's Holly, Holly Metcalfe. I knew his brother.'

She hesitates. 'I'm Mia, his fiancée and I know who you are. You'd better come in.'

I follow her into the flats. The communal hallway still has the original Victorian features including stained glass windows and floor tiles laid out in a geometric pattern. Her heels clip as we climb the staircase to the top floor.

Fear ripples through my brain. Should I follow her? What if she's in on it too? You naturally trust a woman, but it wouldn't be the first time a woman has been used to lure unsuspecting victims to their death. I'm starting to wish I had told someone where I was going today. I try to remember everything Tom taught us in our self-defence classes. Keep a clear route to the door, don't turn your back, scan the room to see if anything can be used as a weapon, listen to your instincts. My instincts are to run in the opposite direction, but I have gone this far; I need to see it through.

The flat is beautifully furnished and obviously cost a bomb. The living room, which is elegantly decorated in white and gold, has floor-to-ceiling windows that overlook the front of the house and the locked communal garden below.

'Coffee?'

'Tea, if you have it.'

'I've only got green tea.'

'That's fine.'

I follow Mia into the kitchen which is spotless and full of expensive gadgets. On the fridge door there is a picture of her and Mark. They are beaming into the camera, with ski goggles on their head.

'Is Mark here?'

'Mark hasn't been here for weeks,' she says, putting the kettle on and popping tea bags into china cups. 'I thought you might know where he is.'

'Me? How would I know?'

She pours the boiling water into the cups and hands me mine. Mia is very beautiful and very intimidating. I can imagine her commanding the attention of a board room, or convincing investors to part with their money.

'He's obsessed with you. He thinks you killed his brother.'

He's wrong. You really don't know where he is?'

Mia sits down opposite me and seems to shrink. All the fire goes out of her eyes and her face exudes misery.

'He's gone missing. He took his phone, his laptop, some clothes and emptied one of our savings accounts. He's not shown up for work. We've all been out of our minds with worry.'

'Did you report him missing?'

'I reported it to the police, but he isn't a high priority apparently. There isn't much they can do if someone voluntarily leaves their home and they're not at risk. They passed on the details to the National Missing Persons Helpline and that was it. I should have told them about you, about how he's been for the past few months, but I didn't want to get him into trouble.'

'He's been threatening me. I think ... I think he wants to kill me.'

I expect Mia to defend him, to accuse me of exaggerating, but instead she nods her head. 'I think so too. Over the past few months his obsession has turned into something else. I begged him to see a doctor.'

'What about his friends and family?'

'I've tried everyone I can think of. I thought he might have killed himself to be honest. Every time the phone rings I think it's the police calling to tell me they've found a body. His mum has been talking about hiring a private investigator.'

'I don't know where he is now, but he has definitely been in Yorkshire. He's been following me, sending me messages. He set fire to my house.'

'I don't know what to do. We have to find him, get him some help.'

I still don't even know I can trust her, but something tells me that she is another victim in all this.

'Mark struggled with his grief, but he was getting better,' she says, tears streaming down her face. 'Then that girl destroyed everything.'

'Meg.'

'She told him that George's death wasn't an accident. That you were all somehow involved. He couldn't let it rest after that.'

'It was an accident, I swear.'

'You told the police that you didn't know anything about George's death. Why did you lie?'

I hesitate. How much has Mark told her?

'Things got out of hand. We panicked. We were young, in a foreign country. We thought we would face the death sentence. I know what we did was terrible, but George was dead, what difference would it have made? It was an accident, a terrible, terrible accident. I loved George. I never meant for any of this to happen.'

'George's death broke his family apart. His mother was devastated. They all were. Mark became obsessed with the idea of putting things right. I begged him to let it go, to get help, to get some counselling but he refused. I'm frightened, I'm frightened of what he's capable of.'

I already know what he's capable of. 'I think Mark killed Meg. And Kristóf. And now he wants to kill me.'

I thought she would be shocked by my accusations, but she doesn't challenge them. She bites her lip and lifts her head with renewed determination.

'Mark is a good man. We were happy together, but he's going to end up in prison, or worse, if we don't stop him. I'll help you. What can I do?'

I take out my phone and hand it to her. 'He's been texting me, so I have his number. You could send him a message? Maybe he will listen to you?'

She nods, takes out her phone, copies the number and types in a message. She sends it before I can see it. Can I trust her? I don't have any choice.

'I'll put my number in your contacts,' I say. 'Text me if he gets back in touch and I'll do the same.'

'I will, I promise.'

'All I want is for him to stop. Move on with his life.'

'Believe me, that's all I want as well.'

'You won't press charges if I help you?'

This man has made my life hell for the past few months, but I shake my head. I don't want the police involved and I certainly don't want to testify in court. 'I just want this to be over.'

Chapter 50

On the way home, I check my messages but there's no text from Mia. I put the phone back in my bag and rest my head against the train window. Now that I have met Mia, Mark seems more real somehow. Not a monster, but a man grieving for his brother. I think back over the decisions we made and what might have happened if we had been honest from the start. Would I have gone to prison? Would I have coped? Would Meg and Kristóf still be alive if we had told the truth? I don't deserve my freedom, I know that, but do I deserve to spend the rest of my life in prison?

I get back into the house after midnight and tiptoe up the stairs, looking in on Jack before making my way to the bedroom. Tom is still awake, catching up with the football scores on his iPad and I get undressed and snuggle up to him, warming my cold feet on his warm legs.

'How was Lisa?'

'Fine,' I lie, feeling guilt wash over me. I must remember to ask her to cover for me.

'Your mum and dad called.'

'Oh?'

'They asked about Christmas. Wanted to know if Jack has any allergies. Have you told them we're going?'

'No, it was just an idea.'

'Only my parents really like to see Jack on Christmas Day. It's special.'

'Of course. Don't worry, we'll go to your parents. Maybe we can do something with mine for New Year.'

There's an awkward silence. 'Thing is, Holly, erm ... Rebecca's going to be there.'

'What?'

'She's coming over for Christmas. She really wants to see Jack again. She's not staying there or anything, she'll be in a hotel, but I've said she could come over for the day, and well, it's going to make things difficult if you're there.'

I'm going to make things difficult? Me? Not the bitch of an ex-wife who walked out on her son and husband? I can feel fury mixed with hurt well up inside me. 'You don't want me there?'

'I'd love you to be there, but it's going to be hard enough. If she knows I've moved on, well, she could make things impossible.'

'But you have moved on. I thought we were serious, Tom. I thought we were a family.'

'We are, but I need to sort this out first.'

In that moment, I hate Tom so much. For being so weak,

so manipulated. Can't he see what she's doing? Using Christmas to soften his resolve against her.

'So, what am I supposed to do? Go to my parents' on my own?'

'Well, that's what you normally do,' he says, as if that is a completely reasonable suggestion. 'And you won't be on your own, you'll have your sister and your mum and dad.'

'I want us to be together. This is our first Christmas.'

He kisses the top of my head. 'But it won't be our last, I promise. And we'll do something really special for New Year instead.'

He switches off his iPad and cuddles me in the dark. Pretty soon, I hear him gently snoring and I shift out of his arms and tiptoe downstairs. I make myself a cup of tea and sit in the living room, seething with rage. Tom has chosen Rebecca over me, and now I have to go to my parents' on my own, like a little girl, while he plays happy families with his ex-wife. Why can't he put me first for a change? Think about what I want? I am sick of always playing second fiddle to another woman. First George, and now Tom. Why can I never be enough?

I switch on the Christmas tree lights and watch the shadows of the branches play on the ceiling. Underneath the tree, Tom has lain out our presents. Jack's pile is huge. At home, we always waited until Christmas Eve before we laid out gifts otherwise prying fingers would be unwrapping them before the big day, but Jack and Tom have different traditions. I see the bulky racing car I bought for Jack at the back of the pile and move it to the front. We won't be opening them together now. I won't get to see Jack's face when he sees his gift and by the time they get back, he will have forgotten all about it. I want him to start thinking of me as his mum, having Rebecca back in his life will only confuse him.

There is a small stack of gifts with my name on the labels. My attention is drawn to a present wrapped in bright pink wrapping paper. I know I shouldn't open it, but curiosity gets the better of me. Inside is a jewellery box made from red velvet. My heart flutters. Maybe I've got this all wrong. Maybe going to his parents' is just a ruse. Is Tom intending to propose? I hardly dare look inside but, listening out for any movement upstairs, I prise it open. There is a ring inside but it's not an engagement ring.

It is a man's ring and I recognise it instantly. It's George's ring, the one I bought for him in Bangkok. He was wearing it the night he died. The police must have given it to the family when they came to identify the body. A cold chill works its way down my spine. Does Mark know the significance of this ring? No, he can't possibly. No-one does.

I check the label but it's not Tom's handwriting, which means Mark must have broken into our house. Tom is intensely security conscious, there's no way he would leave the house unlocked even when he is upstairs, which means

Mark must have a key. He's been here, inside my home, again. I am not safe here; I am not safe anywhere.

I find my phone and check the text messages. Nothing. I type a message to Mark.

You need to stop this, Mark. I know what you did to Kristóf and Meg and my sister. I will go to the police and tell them everything.

It's two in the morning so I am not expecting a reply, but it comes back immediately.

Do it. If the case is re-opened, then I'll leave you alone.

They won't believe me.

Then you'll have to convince them. Show them the picture.

If I do that then it's game over. They will know I lied, that I was there that night. Meg and Kristóf are dead so there's only my word for what happened. I need to convince Mark to let it drop.

I want to talk to you first. There are things you need to know about that night.

I sit looking at the phone waiting for a notification, but nothing comes up. I pace around the room and check again. Nothing. I make a cup of tea. Nothing. Nothing. Nothing. Finally, it beeps.

OK. Where and when?

My mind is racing. I must be crazy, planning to meet someone who wants to kill me, but I need him to under-stand that what happened to George wasn't my fault. I think carefully. I need to pick somewhere safe, where he can't get to me. Where there are plenty of witnesses.

Sarah Linley

Tomorrow. At the park.
Come alone. No funny business.
OK.
Tomorrow, 2pm.

Chapter 51

Mark had been waiting for an opportunity to plant the ring for some time. Modern houses have good security, but everything has a weakness. It just took time and patience and a lot of research to discover the flaw in the patio door lock.

Walking around another man's house in broad daylight makes Mark feel powerful. He understands now the adrenaline rush that burglars feel when they invade someone's home. He feels a desire to smash it up, to destroy all those self-satisfied photographs of family life, the crayoned masterpieces stuck to the fridge door, the expensive bottles nestling in the wine rack. But he has to be cautious. He can't risk getting caught. Not now, not when he is so close.

He walks into their bedroom. The bed is unmade, the duvet half on the floor covering a pile of magazines and some dirty clothes. Disgusting. He plucks a hair from Holly's pillow and holds it up to the light, wondering if the colour is real or fake. A book is laying on the bedside cabinet, its pages forming an upside-down v shape, cracking the spine. He picks it up carefully. Inside the pages are dog-eared and passages are underlined. He puts it back as it was, although he feels it's criminal to allow a book to get into such a state.

The kid's bedroom is full of toys. A Thomas the Tank Engine clock ticks loudly. A row of cars is lined up on a racing track and Mark's heart pulls as he remembers playing the same game with his brother. He hopes that one day, he and Mia might have children. It would make his mother happy and he would enjoy being a father. All in good time, Mia has promised, although he suspects she isn't keen to jeopardise her career by going on maternity leave.

The bathroom is full of the usual crap that people accumulate. Tom has an impressive collection of aftershaves. Holly wears cheap perfume. He takes a note of the brand. It might come in useful one day. Their two toothbrushes kiss in a plastic cup. He pulls them apart.

He makes his way downstairs and places the ring among the presents underneath the plastic Christmas tree. She will probably think that daft sap is going to propose. That's what she wants, isn't it? To play happy families with Tom while Mark is stuck on the outside, looking in like Frankenstein's monster?

Holly has wrecked his family, so now it's time to do the same to hers. The sister was just a start. He wants her to know that he can get to her anytime and anywhere he pleases. The parents are fair game. So proud of their precious daughter. Do they know they've raised a liar? It's about time they found out.

He is just leaving the house when he gets the message from Mia. He can barely contain his fury as he contemplates what this might mean. Mark has underestimated Holly. The bitch has been to his house, spoken to his fiancée. No doubt fed her a pack of lies and proclaimed her innocence. So far, Holly has been running scared. What's changed? She seems less afraid. She should be terrified.

Later, when he is back in the cheap B&B he has booked in Skipton, he receives her invitation to meet him in the park. Her new-found courage intrigues him. Perhaps she is trying to trick him? If he meets her, he could be exposing himself. She could have a hidden recording device or be carrying a weapon. Is it possible that he is as much at risk from her as she is from him?

On the other hand, perhaps she does intend to finally tell him the truth. Isn't that what he's wanted all along? After all this time, can he really walk away from this opportunity to find out what really happened to his brother?

Chapter 52

Thailand, five years ago

We didn't get a chance to report George missing. The Thai police were already at the hostel, speaking to the receptionist, when we walked down to breakfast.

I hadn't slept a wink. Several times in the night I had picked up my phone to ring my dad, to ask him what to do, to help me sort out this terrible mess but this was one situation that even he couldn't rescue me from. I could hear Meg shifting around in the bunk above me, so I knew she wasn't asleep, but I didn't know what to say to her. What happened to Meg was all my fault. If it hadn't been for me, she would never have been down at the beach with George. She would never have been attacked. And Kristóf wouldn't have had to protect her.

The receptionist pointed to us, speaking fast Thai, and the police officer, an older man with huge eyebrows and a pristine uniform, walked over.

'English?' he asked. We nodded. 'You know this man?'

He showed us a photocopy of George's passport. He must have had it on him when he died. We had to register our IDs when we checked in so I guessed they must have been able to trace him quite easily.

Kristóf took control. 'Yes, he's our friend, George Bolton. Has he lost his passport? Stupid idiot, he was pretty pissed last night.'

'Pissed?' The policeman looks confused.

'Drunk.' Kristóf mimed raising a glass to his lips.

The policeman looked Kristóf up and down. 'I need you to come to the station please. About your friend.'

'Why? What's he done now?' I had to admire Kristóf's acting skills, his steady use of the present tense. I couldn't look at Meg. I could feel my left leg shaking and I pressed down hard to try to disguise it.

'Please. Come with me.'

'Of course, no problem. Will you girls be OK while I sort out George?'

'You all together?' the policeman asked. 'Please. Don't leave the hotel.'

Meg and I waited by the pool. Lying on the plastic deckchairs, feeling the hot morning sun dance on our torsos, felt so wrong. I desperately wanted to talk, but Meg had her headphones in and was resolutely ignoring my attempts at conversation. A Myna bird with a mustard coloured beak dipped his head in and out of the pool, shaking water through its feathers. Half an hour turned into an hour turned into two. I tried to concentrate on a magazine, but I was too fidgety, and I kept turning my head to see if Kristóf had returned.

'Act normal,' Meg hissed. 'It'll be OK. Kristóf will handle it.'

'But what if they've found something? A footprint or a piece of clothing or something?'

'Shhh!' Meg looked around, but the pool area was deserted. 'They won't.'

'What if someone saw us? What about CCTV?'

'There wasn't any.'

'How do you know?'

'Because I looked, alright? I checked on the way back and there was no sign of any cameras. Play it cool.'

'We've just killed somebody. How the fuck can I stay cool?'

Meg grabbed me by the shoulders and gave me a steely glare. 'Because if you don't, we're all going to prison. Now grow up and stay focussed.'

I turned my back on her, fuming. How dare she tell me to grow up after what they did last night? Nascent tears pricked my eyes, and my stomach churned. I hadn't eaten anything since last night, but I had no appetite for food. Were we going to go to prison? How would I cope? What would Mum and Dad say? My life was over.

A Kristóf-shaped shadow crept over my sun lounger. I sat up. He looked drained and exhausted, running his fingers through his hair nervously. 'They're upstairs,' he said quietly. 'Going through his things. I said I would break the news to you. They want you both to make a statement.'

'Do they ...?'

'They think it was an accident. Stick to the story and we'll be fine. They're letting his parents know this afternoon.'

It suddenly felt very real. Meg and I gathered our things from the pool area and got dressed in silence. She held my hand as we were driven past bars and restaurants filled with carefree backpackers and tourists. It felt like a parallel universe. There were flecks of neon paint left on my hands from last night. I tried to rub them off in the car. I needed to stay calm, I couldn't afford to get this wrong. What if they used a lie detector test? We were in serious shit.

The police station was hot and claustrophobic. They led us into separate rooms and asked me to wait. A fan whirred lazily above my head circulating the hot air, and the water they gave me in a plastic cup was warm and musty. Finally, a detective came in with a translator, a young Thai woman who spoke English with a beautiful accent and smiled kindly. I felt reassured by her presence as she translated and patiently listened to my answers.

I had never been interviewed by the police before. Never been in any kind of trouble, not even at school. I was surprised how calm I sounded as I lied through my teeth, telling them we had seen George leave the party with a girl. We had agreed to describe someone who looked a bit like Meg in case they had been seen together.

The Beach

The policeman appeared to believe me. After about forty minutes of asking the same questions, they let me go. He handed me back my passport and asked how long we were staying.

'We have another week in Thailand,' I said, wishing I could take the first flight home. He nodded and wrote something down on a piece of paper.

I wanted to ask him what would happen to George. Would they bury him here or take him home? Would there be an autopsy? Would his parents have to come here to identify the body? But I kept my mouth shut. I supposed I would find out everything I needed to know in due course.

'I'm sorry,' the translator said as we stood up to leave.

'Sorry?'

'About your friend. It's very sad.'

I smiled. I was full of emotion, but it hadn't occurred to me to be sad. I was too bloody terrified.

Meg was waiting for me outside the police station, smoking a cigarette like her life depended on it. 'Everything go OK?'

'Yeah, fine. You?'

'Think so.' We hailed a taxi and drove back in silence. I had so many questions, but I didn't think she had any more answers than I did. I just wanted to get the hell out of Thailand.

*

363

I couldn't stop thinking about the photograph I had taken at the beach. The police hadn't asked to go through our phones, but it was the one piece of evidence that would destroy our alibi, that would prove we were there when George died. When we got back to the hostel, I made an excuse to get away from Meg and walked to the promontory. I stood at the edge, watching the waves crash against the rocks, the spray hitting my face and hurled the phone as far as I could into the ocean.

When I got back, the news had broken, and the hostel was rife with gossip. We thought it would arouse too much suspicion if we moved somewhere else. I borrowed Meg's phone and rang my parents to tell them what happened; I didn't want them reading about it in the papers. They wanted to fly out to support me but there was nothing they could do, and they would just have made things worse by fussing. I only had a few more days to get through before we could go home. I spent most of the time in my bunk listening to music and trying to ignore everyone around me.

The story was splashed across the news and over social media. The speculation and faux sympathy were difficult to handle. Several journalists turned up at the hostel, wanting to speak to us, but the management kept them away. They hung about outside, catching backpackers as they left and some of them gave interviews, pretending that they knew George. There were pictures from the party online and official statements from George's family and the Foreign Office, but no-one said anything that contradicted our story. More than once I contemplated breaking the pact and going to the police with the real story, but I was terrified of what might happen if I did.

The media soon lost interest when there was no evidence that a crime had been committed. Just another grieving family, another tragedy on a paradise island. The police collected George's belongings to give to his parents. I kept going over and over that night. I couldn't believe George was dead. I loved him, I thought he loved me, so why would he go off with Meg? Why did he try to hurt her when she pushed him away? Why wasn't I enough for him? How could I have misjudged him so badly?

Kristóf insisted that we went to meet George's parents once they had arrived in Thailand. His mother was a mess, a far cry from the elegant woman we had met at the New Year's Eve party. She looked old and haggard, her skin grey and lined, and she complained miserably about the poor hygiene standards even though the hotel was the height of luxury and the staff were bending over backwards to make them comfortable. George's dad was in touch with the Foreign Office but there wasn't much they could do. There was no suspicion of any crime being committed. Everyone seemed to have accepted that it was an accident, that George was high and drunk, and must have tripped and drowned. There was no evidence and no witnesses to suggest otherwise.

Kristóf was charming, listening politely to their

complaints and talking about George like he was a treasured friend. Lying to the police was one thing, but the way Kristóf coolly lied to George's parents was shocking. At least Meg had the grace to look upset by the whole thing. I wanted to tell them how much I loved him, but it seemed completely inappropriate when they told us how devastated Fiona was. Clearly George hadn't broken it off with her; which was no less than I expected, but it still hurt. Meg barely spoke, but George's parents didn't seem to notice. They were too wrapped up in their own grief to care about our feelings.

'We'll fly the body home, bury him in England,' his father told us. 'It's what he would have wanted.'

I wondered how much that would cost, but I supposed money was no object to them. The thought of George's body being flown back on the same plane as ours filled me with horror. Did they have special planes for this sort of thing?

'George was such a good boy. The police say he had been taking drugs, but I can't believe that.'

'Oh, you know what young boys are like. Mark was no angel at that age either,' his dad said, earning himself a sharp look from his wife. 'But, I'm sure you're right.'

I kept my lips firmly shut, smiling and sipping my mango smoothie politely. The small talk while we waited for food was interminable. When it came, I just picked at it, moving it around with my chopsticks, anything to distract myself from what was, by far, the most painful conversation I had ever had with anyone. Sweat was trickling down my back but I wasn't sure whether that was down to heat or fear. I was terrified I would slip up and drop us all in it.

'We'll let you know about the funeral,' George's mother said as we finally took our leave.

I had already decided I wouldn't go to the funeral. I couldn't bear to watch Fiona usurp my position as George's girlfriend. She didn't love him like I did; how could she? Perhaps he would have gone back to her after the summer, perhaps not. But now I would never get the chance to find out.

Chapter 53

It is a dark overcast day. The rain, embedded in the mist, is soaking through my supposedly waterproof jacket. The weather must have put off the families which normally congregate around the play area and even the teenagers are conspicuously absent from the skate park. A lone dog walker nods as he passes me shivering at the entrance gates of the park.

I haven't thought this through; I should have met Mark at the Black Swan. When he arrives, I will suggest we go somewhere more public. I spent most of last night working out what I'm going to say. I need him to leave me alone. I need to do everything I can to make sure he believes that what happened wasn't my fault.

I'm early. I pace up and down outside the gates to keep warm, grateful that I remembered my scarf and gloves. Every few minutes I check my phone to see if Mark has messaged me. I told Tom I was going to Rhona's, even though she hasn't invited me around since the fire. I'm pretty sure Rob doesn't want me in his house. At best, he probably thinks I am an attention-seeking mad woman; at worst, an arsonist. You can't really blame him for keeping his distance.

I hear the church bells ringing two o' clock and have another look around but I can't see anyone approaching. There are two entrances to the park, but the other one is overgrown, and no-one ever uses it. I suppose Mark might come that way if he wanted the element of surprise but what would be the point? My mind is whirring at a hundred miles an hour thinking about what he wants from me. Is he going to hurt me? Make my death look like another tragic accident?

I check my phone again. Nothing. For something to do, I scroll through my Facebook feed. Everyone seems to be spending their Sunday afternoons in gastro pubs or tucking into mulled wine at German Christmas markets, not meeting murderers in deserted parks. I envy them their easy existence. I am still fuming about Rebecca. I had to call my parents this morning and let them know I was coming for Christmas alone. I feigned a bright cheery tone, but I could tell they could see through my charade. Fortunately, they were too preoccupied with my sister's problems to question me too closely.

Ten past two. Where is he? Should I ring him? Have I made a mistake? I am now absolutely freezing. The pavement is layered with leaves which squelch underneath my boots. The park itself is like a bog. I look down the street and my heart jumps as a figure emerges from the corner and walks towards me but as he approaches, I realise it is an older man with silver hair who is walking with his head down and his hands in his pockets. He grunts a greeting as he passes.

I check my phone again. No messages. Is he already in the park? I don't want to venture too far from civilisation, but I walk through the gates and look around. It is quite a small park which was refurbished some years ago using lottery money. Volunteers keep it neat and tidy but even they can't do battle with the weather which has pulled branches from trees, cascaded litter everywhere and battered the remaining shrubbery. I'll give Mark ten more minutes and then I'm going home.

At half past two I resign myself to the fact that he is not coming. There's no way he could have missed me, even if he did come in through a different entrance. He is playing games again. Frustrated, but also a little relieved, I message the word 'Coward' to him and make my way home.

Tom is cooking dinner and the smell of roast beef fills the house. Jack is playing in the lounge and drags me to look at the latest addition to his extensive Lego collection. I allow myself to be enveloped in this domestic scene and push my problems to the back of my mind. Maybe Mark not turning up is a good thing. Maybe he has come to his senses and gone home. Maybe this is over.

Chapter 54

Holly is not in charge here; she does not get to call the shots. She's been lying through her teeth for years. Why should Mark trust her now? He is ready to hear her confession; but he will choose the place and time. And it's not here, not now.

After all, isn't justice always meted out in public? It's only right that everyone she loves hears the truth about the pain and suffering she has caused. It's only right that she should stand trial. And if the authorities won't do anything, then it's up to him to make it happen.

He makes plans. He will forgo Christmas with his family and follow her to Morecambe. It's a shame that the boyfriend and his son won't be there, but he can find a way to ensure they still witness her shame.

In fact, thanks to modern technology, everyone can tune in. It will make a pleasant change from all the repeats on TV or listening to the Queen's speech with bloated bellies and a glass of sherry.

Judgment day. Otherwise known as Christmas Day.

Chapter 55

The last week of the Christmas term passes quickly. The nativity is dutifully performed to a collection of proud parents, and 'Orrible Oliver defies all expectations by delivering his lines impeccably. My class is relatively well-behaved, and Bilal gets a standing ovation when he takes it upon himself to repeat the last verse of *We Three Kings* as a solo. I spot Emma in the audience, sitting in the back with Samantha and a lean looking man that I assume is Liam. Trevor told me last week that although social services will be monitoring them over the next few months, they seem happy enough with the situation now that Emma's medication is working. Nathan certainly seems to be happier and has made some friends.

Rhona and I celebrate the last performance with a night at the pub which leaves us with blistering hangovers for the final day of term.

'I'm giving up drinking for New Year,' Rhona tells me as I make her an extra strong cup of coffee.

'Yeah, right.'

She looks up at me, her face suddenly serious. 'I mean it. Well, at least cutting it down to weekends. It's got a bit ... out of control, of late.'

I hand her the cup. 'Good for you.'

'Thanks,' she sips the coffee. 'It's just too easy sometimes to reach for the bottle when you've had a bad day. I'll have to try yoga or something in future.'

I try to picture Rhona doing yoga and meditation every night and wonder how long this latest health kick will last. 'Well, good luck.'

'Any news on the house?'

The builders have said that I should be able to move back into my house after Christmas, but I'm hoping that Tom will ask me to stay. 'Might be a while yet. It's still in such a mess.'

'But you'll be moving back eventually, won't you?'

'I don't know, we haven't really discussed it yet.'

She gives me a knowing smile. 'I'm sure whatever happens, it will work out for the best. When do you set off for your mum and dad's?'

'Christmas Eve. What are you up to?'

'Just me and Rob this year so we're going to slob out in front of the telly in our pyjamas and eat cheese!'

'Sounds like a plan.'

Trevor walks in and claps his hands ostentatiously. Rhona rolls her eyes as I sit down beside her to listen to his last day of term speech in which he thanks us for our hard work and wishes us a Happy Christmas. Diane hands out cheap bottles of wine and boxes of Milk Tray that she's obviously bought in bulk at the cash and carry. The kids have all brought in presents: several mugs with 'Best Teacher' written on them to add to my collection and posh boxes of chocolates from Marks & Spencer. The mums always try to outdo each other but we don't complain. Still, it's a relief when the final bell goes, and the kids troop off, all over-excited about their impending visits from Santa.

I leave the school with Rhona. Outside it is freezing and the drizzle is sparkling like glitter on a Christmas card. We part company at the bridge, wishing each other Merry Christmas even though we will be messaging each other throughout the holidays. As I walk over the bridge alone, I watch the sun setting behind the hills. Dusk falls rapidly and I glance backwards to make sure no-one is following me. It seems odd that I haven't heard anything from Mark since he stood me up at the park. Maybe something has happened to him? Maybe he has given up?

Tom and Jack set off early on Christmas Eve morning. They have a long way to travel and I make Tom promise to take it steady. The rain is falling heavily now, and there are weather warnings out for Lancashire. Tom holds me close.

'Are you sure you're OK about me going?'

'It's fine, honestly,' I lie. I'm still cross that he has chosen Rebecca over me, but I do realise it's for Jack's sake. We have the rest of our lives to spend Christmas together. 'Text me when you get there.'

Jack gives me a big hug and wishes me a Happy Christmas. He has made me a card with a badly drawn Santa on the front holding my hand. He has been worried all week that Father Christmas won't know where to deliver his presents. It's lovely to see him so excited, and well behaved. Whoever made up the Naughty and Nice list is a genius. I worry about how he will react to seeing his mother again. Tom hasn't told him she's coming; he doesn't trust her not to let him down again.

I go back inside and finish packing up my things to take with me to my parents'. Tom has left me a pile of presents on the bed; they have obviously been gift wrapped in store and I try not to mind that he hasn't done them himself. I pack them in my suitcase and start to lock up the house, switching off appliances and making sure all the windows are secure. Outside the wind is howling and the trees are battering at the windows. I'm nervous about driving in such terrible weather but I have no choice. I'm too old to ring my dad and ask him to pick me up.

I am about to leave when the phone rings. I am in two minds whether to answer it but, thinking it might be Tom, I pick up the receiver.

'Holly, love. Oh, I'm glad we've caught you.'

'Hi Mum, I'm setting off now.'

'Have you seen the news?'

'No, why?' My heart jolts, thinking something else might have happened to Lisa.

'There's flooding everywhere, love. We're completely cut off.'

'Are you OK?'

'We're fine, your sister's managed to get here alright but all the roads have closed. I don't think you should risk it.'

I look out of the window, hoping to see something that proves Mum is exaggerating but I can see pools of dirty water forming on the estate. The rain is torrential. I bite my lip.

'Is it really that bad?'

'I'm sorry love. Perhaps you could wait until the morning and come up tomorrow? The rain has got to stop at some point.'

'OK, Mum. Well take care, keep me updated.' I put the phone down, my heart sinking. With Tom and Jack away and my parents unreachable, I am going to have to spend Christmas Eve on my own. I think about ringing Rhona and Rob and seeing if they want a visitor, but it feels like such an imposition. I reach for my phone and message Tom to tell him what's happened. No reply, so he must still be driving.

The house feels eerily quiet. I go back around all the rooms and check the windows are secure, drawing the curtains so no-one can see inside. It's only 5 pm but it's already pitch-black outside. I turn on the television for company and select a nice Christmas movie to watch. We don't even have any food in the house because we thought we would be away, and all the shops are closed, but I manage to find myself some pasta and a jar of sauce. It's a miserable meal to match my miserable mood.

At seven o'clock Tom rings me to tell me they've got there OK and that he loves me. He tells me that Rebecca has been in touch with his parents and is coming around in the morning to watch Jack open his presents but has not been invited for lunch. I try not to mind that she will get to share that moment with him and I won't.

I open a bottle of red wine and settle on the sofa feeling sorry for myself. I thought it would be bad enough being back at my parents' for Christmas Eve, but being alone while everyone else is celebrating with family sucks. I scroll through my Facebook feed but that makes me even more depressed, so I shut it down.

Outside the wind has picked up and the trees are bending at dangerous angles. Christmas lights are dangling precariously from the guttering and several bins have over-turned. The road is full of puddles and the drains are regurgitating dirty water like chocolate fountains. It's not long before the lights flicker and then the electricity fails. The street is plunged into darkness. I curse and go into the dining room to retrieve some candles.

The flames cast eerie shadows on the wall. I think about calling Rhona and seeing if I can stay there tonight, but when I pick up the landline there is no signal. I grab my mobile but don't ring her. I'm probably better off staying put. The weather is wild out there and I will get soaked walking through the village. Besides, no-one wants unexpected visitors on Christmas Eve, whatever they might say to the contrary.

I pick up my book, *Wuthering Heights*, but the depiction of departed souls wandering the moorland, creeps me out. Power cuts are like being cast into the dark ages; for want of anything better to do, I might as well go to bed. At least I will be rested for the drive tomorrow morning. As soon as it gets light, I'll set off to my parents'.

I take the candle upstairs, feeling like a character in a Victorian novel. I set it down on the bedside cabinet and look outside. The rain is still bouncing off the pavement. It reminds me of the downpours we experienced in South-East Asia although at least they were warm and usually short-lived. I clean my teeth by candlelight, close the curtains and get into bed. The heating has gone off with the power cut and it's freezing. I lay awake awhile, trying to get warm and thinking about Tom. No doubt he will be putting an over-excited Jack to bed right now, before settling down to a whisky and a few mince pies with his parents. Later, he will be creeping into Jack's room in the middle of the night to place his over-filled stocking at the end of the mattress and take a bite out of the carrot they have left for the reindeers. I think about my parents and Lisa in Morecambe. They will have got the Scrabble board out and will be squabbling over the dictionary. I should have set off earlier. I wish I was there; I wish I was anywhere but here.

Chapter 56

I wake up in the middle of the night convinced I can hear someone downstairs. I lie in bed, trying to steady my breathing as I tell myself that my mind is just playing tricks. The wind has calmed down and it is eerily quiet. I pull myself out of the warm cocoon of my duvet to look out of the window, but the garden is in darkness. The outdoor lights are on a sensor but I have no idea if they work during a power cut. I take a deep breath and listen again. Nothing. Was I dreaming?

I go back to bed, but I can't settle. My mobile phone is downstairs, and I would feel safer if I had it with me. I pull on my dressing gown and creep out into the hallway. I try the light switch, but the electricity is still off. I stand at the top of the stairs, listening out for sounds, telling myself I am being paranoid. I just need to go downstairs, grab my phone and then come straight back to bed. I tiptoe down the stairs, clinging on to the banister, and step into the dark hallway. Everything looks exactly as I left it. I'm being ridiculous.

With a bit more confidence, I walk into the living room and spot my phone on the mantelpiece, the orange light flashing in the darkness to indicate low battery. I am a few centimetres away from it when I hear a sudden movement behind me. As I turn, I see a man dressed entirely in black swinging a metal object towards my head. I try to duck but I'm too late. I hear a thwack as my head explodes with pain and everything goes dark.

I don't know how long I lost consciousness for, but when I come to, I am tied to one of the dining room chairs, my wrists bound behind me and my ankles shackled to the chair legs with green plastic twine, the type you might buy from a garden centre. My head is pounding and I feel disorientated as I try to remember what just happened. I can feel a sticky substance on my forehead which I can only assume is blood. I feel vomit rising but swallow hard and try to focus.

The chair has been placed in the middle of the living room and opposite me is a video camera on a tripod. A man is standing behind the camera, adjusting the settings. The moonlight coming through the window is painting the room monochrome colours and I cannot see his face, but it's not hard to work out who he is.

'Mark?' my voice comes out as a whisper and he doesn't seem to hear me. I try to move my head, but the pain is excruciating. 'Mark?' I try again, louder this time.

He turns his head and quickly walks over to the chair, checking to make sure the restraints around my wrists and ankles are secure. He is so close to me that I can smell his breath. He looks like George, only older and his hair is cut short to disguise his sandy curls.

'Please ...'

He doesn't speak but, satisfied that the bindings are tight, goes back to the camera.

'What do you want from me?'

'You know what I want,' he says, finally. 'I've made that perfectly clear from the start.'

Even his voice reminds me of George, although he would never have spoken to me in such a harsh tone. My head is throbbing, but my mind is surprisingly calm. I just need to think my way out of the situation.

'I'll tell the police everything, I promise.'

'It's a bit too late for that now, Holly. I've given you plenty of chances.' He switches on a button and a red recording light flashes. 'Smile, you're going on Facebook. A nice Christmas Day message for all your friends and family.'

'Please Mark. Stop this, think about Mia. Think about what this will do to her.'

I look at the man behind the camera but there is no mercy in his expression. My brain tries to calculate my next move.

'Come on, your audience is waiting. I want you to tell them everything.'

'My name is Holly Metcalfe,' I say quickly. 'And I am being held hostage at 24 Ashfield Crescent. My attacker's name is Mark –'

He jumps over and slaps me hard across the face. The impact forces the chair to rock and for a minute I think I am going to hit the floor, but I don't.

'I can't trust you to do anything, can I? Certainly not to tell the truth, even if your life depends on it. And believe me, it does. But not to worry, I didn't think we'd get it right the first time, so we'll call that a dress rehearsal.'

He fiddles about with the recording equipment again.

'I'll post our little video tomorrow, after they've tucked into Christmas Dinner and they're in the mood for a good old-fashioned murder mystery. What shall we call it? I know. How about "Who killed George?"'

He glares at me intently. I take a deep breath and try to calm myself down. I think about my family and friends watching this on the internet, powerless to do anything to help me.

'What do you want me to say, Mark?'

'I want you to tell the truth. That you and your friends murdered my brother.'

'We didn't murder your brother. It was an accident. Please Mark, switch the camera off, we can talk about it. I'll tell you everything, I swear.'

'How can I trust you? You've lied from the very beginning. You told the police you weren't even there that night; that you never left the party.'

'I know.'

'But you slipped up, Holly. You should have deleted the photo.'

'I did. Well, I thought I'd destroyed it. I threw the phone in the sea. I don't understand how you found it.'

He smiles at me like I'm a little kid. 'You didn't think to delete it from your cloud though, did you?'

Shit. The cloud. The photo must have automatically backed up when I got back to the hostel. I haven't touched that account in years. I just bought a new phone when I got home and forgot all about it. All this time, that photo was sitting there on the internet like a ticking time bomb. It's too late now. Even if I get out of this alive, Mark will have made copies. I need to make him believe that none of this was my fault; I was just an innocent bystander.

'If you want justice, make me stand trial. Make me go to prison for the rest of my life. Surely killing me won't bring you satisfaction.'

'Nice try, Holly. Now, talk.'

I try to imagine what I must look like in the small screen on the other side of the camera, tied up and covered in blood. I don't want my parents to see me like this. How can he be so cruel?

'Five years ago, I went backpacking with my friends George, Kristóf and Meg. One of my friends, George Bolton, died in a tragic accident.'

'For fuck's sake.' He turns off the camera and kneels in front of me. 'You don't get it, do you, Holly? This isn't a game. I know George's death wasn't an accident. One of you killed him and I want to know who and why. I'm going to stay here all night and get this confession. And if you don't confess, Holly, then I'm going to kill you, slowly, and let your friends and family watch you die.'

He walks out of the room and I take advantage of his absence to look around me for a weapon. Mark walks back into the living room with a knife from the kitchen. It is the one Tom sharpens every week and I know it is razor sharp; I have cut my fingers on it often. He holds it against my throat, and I can feel the cold metal against my skin.

'We can do this the hard way or the easy way. Your choice.'

Tears start to fall down my face and I blink them away.

'Fine, I'll do it. Switch the camera back on.' Mark walks back to his position, still holding the knife in his left hand. The red light blinks. He nods.

'Five years ago, I went on holiday with my friends Meg, Kristóf and George.'

'Go on.'

'We were at a beach party in Thailand. We had all been drinking. Meg and George had taken some pills. They went off together and we – me and Kristóf – followed them.'

'Where did they go?'

'Further down the beach,' I sniff. 'Away from the party.'

'Who killed my brother?'

'Kristóf. He hit him with a rock. It was an accident, I swear, it was an accident. No-one meant to hurt him. I loved George.'

'Why did you kill him?'

'He attacked Meg. I think Kristóf was trying to save her.'

'Why didn't you call the police?'

'We were scared.'

'You were a coward.'

I nod. 'We moved the body so that it would look like he tripped, and we lied to the police and I'm sorry, I'm really sorry. I will regret that decision for the rest of my life.'

Mark seems satisfied. He switches off the camera and takes out the memory card. He unscrews the camera from the tripod and puts it away in his rucksack. I watch him put the memory card into a small plastic case and put it in the top pocket of his leather jacket.

'Please, Mark, I've done everything you asked. Please don't kill me.'

He responds to my pleas with more silence. Mark said he wouldn't kill me if I confessed but why would I believe him? He didn't spare Meg or Kristóf.

'What are you going to do now?'

He walks over to me with the knife in his hand and leans over. His face is inscrutable. Tears are running down my face. I take a deep breath and try to calm my mind. This is it, the end of my life. I close my eyes, waiting for the cut, praying that it will be quick, that it won't hurt too much. At least he has put the camera away. At least my parents won't see me die.

Nothing happens.

I open my eyes again. Mark is sitting on the sofa, his head in his hands. All the energy has drained out of him, he looks like a broken man.

'You're not going to kill me?'

His voice is softer this time, more human. 'It didn't have to be like this. You know you're the only one who's actually apologised? Meg was full of excuses and self-pity.'

'And Kristóf?'

'He wouldn't even give me the time of day. Arrogant prick. All I wanted was to know what happened to my brother. I'm not a bad person, Holly. I didn't set out to hurt anyone, but it was the only way I could get any of you to talk to me.'

'Why didn't you meet me at the park? I would have talked to you then.'

'I thought you were just going to feed me some more bullshit.'

Mark is still holding the knife. I need to get him to put it down and untie me. He seems to be wavering.

'Please let me go, Mark. I won't tell anyone what you did, I promise.'

He looks up at me. 'You still don't get it, do you? What kind of person keeps quiet about stuff like this? What kind of person are you, Holly?'

'A coward, OK? I'm a coward. I should have gone to the police, I should have told them the truth, but I didn't. And I can't change that. But you can change things now. If you post that video, the police will know you attacked me. It'll be over, Mark, we'll both go to prison.'

'Do you think I give a fuck about that? Anyway, it's too late now.'

'It's not too late. I haven't given your name to the police. They don't believe anything I say anyway. They think I'm delusional. Only Mia knows, and she loves you. I won't tell anyone, I swear. You can walk away from this. We both can. Carry on with our lives, agree to leave the past in the past.'

I wonder if I have said enough to change his mind. Surely, if he wanted to kill me, he would have done it by now. Finally, he pulls himself off the sofa. He kneels in front of me and slices through the binds around my wrists and then the ones around my ankles. He looks so pitiful on his knees before me, his head bowed as if he is praying. Using as much strength as I can muster, I kick him as hard as I can in the balls and grab the knife.

Chapter 57

Mark falls to one side, writhing in agony, as I plunge the knife as hard as I can into his side, feeling it hit the rib cage. He howls in pain as blood sprays from the wound and all over my hand. I reach into his jacket pocket and retrieve the memory card. There is no way this is over. Not while he has evidence against me. He makes a grab for my ankle as I stumble towards the door, but his grip is weak, and it's easy to break free.

I run into the hallway and grab my coat and a pair of trainers from the shoe rack. I fumble with the Yale lock and chain on the front door, looking behind me to check that Mark isn't following. I can hear him screaming in the living room, but I don't think the wound will hold him back for long. Finally, I manage to unlock the door and fall outside.

The icy wind is a welcome shock to the system. I pull on my trainers and jacket and look around me. My car is sitting there on the driveway, but I don't have my keys. The whole street is still in darkness and it's impossible to work out which houses are occupied; so many people will have gone away for Christmas. If I try an empty property, Mark will catch me and there's not a chance in hell he'll let me live now. The storm has picked up again and rain is lashing at my face as I make my way down the driveway. I need to get as much distance between me and Mark as possible. Rhona and Rob's house is five minutes away, and at least I know they will definitely be in. It's the best chance I have.

I run down the estate, sticking to the side of the road, close to the hedges, in the hope that Mark won't be able to see me, although there is only one route out of the cul-de-sac so it's going to be pretty obvious which way I went. Huge puddles stretch across the pathway and my pyjama bottoms are already soaked wet through. Glancing back, I see Mark's dark figure behind me. He is clutching his side but, despite his injuries, he's pretty fast. As I reach the end of the estate, I break cover and start to run, turning left towards the river.

My heart is pounding in my chest and my breath feels hot and ragged as I make my way down the dark country road, praying that someone will drive past and rescue me. The wind tears at my clothes, and the rain saturates the thin fabric. I may as well be naked for the protection my clothing is offering. All I can think of is getting to Rhona's house. If I can just make it there before Mark gets hold of me, I will be safe.

The bridge comes in sight, but I am forced to stop sharply. The river has burst its banks and a large stretch of flood water has spread across the carriageway. I know it can only be a few metres before the road rises but it's impossible to tell how deep the water in the dip is. I look back and see that Mark is not far behind me. I don't have a choice.

I take a deep breath and wade through the flood, feeling the ice-cold water filling up my trainers. The water is flowing against me and it's difficult to make much progress. It is now up to my knees, and I still have a couple more metres to go before I reach the other side. I can hear Mark splashing and try to speed up, but I am struggling to stand upright, let alone stride ahead. I'm not going to make it.

I feel a sharp push on my back and topple over onto my knees. Mark grabs the back of my neck and pushes my head down into the filthy water, which fills my mouth and nostrils. Panic streaks through my body as I shake my head as hard as I can to get free. Mark's strong, but I remember what Tom taught me about breakaway techniques. I pause for a split second and then suddenly drop my head even further into the water to release his hold, twist to one side and use all the strength I have to push Mark backwards. He lets go of me as he falls.

I scrabble around in the water, trying to find a rock, a branch, anything I can use for a weapon but there's nothing. I pull myself up and drag myself away from him, using every ounce of energy I have to crawl out of the flood. Mark has recovered quickly and is doing the same. I only manage to get a few steps up the bridge when he grabs me again and smashes me against the wall. Pain reverberates through my hip and I wonder if he has broken it.

'Fucking bitch,' he says.

'Let go of me.'

I kick and struggle like a wildcat, but he has a solid grip of my shoulders. Behind me the river is surging through the valley, faster and more furious than I have ever seen it before, and the roar is deafening. The wall is only waist height and I can feel myself tipping over the edge. Would I be safer taking my chances in the swirling river below than on the bridge with a man who wants to kill me?

'Give me the memory card.' Mark looks like a man possessed, his demonic eyes shining at me in the moonlight.

'I haven't got it. I dropped it in the water.'

'You can't stop lying, can you, Holly? Even now.'

He releases one of my shoulders to search me, his hands fumbling in my jacket pockets. As he frisks me, his grip loosens, and I swing my body weight to one side, knocking him over the bridge and into the river below. I get a momentary glimpse of his face contorted with terror before he is swallowed by the hungry river.

Chapter 58

Mark hits the water with an impact that ricochets through his body. The river is cold, shocking and fast. He forces his eyes open, but his vision is too blurred to see anything under the water. He cannot tell which way is up or down, but his survival instincts kick in and, almost on autopilot, his fingers stretch towards a patch of silvery moonlight and force his body to follow their lead.

He surfaces, spluttering and coughing, and gasps the clean crisp air. His lungs are burning, and his ears are blocked. Behind him, the bridge is already a faint outline in the distance. The bitch has won.

He concentrates on staying alive. Thinks about Mia and his mother. What it would do to them if they lost him too. His body has started to shut down, his feet are already numb, but he doesn't think he is injured. If he can get to the side, grab a branch, he may have enough strength left to pull himself out. He tries to swim to the bank, but the current is too strong and it's all he can do to keep his head above water.

It is as if the river has heard his thoughts. It sucks him back under, pulling him down until his lungs are screaming for mercy, before throwing him upwards again like a piece of jetsam. It is toying with him, demonstrating its power, like a particularly cruel cat playing with a mouse.

The river crashes through the valley, taking him with it. Above his head, lightning flashes and the dark clouds hang like ominous shadows. He tries to clutch on to the debris that sweeps past him, but his fingers are frozen. Branches tear at his face as he is tossed from one unforgiving rock to another. He knows with absolute certainty he is going to die and feels a strange sense of calm as he lets the river take him.

Chapter 59

I look over the bridge but there is no sign of Mark. The river is vicious – plunging down the valley, crashing against the rocks and depositing debris in its wake. Even if he survives the fall, he will be sucked under by the current and slammed against the rocks. Hardly daring to believe it's finally over, I sink to the ground and allow my heart rate to return to normal, hot tears streaming down my face. Another man is dead because of me, but I'm safe. My family are safe. And that's all that matters to me right now.

I take the memory card out of my pocket. I know it contains the video but what else is on it? I could give it to the police, tell them everything, and spend the rest of my life in prison. Or I could take the chance and destroy it. I pull myself up to a standing position and let it fall into the swirling river below.

I can't stay here much longer; I need to get warm. I limp down the road, the rain strafing my face, praying I won't hit any more flood water. I wish that I had my mobile phone with me and could call for help. I check behind me from time to time, more through paranoia than genuine fear, but the road is empty. As I reach the village, I see lights in windows; either the electricity is back on or they haven't suffered the same power cut. I can hear convivial noises emanating from the Black Swan; there must be a Christmas Eve lock-in, but the urgency is over. I can make it to Rhona's house.

I hammer on the iron door knocker and keep my finger pressed on the bell, resting my head against the stone wall. It feels like an eternity before Rob opens the door, dressed in a fluffy grey dressing gown and Homer Simpson slippers. He takes one look at me and pulls me inside, yelling for Rhona. She appears at the top of the stairs. 'Holly? Oh my God, what happened?'

I am so relieved to be inside, in the warmth, that for a few seconds I can't speak. Rhona grabs a blanket from the living room and wraps it around me, rubbing my arms and legs for warmth.

'What the hell, Holly. Look at you. You're soaked and freezing. What happened?'

'He broke into my house. He attacked me.'

'Who did? George?'

'No. Not George. It was Mark, his brother. It's been Mark all along. He sent those messages.'

'Where is he now, Holly?' Rob asks urgently, already in police mode.

'He fell into the river. I think he's … I'm sorry, I'm so sorry.'

Rhona holds me close and shushes me as I start to cry.

'It's OK, you're safe now. We won't let anything happen to you.'

'I'll call control. Where exactly did he fall, Holly?'

'At the bridge.'

Rhona leads me into the living room, dripping water and God knows what else into her carpet. She puts on a small electric heater and directs it towards my feet. I can feel the warmth start to return to my body.

'I'll get you some clean clothes,' she says. 'And a cup of tea.'

I grab her hand. 'Please don't leave me.'

She looks torn but returns to the sofa. On the coffee table there is an empty bottle of wine and a half-eaten box of chocolates. The bookcase is adorned with Christmas cards and copper reindeer decorations. Everything looks so ordinary; it's hard to believe that a few minutes ago I was fighting for my life. Rob comes back into the living room.

'They're having a busy night and the road is blocked, but they're going to try and get the search and rescue helicopter out. How are you doing, Holly? Are you hurt? Do you need to go to the hospital?'

I shake my head. My hip is still throbbing, but the pain has subsided. I decide not to tell him about the blow to the head. I don't want them thinking I'm confused. 'Just bruised, I think.'

Rhona leaves me with Rob as she goes to make a cup

of tea. He sits beside me on the sofa and pulls out his police notebook. I force myself to concentrate.

'Now, tell me exactly what happened.'

I tell him how Mark broke into my house and how he attacked me. I told him I stabbed him in self-defence before running to the river and that in the tussle he fell into the water. It's not hard to cry; in fact, it's a relief.

Rob's face is inscrutable and I'm wondering whether he is worried about his role in all of this. He should have taken me more seriously when I reported the messages.

'This is way beyond my pay grade, Holly. I'm going to have to call in the big boys.'

Rhona comes back in with a cup of tea and some biscuits. She hands me her mobile phone. 'I rang Tom. I've told him what happened.'

I take the phone and feel a rush of love as I hear his voice. 'Holly, are you OK?'

'I'm fine, please don't worry. Rob and Rhona are looking after me.'

'I'll come back.'

'No, Tom, it's Christmas Eve. Besides the road is blocked, you won't get through. I'm fine, honestly.'

'Why didn't you tell me all this was going on? I would never have left you alone like that if I'd known.'

'I didn't want to worry you. I'm alright, I promise.'

'I love you, Holly.'

'I love you too.'

'Everything's going to be OK.'

I nod my head but can't answer as I shut down the phone and hand it back to Rhona. The fact that he still loves me despite everything makes me feel better. Maybe things will be OK now that Mark has gone?

Rob excuses himself to get dressed and it's not long before there is a knock on the door. I catch fragments of their conversation as Rob briefs someone in the hallway. I overhear the words 'self-defence' and 'stalking'.

A woman in her late fifties with a strong West Midlands accent walks into the room and introduces herself as DS Elaine Briggs. Rob looks terrified of her. She asks me the same questions but presses me every time for more detail. Elaine has a no-nonsense attitude about her which makes me trust her immediately and I can tell that she is not best pleased about the way Rob has handled my case.

Elaine asks me for the keys to Tom's house even though the door is probably still unlocked. 'We'll send over a SOCO unit,' she explains.

I picture families on our estate waking up on Christmas Day morning to see police tape around the garden, the officers in white suits coming out with evidence bags and wondering what on earth has happened overnight. If Tom and I weren't the talk of the village before, we certainly will be now.

I spend Christmas Day at the police station in Harrogate, answering more questions about Mark, George, and my suspicions about Kristóf's and Meg's deaths. I realise that, even though I've destroyed the memory card, I'm going to have to tell them I was a witness to George's death. Mark has been tracking us for months, he will have gathered all the evidence against us, and the police will only have to look on his computer to find it. So, I break the pact, telling them that Kristóf killed George, that Meg and I moved the body, and that we agreed to keep quiet so that he wouldn't be prosecuted for murder. I tell them that I wanted to confess but that Kristóf put me under duress to keep quiet, threatening to tell the police that I was responsible for George's death. I am forced to repeat myself over and over again, but I keep my story consistent and I think they believe me.

I have not been arrested. Yet. Officially, I am just helping them with their enquiries. I'm not sure if I am being treated as a victim or a perpetrator, perhaps both. Elaine shows me the knife they retrieved from the house. It is stained with rust coloured blood and it makes me feel a bit sick to look at it. I confirm it is the one that I used to stab Mark.

A doctor examines me and confirms that my hip is not broken. She asks me a series of questions to check my mental health and says she will refer me to a specialist to deal with any trauma. She prescribes me some sleeping pills, but I need to keep my head clear. They take away my clothes as evidence and Rhona has to bring some of hers for me to change into. Rob doesn't seem to be part of the investigation, and I wonder if he is in trouble. Elaine doesn't look like the type of person that would stand for anything less than one hundred per cent perfection.

The Beach

At lunchtime, they bring me a ham and cheese sandwich and a mince pie. I picture families around the country tucking into turkey with all the trimmings, pulling crackers and drinking sherry, while I am stuck in a tiny interview room, reliving my ordeal. The police station is busy, and I feel a fresh wave of guilt when I think of all those officers missing out on Christmas Day with their families to sort out my mess. Mum and Dad will be wondering why I haven't called. I haven't had a chance to tell them what happened; where do I start? How are they going to feel that I have been lying to them all these years?

The storm has worn itself out and, from what I can see through the station's windows, the day is relatively benign. They tell me the flood water has begun to recede, so Tom should be able to get through later today. Lancashire is still cut off. They still haven't found Mark's body, but they are pretty confident they will once the river levels go down. I suppose they are waiting for the body to turn up before they charge me, see if my version of events matches up with the evidence.

By the time they finally release me, I haven't slept for nearly twenty-four hours. Tom picks me up from the station. I am so relieved to see him that I burst into tears and cry all the way home. In between changing gears, he holds my hand. He makes small talk about the weather and Christmas but I'm not really listening. I still haven't asked him about Rebecca. I close my eyes as we approach the bridge, I don't want to see it again. I can hear the splash of floodwater against the tyres as we drive over and that is bad enough. We will stay at my house until we can go back home.

'Where's Jack?' I ask, as we get out of the car. 'Is he alright?'

'He's staying with Mum and Dad for a few days. Rebecca's there.'

I wonder if Tom is OK with that, whether he was happy leaving him alone with her again, or worried that she might try to win him back in his absence.

'I'm sorry. You should be with him.'

He strokes my hair. 'It's more important that I'm here right now. Jack is safe. I'll go back and pick him up in a few days and you can come with me. I'm not going to let you out of my sight from now on.'

'You want me to meet your parents?'

He nods. 'Besides, I want to see Rebecca.'

My heart plummets.

'I'm going to ask her for a divorce.'

'Really?'

He looks me intently in the eyes. 'It's time I moved on, properly. I've been scared to commit again, scared of getting hurt. But I love you, Holly. I want us to be a proper family.'

'I want that too, but Tom, I'm going to prison.'

He shakes his head. 'That won't happen. It was an accident. Besides, the man was trying to kill you. If that isn't self-defence, then what is?'

'But I stabbed him, Tom. What if they don't believe me?'

'They will. Holly, you did nothing wrong.'

'That's not what they'll make out in court. They're going to pull me to pieces. And what about George?'

'Let's take it a step at a time, shall we? And make the most of our time together, however long that might be.'

He holds me for a very long time.

'Holly,' he says eventually.

'Mmm?'

'I hate to tell you this, but you really need a shower.'

Chapter 60

They find Mark's body a mile downstream, trapped in a narrow channel amid a labyrinth of rocks. Elaine shows me photos on her iPad.

'Is this the man who attacked you? Is this Mark Bolton?'

His face is swollen and heavily bruised, discoloured by the water, but it is still clearly Mark. She takes yet another statement from me. I wonder if they have told his mother yet and whether she will have to identify the body. Surely there must be a way of saving her that ordeal.

Rhona comes around to tell me that Rob has been suspended and is facing disciplinary action at work.

'They're not happy with the way he handled your case. He should have reported the stalking straight away, even without any evidence. Apparently, he told them you were "hysterical".'

Rhona delivers this last adjective with a look of contempt that tells me Rob is probably suffering as much at home as he is at work.

'Will he lose his job?'

'I don't know. It's not looking good.'

'I'm sorry.'

'You have nothing to apologise for. None of this is your fault. How are you feeling anyway? You look wrecked.'

I do look a mess. I'm not sleeping properly, my brain is plagued with nightmares, and I have to force myself to eat. Everything tastes rancid, like the floodwater I was forced to ingest.

It's a relief to get out of the village a few days later and drive down to Tom's parents to pick up Jack. I don't know how much he has told his mum and dad or what impression they must have got of me from everything that has happened over the past few days, but they are either genuinely pleased to meet me or very good actors. Jack gives me a big hug and drags me into the living room to examine everything Santa brought him. I can hear Tom talking quietly to his parents about Rebecca. The look on his mother's face says everything I need to know about how she feels about his ex-wife.

'Will you guys be alright if I leave you for a little while?' he asks, his face tight with anger.

'Do you want me to come with you?' I am a little alarmed about being left alone with his parents so soon after meeting them.

He kisses my forehead. 'No, I won't be long.'

Tom's mum offers me a cup of tea and I follow her into the kitchen. Fussing over tea bags and whether the milk is fresh, she confides that Rebecca is going back to America today. She hasn't even said goodbye to Jack. She told them over the phone it would be easier that way.

'Has Tom gone to stop her?'

'Not likely. I think he's gone to check she's got a one-way ticket. Sorry, I probably shouldn't badmouth her, she is Jack's mother after all, but when I think about that little boy ...'

'He's got Tom.'

'And you. You're all he ever talks about. I think it might have got up Rebecca's nose to be honest. Holly this, Holly that.' Tom's mother laughs, carrying the tray back into the living room. Jack settles down on my knee and I read him one of his new storybooks. It is a silly story about aliens meeting Father Christmas and he makes me read it twice through. As I tuck him into bed he asks where his dad is, and I tell him he will be back soon. He doesn't even mention Rebecca.

Mark's death is on the national news. There aren't many details, but they name him and show a picture of him with Mia, looking happy and relaxed on holiday. They don't mention me at all. We watch the whole piece in silence and then Tom's mum quietly switches it off without comment.

Tom finally returns shortly after midnight, stinking of whisky. He climbs into bed, buries his head in my chest and I rock him to sleep like a baby. The next day we drive back home. No-one mentions Rebecca and I can only assume that she has disappeared back to America.

Eventually they let us back into Tom's house. A section of the living room carpet has been cut out and I realise it must have been covered in Mark's blood. There are traces of silver fingerprint powder on the window ledges and door frames. We clean up the living room as best we can and buy a new rug to cover the patch in the carpet, but the house still feels tainted. I can feel Mark's presence everywhere. I don't think I will ever want to be alone in that house again. Tom understands that we need a fresh start and begins looking at properties on Rightmove.

In January, I am called to give evidence at the inquest. I stick to the statement I gave the police and answer the coroner's questions as best I can. I don't look at the area where Mark's family and Mia are sitting. Several weeks later, with the possibility of prosecution still hanging over me, I get a call from the police.

'The coroner has recorded a verdict of accidental death,' she said. 'Mark drowned in the river, not from the stab wound.'

'And what about George?'

She pauses. 'With the perpetrator and the only other witness dead, the prosecutors have decided not to pursue the case. There's simply not enough evidence to make a case against you.' She doesn't sound happy about their decision.

'So, I'm free?'

'You're free.'

Epilogue

The seasons are changing. Nature continues its cycle of decay and rebirth. There are daffodils along the riverbank and tiny crocus heads emerging from green leaves. The fields are full of baby lambs. I stand on the bridge, watching the river gently wind its way down the valley, the surface smooth and glittering in the spring sunshine. It looks picturesque, innocent. You would have to know its deepest, darkest secrets to understand its capacity for murder.

Everything is perfect. Tom and I have moved into our new home at the other side of the village and pretty soon we will be able to tell Jack that he has a new brother or sister on the way. I was over the moon when I found out I was pregnant. It's all I've ever wanted: a family of my own and it's going to be perfect.

We've put the past behind us, promising never to talk about what happened in Thailand or that night on the bridge. Mum and Dad had plenty of questions, particularly after the inquest, but seemed satisfied with my version of events. I felt a bit bad about lying to them but when it comes down to it, we all lie sometimes to get what we want.

It's not like I set out to kill George. He was my first love. I never thought for one minute he would hurt Meg. I should have listened to her; I should never have put her in that position. When I saw George lying there in the water, blood seeping from his head wound, I really thought Kristóf had killed him. That there was nothing more we could do. I didn't know whether to be sad or happy that he could never hurt me, or another woman, again.

Then I heard him groan.

Kristóf and Meg were in the sea, washing her t-shirt, their backs turned to me. I bent my head over George's face and felt his breath on my cheek. He was dazed and confused, struggling to say something. I held his hand and looked into his eyes, expecting him to tell me that he was sorry, that he made a mistake, but all he said was 'Help me.'

Typical George. Always thinking about himself.

Gently, I covered his mouth with my hand and pushed his head under the water, feeling a slight resistance as he struggled against me. His eyes widened as he realised what I was doing but he was weak, he couldn't fight back. Tears fell down my cheeks as the waves crashed over his face again and again, washing away his sins. When I was sure he was really dead, I slipped the ring on his wedding finger. I couldn't keep him in life, but he would be mine in death.

The Beach

George would probably have died anyway but I wasn't going to take that chance. He had hurt my best friend and betrayed me in the worst possible way. He had strung me along, stolen my heart. He was never going to leave Fiona and commit to me. I was just a bit on the side.

It isn't much to ask, is it? To be someone's number one?

At least I have Tom now. And Jack. A lovely home. And, after the baby is born, we will get married and I'll have everything I've always wanted. A happy ending. I'm not going to be second best ever again.

I'll make sure of it.

Acknowledgements

To my long-suffering husband, Adam, who has spent many hours walking along beaches with me working out how to get away with murder.

To my family and friends, who always believed this would happen one day.

To Kathryn Cheshire from One More Chapter for taking a chance on this book and making my dreams come true.

My beta readers for not laughing at my first drafts and offering constructive advice on how to develop the characters. Mum and Mandy for always wanting to be the first people to see my stories (even when they're not finished, Mum).

A shout out to my Curtis Brown Creative colleague and the best critique partner in the world, Phil Parker, who has encouraged me to keep going in the face of many rejections.

Think Forensic in Huddersfield for their advice on fire investigations and answering my many, many questions during, and following, their authors' workshop. Jo Mallard for your brilliant insight into Crime Scene Investigation. All mistakes are mine.

Phil Payne from Total Warriors in Halifax and Mark Spencer for their advice about ju-jitsu and self-defence techniques.

Margaret Roberts, Joan Stroud and Eleanor Whiteley for their sage insights into teaching.

To my godson Jacob Bailey, social media consultant extraordinaire, even though he thinks I'm too old to learn Snapchat. Jenny Hakney for checking all my references to nature and James Bate for filling a plot hole at the 11th hour with his IT know-how.

To all the team at the Festival of Writing in York. Without your support, advice and encouragement, this book would not exist.

Matt Harmon, Amanda Huggins, Sophie Barker and Gemma Allen for your constructive criticism and encouragement throughout many drafts of this novel and to my good friend Kay Sanders, who loved books. I wish you were here to see this being published.

To the writing community on Twitter and all my Twitter friends who have encouraged me throughout the process of writing this book *waves*.

And last, but certainly not least, I would like to thank you for buying this book. I hope you enjoyed reading it as much as I enjoyed writing it.